PRAISE FOR

SIX DAYS

"Kelli Owen has pulled off a kind of dark magic with this book and done so with an assurance rarely seen in a first novel. She's made us care deeply about a flawed character completely alone in the dark, a scary one-character play peopled with everyone she's close to… which is no mean feat for any magician. And the ending packs a hell of a wallop." —Jack Ketchum

"This is one HELL of macabre, psychological mystery. Owen has a terrifying talent for pushing the reader's buttons, one right after another, until you're trapped in the same lightless, inescapable cloak of HORROR as the main character. One of the most suspenseful books I've read in long time, and a stellar debut." —Edward Lee

ALSO BY KELLI OWEN

Novels
The Headless Boy
Teeth
Floaters
Live Specimens
White Picket Prisons

Novellas
Forgotten
The Hatch
Wilted Lilies
Deceiver
Grave Wax
Buried Memories
Survivor's Guilt
Crossroads
The Neighborhood
Waiting Out Winter
Passages

Other
Black Bubbles (collection)
Atrocious Alphabet (coloring book)
Left for Dead/Fall from Grace (chapbook)

SIX DAYS

KELLI OWEN

CEMETERY DANCE PUBLICATIONS

Baltimore

— 2023 —

Six Days
Copyright © 2010-2023 by Kelli Owen

Cover Design © 2023 by Kealan Patrick Burke | Elderlemon Design
Interior formatting © 2023 by Todd Keisling | Dullington Design Co.

All rights reserved. No part of this book may be reproduced in any form or by any electronic or mechanical means, including information storage or retrieval systems, without permission in writing from the publisher, except by a reviewer who may quote brief passages in a review.

Third Trade Paperback Edition

Paperback ISBN: 978-1-58767-898-1

Originally published in hardcover by Thunderstorm Books (2010) with a foreword from James Moore. First edition paperback included said foreword and/or an afterword by the author.

This book is a work of fiction. Names, characters, places, and incidents either are products of the author's imagination or are used fictitiously. Any resemblance to actual events or locales or persons, living or dead, is entirely coincidental.

Cemetery Dance Publications
132B Industry Lane, Unit #7
Forest Hill, MD 21050

www.cemeterydance.com

To Mom—
for always insisting on a day job, but never suggesting I not dream.

"In darkness one may be ashamed of what one does, without the shame of disgrace."
—Sophocles

"Character is what you are in the dark."
—Dwight L. Moody

SIX DAYS

CHAPTER ONE

Jenny opened her eyes, saw nothing and closed them again. She rubbed unnatural sleep away and blinked several times. Still nothing. Looking for her alarm clock on the left, she found only inky blackness. This wasn't her room. The darkness was different—without edges or shades. Empty and consuming it enveloped her and alerted Jenny to full consciousness.

She heard her breath catch. The soft echo was absorbed and the renewed silence startled her. Jenny squeezed her eyes shut, willed them to work, and reopened them with a prayer on her lips.

Hope was swallowed by the nothing.

I'm blind. The thought screamed through Jenny's mind as her eyes danced from side to side in an unfocused flutter of movement, a conscious pantomime of deep-sleep REM. There was nothing for them to focus on and she inhaled panic, holding it a moment while she collected herself. *Blind?* She waved her hands in front of her face. Perhaps the black was relative. Perhaps she had an outline, a shadow—a something. She couldn't see the fingers she wiggled in front of herself. She couldn't see the shape of her hands. Jenny turned her palms away from her and the faint glow of her watch caught her attention, a subtle blur in the darkness. *Not blind,* she sighed. The fading incandescent blue was too weak for her to see the numbers on the watch's face in contrast.

"Damn." Her frustration bounced lightly in the air, and her eyes widened.

Sucking saliva from her parched mouth, she swallowed hard and tried to calm down, to remain rational. Jenny realized she was lying flat on her back. *I'm dreaming. Lucid dreaming?* She'd never been able to figure out she was *having* a dream, let alone how to control them. No, not dreaming. And not in her bed either. She reached straight up, fearing she had been buried alive, but found no coffin lid above her. She opened her mouth to scream, and stopped—*who might answer?*

Jenny pushed herself to a sitting position with one arm. Her hand felt the rough terrain under her and her mind registered dirt and rocks. *Not blind, not dreaming.* Relief was momentary as she tried to grasp the meaning behind the bare ground beneath her. *In the dark. But where? Why?*

Jenny tried to remember where she had been before waking up. She pulled her legs tight to her chest and wrapped her arms around her shins. A sunburst of color lit up the darkness as pain shot through her body. She reflexively let go of her legs and looked at them. The rainbow of agony faded to black and her mind reeled. New questions replaced those still unanswered.

With trepidation, she felt her knee and noticed the heat of her skin where material should have been. She remembered wearing jeans and traced around the exposed flesh, roaming cautiously with her home-manicured fingertips while tilting her head to the side in concentration. She found the edge of the denim and noted the thick, cool gel coating it. Her brows furrowed.

The ink around her became oppressive, thicker, as the air grew heavy. Her breathing became labored with stress, and she felt the moisture of fear in the corner of her eye.

My God, she thought. *Is it blood? Am I bleeding? Am I dying?*

Panic flushed her face.

Am I dead?

"Beth?" She whispered her friend's name, feigning belief in the rumors that claimed your loved ones greeted you in the afterlife and hoping Beth would be the guide assigned to her. Unless Jenny considered the sound of her beating heart and staccato breaths, no one answered.

Dead? The thought rolled around her tongue as Jenny mouthed the word, absorbing its meaning. No. She was conscious and in pain. Even with her split from the church, Jenny couldn't believe blood would follow you to whatever afterlife there might be. She was injured. She was alive, but somewhere unfamiliar. And the truth finally registered—she was in trouble. Jenny stopped thinking about the gelatinous substance on her leg and began to worry about Alan.

Although precocious for ten, Jenny reminded herself Alan was still a child—complete with fears, irrational or otherwise. The fact she and Dan had divorced the year before escalated the normally erratic boyhood behavior. Now Alan spent his time bouncing between parents, emotions, expectations, and attitudes. Some days he seemed to understand his parents being apart, other days he obviously missed the family unit, blamed them or himself, and lashed out—breaking heirlooms, running off for hours at a time, and he'd even shoplifted once.

Dan and Jenny tried the best they could. For the most part, they had separated on good terms, but the divorce wasn't a friendly goodbye for either of them. Jenny had a hard time hiding her disgust at Dan's logic.

Jenny had taken care of them and their house for years, having quit college when she found herself pregnant. When she decided to finish her marketing degree, she hadn't expected Dan to see her as a threat. Oh sure, he'd been supportive through her final year of night courses, but when she graduated and found a great midlevel position with decent pay, rather than an entry-level position and inappropriate wages, things changed.

She was still taking care of the house, the family, and then added working a full-time job she enjoyed at the town newspaper. As an advertising sales rep, she spent her mornings soliciting ads from the local businesses, her afternoons bringing proofs back to the business owners, and left her work at the office to spend her evenings with her boys. She was happy.

Dan had felt unneeded.

With an income of her own, a satisfying career, and a loving son, Jenny had everything she needed according to Dan, and he couldn't validate his position in the equation any longer. Once that negative thought had planted itself in his mind, Dan began to fall out of love with her, and his eyes wandered. He claimed he never acted on his impulses, out of respect, but he admitted those urges were, more often than not, toward women who mirrored what Jenny used to be. And while he claimed to be saddened by this, he never tried to overcome it. In early March, two years ago, his "World's Best Dad" coffee cup in hand and daily newspaper—her paper—tucked under his arm, he announced he was leaving.

"What?" She'd heard him but couldn't believe he was serious.

"I'm leaving. It's ridiculous for us to continue this."

Realizing he was serious, Jenny assumed the worst. "Do I know her?"

"Her? No. There is no one."

"Bullshit." Jenny's voice cracked as it rose in emphasis, shock pushing its way into her vocal cords. "Do *you* even know her? Or is she just some stray you picked up? Some faceless, convenient excuse—"

"I'm telling the truth. There's no one." He matched her shock and assumption with both volume and angry defensiveness. "Yet."

"*Yet?*" She stared at him, eyes wide and mouth agape. Her mind spun at the insinuations and boldness. This was not the man she'd lived with for over a decade.

"Oh, there have been *plenty* to look at." His volume further increased, and his eyes took on the expression she'd seen in every argument they'd ever had—letting her know he was planning what he was saying rather than listening to what she said. "Lots of fish in the sea to pay attention to me, or need me."

"*Need* you? That's what it boils down to? I don't fucking *need* you?"

"You don't." His deadpan eyes echoed his curt answer.

"Bullshit. Who is she?"

"I haven't cheated on you." He took a quick sip from his coffee. "Oh, but I *have* thought about it. Doesn't that say something?"

She wasn't sure if he presumed honesty was best delivered in volume and cruelty, or if he really didn't care anymore. "Yeah, it says you're an asshole who's about half a step from cheating on your wife and ruining your family."

"No. It says I'm unhappy."

"And happiness is something you can find in another woman's

bed? You shallow sonuvabitch…" Anger began to roll behind her eyes and she couldn't finish her thought.

"It's not like that. It's not about sex. It's about being a partner—a team. You just don't need me to win. I'm no longer necessary. It's unfair *to you* to keep doing this."

"Me? Unfair to *me?*"

He ignored her and continued. "It's no longer mutual, or pure. It's convenience, not passion."

Anger gave way to confusion and pain, and Jenny crumpled into one of the kitchen chairs, gripping the table to keep herself off the floor. She stared at him, unsure what to say, uncertain how to react, and fought the pressure of hot tears in a dumbfounded silence for several minutes.

"Jen, I love you. I always will on some level. But this is just not what I signed up for." Without another word, he put his coffee cup on the counter and left the house.

And the dam burst.

She sobbed uncontrollably until her mouth was as dry as one of her failed turkeys, her throat hoarse as a teenager's after an AC/DC concert, and her eyes puffed all but shut. Sometime after noon, she found her strength and stood up, wiped her face on a nearby dishtowel, and grabbed the phone to call in to work. They had tried to reach her several times and left messages she had heard but couldn't respond to in her shocked mental state. She needed to contact them, before their annoyance turned into worry, or panic, or they called 911. As the company golden child, there were no repercussions for Jenny's absence, just concern and an offer to help. She thanked her boss and promised to be back the next day.

By the time Dan got home that evening she had power-cleaned the house, finished all the laundry, and separated their belongings right down to the spices in the kitchen cabinets. After sorting heirlooms and memories, her tenacious rage vented through the little things. Jenny took the larger containers whenever there were duplicates. After all, he didn't cook and she wasn't supplying the ingredients for her replacement. She had already fed Alan and sent him to her sister-in-law's to sleep over with his cousin Michael for the night. Alan had eyeballed her askance, stealing furtive glances at the various piles around the house, but never questioned anything out loud.

Jenny waited for Dan in the same kitchen chair he'd last seen her. He didn't appear shocked she was there, but was noticeably taken off guard by her preparation—his self doubt transparent. Jenny kept her composure and used an aloof tone to ask who should pack, who was leaving, and demanded he sign over the title of the car. He grabbed a beer from the fridge and the pen from her hand.

Everything that followed, from separating their bank accounts to agreeing on visitation rights, was civil—almost too calm—especially in front of Alan. Through it all, there was a constant hint of hatred in her voice and a touch of bitterness in her eyes. The judge had tried to give her alimony but she'd refused it. She stood tall in her expensive-looking suit from the bargain rack and said no. She stated one of the reasons for the divorce was his anger at her self-sufficiency and she therefore could not accept court-ordered stipends. Her sarcasm did not go unnoticed.

They dealt with Alan's child support, with little to no arguing. An outsider would have thought they were sorting socks for all the emotion they showed. Both trying to be the bigger person, they battled for the crown with an assassin's stealth and a debutante's grace. Dan said he didn't want to upset her. Jenny knew she didn't want to criticize him publicly, and neither wanted to hurt Alan nor give the other any ammunition.

Thinking of Alan and the independence she had used to keep them going returned her to her surroundings. The images of her life—displayed in vibrant detail across her mind, as if she were watching a film—dissipated and Jenny blinked back into the unknown darkness.

How long had she been gone? Was Alan worried yet? Was he okay? Was *he* in a similar dark room? She'd left him at school this morning on her way to work, just like any other day.

If today was still today.

There was a strong possibility Alan would call Dan after chores and homework, not meaning to tattle but to talk to someone out of loneliness. When he wasn't angry, Alan bordered on being clingy—almost as if he expected them to take the divorce another step and leave him. Dan, comfortable in his everlasting conviction that she could take care of herself, wouldn't worry until the next morning. If *worry* was even the right word for it. Alan, however, would watch the clock, and check both the oven and fridge for a precooked meal. Sooner or later, he would give in, make macaroni and cheese for himself, and if he got bored enough, he'd do the dishes. Alan had grown accustomed to the occasional late night her position required, and wouldn't worry about her until nine o'clock, when he was supposed to go to bed. If history and habit meant anything, he'd love the extra time and take full advantage of it for an hour or so. Then the pacing would start—she'd come home during this stage once and was both touched and saddened at the frantic state she found him in—and in the end, he'd call Dan.

She glanced at her wristwatch again, but the luminescent face was now completely black. She'd never paid attention to how long it took it to go out before, so it told her nothing—not the time, not how long she'd been missing, and not how she'd gotten here. The blackness yawned around her as she looked up. "Nothing" was becoming the status quo.

She looked toward her leg again, realizing she needed to make sure her wounds were not life threatening. Shallow breaths escaped as she resumed her blind exploration. Thick, coagulating blood aged the wound by at least a few hours. The surrounding flesh had variations of tenderness and she presumed whatever tore her leg open must have bruised it in the process. The remainder of her right leg was intact and pain free, so she moved to her left leg.

Her mind wandered in a lazy, casual fashion, as she moved her hands over her clothing and bare flesh. Jenny clearly remembered her 5 a.m. alarm and pouring herself into her sweat pants for her sunrise jog. A quick breakfast of cream cheese on toast and a shower followed her twenty-minute, two-mile run. She woke Alan at seven and, after his own version of a morning routine, dropped him off at Franklin Middle School. She parked in the bank parking lot across from the small town's old post office, which now housed the Harding Harold News.

She noted she had no shoes on and shook her head. Jenny knew she'd chosen jeans and a beige blouse with her brown boots and matching leather jacket—her attempt to fit into the businesses on her schedule that day, the local sports shops. Lines stretched across her forehead as she furrowed her brow, thinking and chastising herself at the same time. It was asinine to try to retrace her steps in minute by minute increments. Jenny attempted to fast forward her memory of the day. Morning meetings at the office, phone calls, five stops around town, and a late lunch with Jack were all clear in her mind. After lunch she—

Jenny paused, the clarity of her day clouded over. The mundane activities were filled with doubt and far less detail.

Oh yes, she stopped at the pharmacy for—

For what?

She remembered the pharmacy, busy for the middle of the day and overrun with older women. The elderly doctor was on duty and handed her the bag—

Bag of what?

What was wrong with her? Why couldn't she remember specifics? She went to the pharmacy to get—

Nothing. She could not remember. She couldn't even remember whose prescription had sent her there. Hers? Alan's? Was she picking it up for a co-worker during her lunch hour as she had in the past? Jenny had no idea.

Now she was annoyed. She'd stopped tracing her body for damage and studied the darkness in front of her, trying to picture the locations and people.

Lunch, she thought, *let's back up to lunch.* Jack had been there before her. They met at Sam's, the local deli owned and operated by two retired high school teachers. The meal had been the soup and sandwich special. The sandwich was tuna. The soup was—

"Damn it." She huffed through her teeth, not quite restraining the building frustration. *What was the soup? Never mind. Move forward.*

Jack had been wearing a suit. *Why?* A gray suit with no tie, but why?

"Think." She scolded herself aloud and looked up at the sound of her voice. It bounced once and was consumed, again making her believe she was in a finite space—an enclosed room or possibly a cave.

A meeting—Jenny's memories interrupted her thoughts of locale—Jack had been dressed for a meeting. *For what? It doesn't matter. Keep going.*

They ate and he walked her back to her car. He opened her door and bent down to kiss her. They made a date for lunch on Thursday.

"Oh," she gasped. "Thursday. Which means today is Tuesday—*was* Tuesday?" Jenny smiled, happy to have a starting point. "So lunch and then the pharmacy. I got a prescription and then I—"

Again her mind froze. She found it interesting that tidbits were missing along the way to the mental block, but it intrigued her more than frightened. Backing up into the pharmacy, she ran through the checkout. The details of the stretched faux leather shoes and faded skirt of the woman in front of her were clear. The Muzak playing overhead—a wordless bastardization of Aerosmith. She and old man Adams had discussed Alan's ball game from the previous weekend, a simple, polite conversation. She'd paid and left, walking into the bright sun.

"That's right," she squinted, as if either speaking directly to someone or searching the air around her for answers. Jenny remembered rummaging through her purse for her sunglasses. She was rifling through the contents as she walked across the parking lot to her car and then—

She sighed, gritting her teeth, and starting to feel the exasperation of the amnesia episode build along her jawline. Jenny tried to fast-forward her memory, but the only thing she could remember after opening her purse was waking up here. In the dark.

Alone?

The lack of memory made her believe she'd been drugged, knocked over the head, or abducted in some similarly trite television fashion. This wasn't somewhere she'd go of her own free will. She didn't know where *here* even was. The freshness of the bruises, not recalled as events of the day, meant they were most likely a by-product of the attack. But why? Who? What did she have to offer up as ransom? It dawned on her she'd stopped perusing for injuries and resumed her search for traces of brutality, blood, or bandages.

Three injury-free limbs later, Jenny braved moving her hands across her head, face, and neck. The back of her head was the only place other than her leg Jenny flinched at. A thick mat of dirt-peppered, gummy residue encased her hair where her head had been resting on the floor. There was no tenderness, but further burrowing through the sticky mess revealed a thin trickle of fluid she assumed was blood. The alternative was unimaginable.

Jenny pushed hard on the area, hoping to both stop the bleeding, and to force her scalp out of shock and feel something other than pressure. She raised an eyebrow and thought for a moment before understanding the true motive. In the dark, she welcomed pain to let her know what was going on because her eyes were useless.

Realizing this, Jenny opened her other senses to her visually thwarted surroundings in hopes of figuring out where she was and how to escape. She had already discovered her boots were missing and now she acknowledged her jacket was also gone. She used her free hand to search the area around her, looking for her missing articles and found nothing. Again, she recognized the material of the floor to be dirt and rock, perhaps a rough-cut root cellar or cave. She paused, unsure why she kept thinking cave and decided it was less confining than the alternatives and it was just hope attempting to twist her logic. She felt the dirt around her. It wasn't cold or wet, nor was it uncomfortably warm. The temperature felt almost fixed, like the office.

And there was a smell.

Musky, rotten, something similar to fallen autumn leaves after it rained, but something else, too. Some clumps of the ground around her were thicker than others were, and she picked up a handful to get a closer look. As Jenny's hand drew near her face, she laughed aloud at the habitual act of trying to see. Closing her eyes, she concentrated as she brought it to her nose and inhaled. Old dirt. It smelled like stale dirt, dust, a recently opened bag of sandbox gravel—not fresh as if the rain had soaked into it.

Filtering the material through her fingers like a sieve, Jenny noticed tiny granules like sand mixed among the larger pebbles. Sharp edges and irregularity made her think of dirt roads rather than water smoothed beach sand.

The larger clumps were more than dirt. A softer, egg-sized piece compressed without difficulty and gave off several drops of liquid before her mind registered the almost greasy feel the substance had. Clay. *All right,* she thought, *we're still near the lake.*

Hard red clay marbled every bit of land in a twenty-mile radius from the small inland lake. Gardeners hated the stuff. It cost them extra money to dig deeper and remove the clay in lieu of store-bought or farm-found compost and fertilized dirt. After a heavy rain, the clay colored the runoff, dirtied the roads, covered vehicles, and gave the area a dingy rust-hued overtone. Being neither a gardener nor an immaculate car owner, the clay didn't normally bother her—she'd actually dug it up on occasion and made sunbaked pots with Alan. She threw the wet mud off to her left and heard it land with a dull thud.

Another filtered fistful yielded a medium-sized rock. Something about the weight of it and the way it fit in her hand made it seem like a good weapon, and instinct moved her as Jenny tucked it behind her for safekeeping. She thought of screaming again, or rather why she hadn't. Wary of the situation, fearful of the circumstances that had brought her here, Jenny continued to follow instinct. She'd always trusted her instinct and if it suggested she remain quiet and arm herself, then that was *exactly* what she was going to do.

Jenny leaned forward onto her knees, careful to avoid direct contact with her injury and wincing when she failed. Another sunburst filled her vision as sharp rocks and tiny grains embedded themselves in her wound. The bruised area around the gash felt like tenderized steak and she sniffed back a cry of pain, while sarcastically wondering what spices to use. She sighed, recognizing the black humor her mind had turned to in a moment of panic and fear.

She felt the gravel in front of her, passing her hands in light sweeping motions across the surface. The side of her pinky hit something solid and she stopped. Picking around it, Jenny used a fingertip to dig and trace at the same time. It felt like a brick, or rather a broken brick in size, but the texture was wrong. Digging into the soft dirt along the edges, she pulled the piece free and brushed it off. Cement? It was colder than the rest with small nodules sticking out in random places. She remembered the broken cement pieces in the alley behind Dan's apartment and concluded it had to be the same material. She put it down behind her with the other and inched forward for more exploration. On one knee and the other foot, she pulled herself along and felt the ground below her.

Her hand stopped. Or rather, something solid stopped her.

Running up along the base as far as she could to either side without moving, Jenny felt the cold, rough surface of ancient foundation. Rather than the smooth poured cement of modern foundations, this felt like the stone-and-mortar style you would find in the older buildings and farmsteads of the area. It wasn't a cave. She was in a basement. She had to be.

As she moved to the left along the bottom of the wall, her wrist rubbed against another larger rock sticking out of the dirt floor. Jenny dug around the edges to pull it free, but it went deeper than the other had and she had to put more effort into it, creating a small hole into the floor in the process. Finally pulling the elongated lump free of the ground, she felt her way back to her starting point, careful to keep track of her movements and avoid getting lost.

Sitting with her legs bent in front of her, she examined her newest acquisition with her fingertips. It was long, and would work well as a club. The surface was somewhat warmer than the cement and far smoother than the rocks—perhaps driftwood? Broken and jagged at one end, the object widened slightly as she traveled the length of it. The top mushroomed and she smiled—it really was club shaped.

The top of it had a slight indent and as she adjusted her grip on it, her grin vanished. Narrow in her left hand, bulbous in her right, she realized the length of rock was bone. A large bone.

A human bone?

CHAPTER TWO

Jenny gasped. She threw the bone and scooted backward in a crab-walk as if the broken remains were going to explode. She slammed into something behind her and her injured knee throbbed at the sudden movement. The bone clattered against a solid surface somewhere to her left, before falling in what sounded like two distinct pieces to the dirt below.

She listened to her ragged breath, and let the idea of walls soak past her fear. Wet with tears, her face swirled with heat. Her wrists began to ache from the trembling she couldn't control. Too many questions and having no answers made it worse—jerking sobs replaced her tears as her throat tightened and her mouth dried up. Jenny's bottom jaw quivered as a tiny voice in her mind tried to calm her with reason. She was having none of that for the moment and ignored her inner strength. She hadn't felt pure adrenaline-laced fear like this since she'd driven away from the scene of an accident long ago.

She was sixteen when it happened and had thought she'd forgotten about it, but for whatever reason, the memory pushed its way past the panic and claustrophobia. It erased her surroundings, engulfed her mind, and replayed itself in vivid details.

Jenny had managed to get the old Buick from her mother to attend the party. She rarely got permission to go to the mall, movies or even store, let alone a party—or as her mother would say, "A gathering of teens, with boys and music and God knows what else." Maybe her mom's tyrannical reign was loosening. Jenny wasn't sure, but planned to enjoy it for one night.

The party had been at Vivian's house, a senior whose opinion could make or break anyone in the ring of high school politics and power—Jenny had both witnessed it and feared it since her freshman year. But she wasn't going because a friend was, or a friend of a friend had invited her. No, the queen of popularity herself had personally asked Jenny to attend. Hesitant, trying to figure out what game Vivian might be playing, Jenny hadn't answered right away. Jabbing Jenny's arm, Vivian had laughed that infectious chuckle of hers, which meant she was up to no good. But the invite was genuine, and Vivian claimed no jokes or cruelty were planned. And none had come to pass after the party either—perhaps forgotten in the aftermath of the night's events.

Beth hadn't just been *not* invited, Vivian had specifically requested, no ordered, Jenny not bring her best friend. Beth told her to go, and a few unsure moments into the party—when people began talking to her just because she was there and therefore somehow cool—Jenny forgot all about her guilt. She spent the evening roaming from circle to circle, mingling with as many classmates as possible, and making sure there were witnesses to attest to her presence. She chatted with cheerleaders and jocks, pep members and non-spirited but popular students, including the cutest guy in school, Tim Brayman.

Waiting in line for the bathroom, Jenny found herself face-to-face with her wildest dream, and was stunned silent by Tim's decision to strike up a conversation. They passed their turns to others in line in order to continue their conversation, and those twenty minutes of heaven in his company overrode her bladder's insistent warnings of explosion.

Still thinking about him on the way home, she drove with a permanent grin, as she mulled over his opinions on parties, the attendees and hosts.

"What? You've never noticed that?" Tim had glanced around them to see who may be within earshot.

"Well, I always figured popularity often comes with the means to throw the best parties."

"Oh hell no. I mean, sure, they're usually from wealthy families, but break it down beyond that."

She stared at his perfect teeth as he spoke and lost track of his voice for a moment. "What?"

"The ones that show up either want to become popular and plan on riding the coattails of those that are, or are desperate to prove the invitation means they already are."

"So I'm on the coattails?"

"Nah. At first, I would have said yes. But it seems to me that you're like me and just here out of curiosity. You're wondering what the big deal is and nervous being here. I'm expected to show up, but I only do so I can watch the entertainment as they fall over themselves. Holding court, drooling over those more popular than them, using key words or phrases or referencing other parties to further prove their worthiness. It's a free show, and a damn good one."

"Oh." Relief washed over her as Jenny escaped his judgment and leaned in closer.

"Now, the one throwing the party—that's the best entertainment. They have to work harder to *stay* on top than they did to get there. Who they invite, what they wear, the music played, the refreshments—it will all be judged. But more important, no matter how perfectly they plan, some will still frown on it. So watching them is always good entertainment. And this particular party? This is the dying cry of a girl who's realized graduation will mean the end of the only thing she's ever known."

The jabs at Vivian had made Jenny like Tim even more and he held her attention rapt until he could hold his bladder no more. He excused himself to enter the bathroom. When she followed suit and then exited the bathroom, he was talking to others and she didn't want to interrupt.

Her mind was elsewhere as she drove home, reliving his breakdown of the various clichés and their supposed powers, when the man walked out of nowhere.

She registered movement too late and stomped on the brake with both feet.

The force slammed Jenny forward. The steering wheel smashed into her chest, collarbone, and chin. Her seat belt pulled at her neck with abrupt force and felt like it tore flesh.

The man bounced onto her hood and slid off the driver's side to lie on the ground below her window.

Her attention had been diverted. She'd been daydreaming, but not speeding. She hadn't touched a drop of alcohol at the party—she knew better than to push her mother's leniency. She hadn't broken any laws. She had just turned sixteen. She couldn't go to jail for manslaughter.

Her thoughts sped up and kept time with her breathing.

She'd watched this scenario in hundreds of television shows and movies and always yelled at the screen for the characters to call the cops, *you did nothing wrong*. But there was no one here to scream logic at her and it never crossed her mind. She could only think of self-preservation and tried to swallow her panic long enough to act.

The fear knotted inside her chest and flowed from her eyes. Jenny wasn't sure if she was crying because of the injuries the steering wheel may have caused, or the shock of the situation. She couldn't even remember when she started crying, only noticing because the wetness dripped from her chin and left a cold spot as it absorbed into her shirt.

She didn't check for a pulse. She didn't get out of the car. She sat frozen, belted in place, and stared at him through her open window. She shook and cried and screamed the unfairness of it all to the empty car and soundless night outside. Jenny cursed the unmoving body, her mother, Vivian, and everyone else who came to her, sparing no one—including her dead father. When she'd gotten it out of her system, autopilot made the decision for her.

She drove away.

Looking into the rearview mirror, she watched the limp body fade from the glow of the taillights into the blackness beyond. The man never moved.

Jenny stopped at the twenty-four-hour gas station by her house, pulling into the back near the bathrooms. There were no other cars and she was certain the clerk, visible by the very top of his head, hadn't noticed her. She used toilet paper to wipe the hood of the car off and flushed the bloody evidence. Jenny's shoulders resumed their wracking motion, but her eyes remained dry as she washed the experience from her own face, fixing her makeup the best she could in the meager, pulsating light of the dying florescent bulb.

Further inspection of the car found the headlight broken and a small dent across the fender and hood. Her mother would notice. She needed to explain it—or better yet, cover it up. Pulling into her driveway, she missed the garage opening and smashed the already damaged car into the corner of the garage, *accidentally* hitting the horn as she did so. She knew her mother would scream bloody murder, make her pay for damages, grill her about whether she'd been drinking—but it was all preferable to the truth, and Jenny faced her mother without fear as she came storming out of the house.

Autopilot dissipated like fog as she hit the pillow two hours later and rapidly broke down. She cried until her mind's numbness matched her body's fatigue. Vowing to forget all the events after she left the party, Jenny fell asleep.

Had the man not become the talk of town, she might never have thought of him again. He would have been tucked deep inside, hiding somewhere near her father and the narrowly avoided date rape from the previous summer. But someone found the old man and brought him to a hospital where he lay in a coma for three weeks before succumbing to his injuries. The newspapers covered the hit-and-run of the local old-timer as if he had been the president of the United States. Jenny tired of hearing about him long before his funeral. The part of her that had not turned cold in order to protect herself found relief when he was put into the ground. And put to rest in her conscience.

The same autopilot that had taken over at sixteen now begged for attention in the darkness of both Jenny's surroundings and subconscious. Breaking through to the surface, the tears of fear and shock slowed and the cautionary critic came to life, assessing the situation.

A bone.

A human bone?

Here. Why?

How?

Could it have been an old animal bone dragged in by a scavenger?

Was it really human? What made her jump to that conclusion?

She didn't want to retrieve it for further examination and continued to consider other possibilities. Her mind reeled even as she felt her eyes dry up.

The anxiety of shock wore off, but the implications were just beginning to sink in.

She was in danger. That was evident now. How much danger could be presumed by the bone, but that was unproven and pessimistic. The eminence of danger, or the outcome of it, was the question.

She folded her hands, lacing her fingers together to help them stay steady. Jenny squeezed the nervousness out of them, wringing them as she thought. Traveling back to the accident with the old man, she had found guilt hiding under the surface after all these years and rubbed the long-forgotten seatbelt bruise on her collarbone.

The cold calculation that had gotten her through most troubles in her life neighbored the remorse, attempted to overshadow it. This inside strength helped her carry on when the circumstances were too much for her mental or physical limits. The first time survival mode had taken over she'd been on the playground in fifth grade. It had scared her then, and made her nervous still, but she'd never been able to control it. In a sense, she welcomed it and often wished it would appear.

The girl, Heidi, was a sixth-grader with what Jenny figured were aspirations of becoming a professional bully—or perhaps a successful female hit man. All rumors indicated Heidi's family life was less than perfect. There were claims her father beat her mother and maybe Heidi as well. The rumor mill thrived on talk of foster homes, alcoholism, and a sibling who had run away from the chaos. That day, for whatever reason made sense to her, Heidi had felt the need to take it out on someone else. Jenny turned out to be the someone.

"Jenn-*it*-fur..." Heidi taunted her from the swing, her voice carrying to the top of the jungle gym. In general, the fifth and sixth-graders belonged to one of two camps—those gathered on the playground equipment to gossip in hushed tones, and those who viewed the geometric dome as a battling cage. Heidi followed, if not led, the second philosophy.

Changing the second syllable of Jennifer's name was Heidi's favorite taunt—it rubbed in the fact no one called her Jenny. Earlier in the school year, Heidi had told her only people with friends had nicknames and claimed it spoke volumes about her personality and popularity. Jenny tried not to care, she knew she had friends—Beth always called her Jen, and that had to count for something. It didn't to Heidi and she persisted, using the taunt as her opening act every time.

"Ignore her." Beth put a hand on Jenny's knee and resumed talking about the latest gossip. "So do you think Kevin really did it?"

"Jenn-*it*-fur!" Heidi stomped her way from the swing set. "Get down here, crybaby."

Jenny winced, and Beth's eyes went wide. The week before, Heidi had trapped Jenny in the boys' bathroom by tying a shoelace from the doorknob to the handle on the fire extinguisher cage on the wall. By the time someone saw the shoelace and undid it, Jenny had curled into the fetal position underneath one of the sinks. They found her sobbing and half-asleep from exertion. Of course, the whole school knew she'd been crying before the end of the day. Now Heidi reminded everyone at the top of her lungs, and everyone on the playground turned to watch.

Jenny and Beth looked to each other with wide eyes, planning their escape using silent expressions and private sign language only best friends could develop. But they weren't quick enough and Heidi appeared below them.

A hand reached up and grabbed Jenny's ankle. Her balance tipped on the precarious metal bar below her and Jenny's arms flailed through the air in vain. If not for Beth's reflexive grab, Jenny would have gone down headfirst. Instead, as Beth held on to her shirt, Jenny had time to grab the bar with both hands and kept her higher vantage point.

For the time being.

"Jenn-*it*!" Heidi looked around to make sure she had an audience. "I said get *down* here." Heidi put a foot up against the first cross bar on the jungle gym for traction and pulled Jenny's ankle.

The stress of everyone watching caused Jenny's palms to sweat, but the fear of entering the fray kept her grip sure.

For a moment.

Jenny watched, rather than felt, as her fingers popped free one by one, like some Saturday morning cartoon. As her left hand came loose, Jenny felt the jerking motion of weakened resistance and attempted to kick out with her free leg. As her right hand came down, she wished someone would wake her up and knew by the end of recess that, "Crybaby" would be an outdated nickname.

Sliding down the side of the structure, Jenny watched as Beth hurried to scramble through the center. Beth dropped from sight, trying to get to the ground, and Jenny's world went into slow motion.

She felt each rail against her shin, knees, rib cage and chin, as Heidi pulled her toward the gathering crowd. Jenny tried to hold her head up to prevent her face from bouncing its way across the surface, but couldn't concentrate on it as she reached, time and again, for the handholds seemingly made of smoke.

She landed with a crumbled thud on the ground. Her head jerked forward one last time and metal caught her right across the nose. The world spun. Her eyes danced. Jenny tasted blood.

Spitting crimson saliva, she glanced around. The pain-induced visual merry-go-round her vision had become blurred her classmates. She felt defeated.

Somewhere deep inside her pain, Jenny could hear the muffled taunts as Heidi continued to build up her audience, the bolder students joining in, tossing their own insults at the already damaged girl. At the edge of her vision, Jenny saw Beth slip into the school to retrieve help from the teachers' lounge. Inside her blood-tainted mouth, she could taste the sour mingle of fear and anger. And from the dark recesses of her mind, she heard a snap.

Jenny blinked a few times, wiped the blood from her nose and upper lip, and grabbed onto a bar to help her stand. She pulled herself up and turned to face Heidi. Jenny's emotions seemed to vanish and she smiled.

"Did you want something, Heidi?"

Heidi stood taller and exhaled her anger in an exaggerated breath, but concern and confusion had slipped into her eyes and let Jenny know she'd taken her off guard. A hush traveled across the playground and Jenny wondered if they thought she was stalling. She wondered herself for a moment.

"Did you hit your head on the way down?" Heidi forced a loud guffaw meant to get the silenced crowd to rally on her side once again, but they were all staring at Jenny with the same glint in their eyes Jenny had seen Heidi struggle to cover. "Of course you did."

"Matter of fact, I did." Jenny stepped closer and the crowd gasped. No one had ever challenged Heidi, and Jenny was the last person anyone would have volunteered. "You should try it sometime."

Jenny reached up with the speed of a viper and grabbed a handful of hair on the taller girl. The silky-looking style registered as stiff and scratchy as Jenny wrapped it around her wrist. She pulled at the roots while swinging her arm back toward the jungle gym. Before Heidi could adjust for the unexpected attack, she was on her knees, her face closing in on metal.

The audible crack the bar made against Heidi's face was loud enough to visibly startle everyone near enough to hear it.

Jenny didn't flinch. She didn't hear her pounding heart or deep, angry breaths. Her emotions had shut down.

A muffled yelp foreshadowed the tears that ran down Heidi's face for all to see.

Jenny yanked the larger girl's head back and slammed it forward again. This time the bar connected with Heidi's eyebrow. Blood splattered as the skin split on impact.

The third time she pulled Heidi back, Jenny unwound her hand from the girl's hair and used an open palm to push her into the structure one last time, her anger satisfied.

Heidi's head turned from the force of the shove. Her temple slammed against the frame, and she flopped to the ground like a rag doll. Blood leaked from her nose, lip and ear toward the ground. Her eyes did not match. One was puffed shut and already showing traces of color that would become a bruise. The other was half-open but only showed the white of the eyeball beneath the lid.

Jenny had turned away before Heidi hit the ground and headed toward the school without a word. Heidi's audience stood in silent awe for several seconds before someone screamed.

Inside, Jenny made her way to the bathroom. Leaning over the sink, she spat blood into the basin and turned on the cold water. Gazing into the mirror, she ran a finger inside her lip and along her gums, checking her teeth. She didn't recognize the girl looking back at her. She cupped a handful of cold water, swished it around her mouth and spit it out. Grabbing a paper towel to wipe her face and hands. Jenny never took her eyes off the stranger in the mirror.

"Did that just happen?" She asked the reflection in a strong voice, cracked with uncertainty. A light echo of her question was all that bothered to answer.

Walking to the last stall, she went inside and pulled the door shut. Jenny pulled down her pants and sat, leaning forward with her elbows on her knees. As she urinated, she heard the snap deep inside her mind again. The sudden rush of tears scared her. She wrapped her arms around herself as she cried, adrenaline releasing its hold on her. She used toilet paper to wipe her face, grabbed more for her bottom, stood, flushed, and left the room.

The call to the principal's office came over the loudspeaker moments later.

The principal and guidance counselor greeted her with grim expressions. They believed her without question when Jenny said she didn't know what had happened. They presumed the constant harassment had at last pushed her over the edge. They dropped it with little more than a call to her mother and a stop at the nurse's office.

Her mother didn't. Grounded for a month, her mother handed her a list of time-consuming chores to keep her busy. Jenny didn't care.

The other students didn't drop it either. Overnight, she became Jen or Jenny to everyone, whether familiar with her or not. No one mentioned what she'd done, but greeted her with a sudden barrage of friendly faces and wide smiles. She ran into Heidi the following Monday outside of the gymnasium.

"Hey." Heidi looked at her with hatred in her eyes, and Jenny expected her to say something about a rematch.

Jenny smiled with the coldest look she could muster.

Heidi swallowed and forced a crooked grin. "You and me are okay." The words were acceptance, the meaning truce, and the difference didn't matter to Jenny.

The two of them seldom spoke after that, passing perhaps ten words right up until graduation.

That was the first time her survival instinct had set in.

Jenny needed it to return now. She needed her emotions checked, her fears overridden.

She listened to the darkness around her with the ears of a hunter stalking its prey. She craved that inner snap and concentrated. She heard nothing for long moments. Then, instead of an imagined internal noise, actual sound invaded.

Through the inky blackness, a faint whine filtered down to her. Mechanical—a motor perhaps. It teased her with its familiarity.

CHAPTER THREE

Jenny's eyes flitted uselessly in the blackness, scanning the unseen area as she tried to locate the source of the sound. It came from everywhere, filling the void with its subtle whisper.

She stood, reaching above her in case the ceiling was low, and favoring her torn leg. Her hand found nothing but tepid air. She sidestepped to where she judged the wall to be, her arms a bad rendition of an early Hollywood mummy, and shuffling her feet to find any holes or hazards. She swung in a wide arc and made contact with a rock foundation on her left.

Jenny leaned in, pressed her ear to the cold stone, and listened. Tiny noises vibrated through the wall, barely perceptible above her pounding heartbeat. The mechanical sound was almost a whirring, reminding her of fan blades in a quiet room. She closed her eyes and concentrated. Its familiarity bothered her.

"What *is* that?" She asked the unresponsive nothing. Her eyes hurt and it dawned on her she was squeezing the lids closed. She opened them and a brief starfield greeted her as the pressure released.

The noise reminded her somewhat of the standing rotary fan she had in her bedroom, but not quite. Something deep inside her didn't like the sound, but she couldn't fathom why without understanding the source. She didn't have any irrational fears she could think of—other than leeches, and she didn't think she'd run into them here. Or rather, hoped. She heard no running water and paused to consider stagnant leech-filled pools hiding in the darkness, lying in wait for her to stumble onto or fall into—placed there by a captor with knowledge of her fears. And what *did* hundreds, or thousands, of leeches sound like? A shudder shook her physically and mentally back to the situation at hand and she chuckled uncomfortably—her childhood See 'n Say didn't have leeches and Jenny told herself her current prison didn't either.

Again, she heard her breath and thought it odd she paid so much attention to her own breathing. But there wasn't much else to hear, outside her pounding heart, so she noticed it and listened. Its ragged, panicked sound made her realize an unhealthy fear of the dark was in the making. She straightened up, fighting the sudden urge to cry.

Where had that come from? Jenny couldn't abide weakness in others, and didn't allow it in herself—not now—and hated the times in her life when she had shown weakness. Jenny reminded herself it was an uncontrollable chemical and emotional response to her situation, made worse by her wandering mind. She was determined to overcome instinct and reflex, yet here she sat with moist eyes, and, she reminded herself, had cried only moments before. She had to keep busy or risk losing it. An emotional breakdown of strength could reduce her to sobbing like a child, inactive in a stunned state of shock. Cracking would mean she risked losing herself inside her own mind, rocking in a corner, waiting for the inevitable.

Whatever that meant.

Inevitable. The word itself scared her. It removed her control over the situation. It made her a victim. She was better than that. Life had given her plenty of opportunities to turn into a sniveling whiner who blamed fate—she hadn't buckled under the pressure of her childhood, or the oppression of her marriage and subsequent divorce, and she wouldn't now. Period.

She smeared the spilled tears across her face with the back of her hand and took a deep breath. Although filled with the stench of autumn and taste of dirt, the motion cleansed her thoughts, strengthened her resolve and pushed her into action.

Keeping her hand on the cold stone, she stood upright and listened intently as she moved down the wall, making note of whether the sound grew louder or faded into oblivion as she moved. She found a rough-cut corner as the foundation turned ninety degrees, and felt some small exhilaration. To map out where she was and how to get out she'd need a starting point, and this looked to be it.

She reached above her again, her hands creeping up, as she searched for the ceiling. At five-foot-eight, she could touch the top of most lower-basements and root cellars—even if just brushed with her fingertips—and found herself mildly surprised there was no upper limitation within her reach. Jenny chewed on her lip and spun around to face the expanse, leaning against the corner behind her.

"Hello." She called out with trepidation. She didn't actually want to get anyone's attention, especially the person responsible for putting her here, but thought an echo might help her judge the size of the cavern. Her greeting reverberated briefly, but like all other noises she had issued, was swallowed up after only seconds of freedom.

Jenny stood for a moment. An apprehensive shudder passed through her body and she tried to figure out a way to mark this spot.

The bone.

She didn't want to comprehend the meaning of the remains—

human or otherwise—and hoped it was the only one, but knew it would make a good marker and set her worries aside. She had thrown it to her left while sitting, but hadn't passed it on the way to the corner. It must be farther out. She bent down and swept the ground lightly with her right hand, keeping her left on the wall, and walked forward along the foundation. Nine steps later, her fingers ran from cool earth to lukewarm smoothness, as she felt the bulbous end of the bone and stopped.

She had indeed broken it when she tossed it, but the club end of it was still plenty long enough. If it was the same bone. One meant the probability of others—not to mention, the possibility of finding the body it had come from. She grabbed it, trying not to overanalyze, and followed the wall back to the corner.

Holding the mushroomed end in her hand, she pushed the jagged end down into the ground at the juncture. It sunk about two inches before meeting resistance. It didn't matter if it was a rock blocking the way or a layer of thick red clay, Jenny didn't need it to sink any farther. The thought of digging in the dirt brought dark ideas of what else she may find in it, and she tipped the remaining portion against the corner.

"There." She smiled, feeling as if she'd done something productive, proactive.

Counting her steps and tracing the wall with her fingertips, Jenny walked forward. She felt the foundation change several times and presumed the changes were repairs using various materials over the years. She imagined the smooth and damp interior of the thick, jagged outlines consisted of some sort of Home Depot cement or sealant, smeared into place to block pressure cracks but prone to condensation. She could feel sections of bare earth on the wall where stones had come loose and fallen out, warning her mere moments before those very chunks of mortar and rock threatened to trip her. Several times, she found herself pulling spiderwebbing free from the wall with her hand and thanked her mother for making sure she grew up without arachnophobia. However, her mother never bothered covering grubs, worms, and centipedes. When her hand found a soft spot in the wall and she paused to examine it, she never imagined it would cave in like wet paper and spill its earthy inhabitants onto her. Jumping back from the wall and brushing creatures and crumbs off her arms, Jenny stepped onto a sharp rock and felt it pierce both sock and skin.

She cried out in surprise, and her voice carried further than her previous echoes had proven possible. Leaning against the wall, she lifted her foot up to inspect it. She couldn't feel a tear in the fabric and figured it must have been small enough to force its way through the weave without stretching or ripping the cotton. Pulling her sock free from her foot, she located the wound by touch without any trouble.

The small puncture had no tears radiating from it, and she used her fingernail to scrape the edges of it to make sure there was nothing still in her flesh. It felt free of foreign bodies, but true to the nature of punctures, was extremely sensitive, with what felt like just a little blood slicking her finger.

Jenny sat on the floor and retrieved her sock. As she worked it back onto her foot with care, she thought, *Whenever I step on something, it hits the tender arch area rather than the callused heel or ball.* Pressing lightly on the sole, she tested the sensitivity and winced, knowing she'd be walking with a slight limp to keep further pressure off.

A part of her was mad she had wounded herself. She knew the floor was earthen and she should have been more careful, but she'd already felt several rocks under her feet and wondered why this particular one had broken through.

She furrowed her brows. She was at step seventeen, diligently counting her paces to measure her prison, and she'd broken the bone way back at nine, so she didn't think a shard had gone this far. Relief passed through her like a chill. Jenny didn't want to imagine someone else's remains touching her. However, the comfort evaporated at once as she thought, *God knows what else could be lying around down here.* Jenny decided she had better find out what it had been for her own peace of mind, and felt the floor around her, looking for sharp objects.

Her hand stopped over a three-pronged item no bigger than a pushpin. She picked it up, rolled the pebble-sized lump between her fingers and let it fall into her open palm. She went over the surface with the fingertips of her other hand. It was hard. The left end was rounded and smooth, like surf-hammered glass. That, along with the clay, all but convinced her she must be close to the lake. Tapering toward the prongs, she felt it split into three pointed tips. Slight variations and bumps ran the length of each of them. Two ended in smooth tips, the other jagged abruptly and she almost cut herself on the edge.

The broken part was cleaner than the rest, bits of dirt clung to the moisture on it, and she decided it must have been the portion that went into her foot. Jenny raised it to her nose trying to detect blood on the end of it. As it neared her face, the size and shape of it became obvious in the back of her mind and flowed forward to her conscious thought like a ripple across an otherwise calm pond. She choked back a scream. Her hand stopped its ascent. Her body froze.

She let her mind wrap around the idea, tested the validity of her imagination, and swallowed what little saliva her mouth contained. It was a tooth.

In what felt like slow motion, Jenny put her index finger to her cheek, as her tongue followed along inside her mouth. She ran over the surface of her own tooth, feeling the texture and contours, and comparing it to the one still trapped in her immobile grasp.

"Oh God," she whimpered as her hand began to shake.

First the bone, now a tooth. Her imagination spun out of control. The gravel floor became graveyard dirt. The stone foundation transformed into a crypt. The moisture on the walls was blood. The blackness around her became hell and then darkened further at the edges of her vision. Fragments of memory exploded in her mind as she remembered the last tomb she'd been in—the ashes of her mother's house.

CHAPTER FOUR

Jenny had been at work, flipping burgers at a local fast-food restaurant, when the fire started. Between her junior and senior year, her summer job had allowed more than her meager allowance. Now that her mother was back on her feet, the part-time paycheck was hers to keep and it opened her world to movies with her friends, shopping sprees at the mall, and impulse purchase power at the bookstore. Now all it offered was guilt. If only she'd been home, Jenny could have saved some of their belongings, or her mother—something the neighbors hadn't managed to do.

The neighborhood.

Mrs. Sweeney, next door, was there throughout the fire, holding Jenny's shoulders and attempting to console and comfort her as they watched the firefighters drown what was left of her life.

Old man Sims stood curbside in the light of the blaze, watching her with solemn eyes and a strange smile. He never offered her a word of sympathy, but said plenty with his narrowed gazes. He'd always thought Jenny and her mother were trash, and while only one of them was dead, he knew both would be out of the neighborhood now. He tried to hide his satisfaction and smug approval, but it leaked out of his expression and poured off his presence until he finally turned and walked back into his house. Jenny was fairly certain he had been the one to start the rumors that traveled faster than the fire itself.

Dean and Glenn, twins a year younger than she was, and still in high school, sat on their porch across the street and watched. Their parents never came out of the house and Jenny wondered if they were even aware of the commotion. Either the boys hadn't bothered to tell them or their nightly drunk had kicked in early and they both lay unconscious in front of the television. Glenn proffered a weak smile of comfort from across the yards. Dean made a subtle motion with his hand, which she took to be a wave nearly as weak as his brother's smile. She acknowledged neither of them with her glazed-over eyes, puffed almost shut from the combination of tears and smoke. When the flames died down and she turned back toward them, they had vanished into the house.

The rest of the neighbors, and several from the surrounding streets, huddled in small circles and watched the activity as if entertained by the horror and drama in front of them. Jenny's life had become the archetypical car wreck everyone slowed down for, to get a better look. None of them made an effort to talk directly to her, though she overheard several whispered questions regarding her health, well-being, state of mind, and sleeping arrangements.

The police were busy keeping the circles of onlookers back and the paramedics waited patiently to run inside once the flames had died down. They had given her a cursory exam when they'd arrived and found her crumpled mass in the front yard. When they discerned it was shock and she hadn't in fact been in the house, they simply wrapped her with a blanket and offered her something to help calm down. She took the blanket, refused the medication, and they never said another word to her.

The firemen had attempted to go into the house after her mother twice, but the heat was too intense, the smoke too thick. When they arrived, the fire had already punched a hole into the roof to feed itself a never-ending supply of night air. It sustained its intensity, until the last bit of shingle, siding, and memories were changed forever.

As the first rays of dawn crept across the street behind her, the rushing sound of flames was finally silenced by the growl of gallons upon gallons of water. When they turned the hoses off, the ensuing hush seemed louder than the noises it had replaced. The scattered onlookers stopped whispering and quietly entered their homes, closing their doors on her turmoil. The birds returned to the trees in surrounding yards, but made no morning chatter as the paramedics exchanged places with the firefighters. Small crackling sounds, creaks and groans, and an occasional sputter echoed in the hollowed-out structure. Jenny's sobs seemed like screams in the predawn stillness.

The firemen had already left when the young police officer woke Jenny from her huddled position on the front lawn. She hadn't remembered closing her eyes, and assumed exhaustion had taken over and shut down her system for sanity's sake. He smiled politely and let her know the paramedics found her mother in the bedroom and had removed her from the premises. They would require her to identify the body at the morgue as soon as she could and he offered to give her a ride.

"What now?"

"Pardon me?" The young man's blue eyes were vibrant in the morning light, yet a hint of sadness rimmed them in worried, furrowed brows.

"What do I do? Where do I go? What next?"

"Ma'am, if you'll come with me, we can get the worst of it over with. We'll get you cleaned up, let the chief do his job, call your insurance company, and begin making arrangements for your mother. We have a psychologist on staff at the station if you'd like to speak with someone."

"Insurance?" Jenny's eyes swam into focus. "I don't even know if she had any. All of that would be in there, wouldn't it?" She raised an arm and gestured at the smoking remains behind him.

"First things first, ma'am. You're in shock and we need to get you downtown. Let me help you." He held out a hand to help her stand. "Are you sure you don't want to stop by the hospital and get checked out more thoroughly?" She shook her head and silently followed him to his squad car.

She didn't remember the car ride, the paperwork, or any of the people she spoke to that morning. She barely remembered the older man from the insurance company, and was too tired to think it odd when he said he'd seen it on the news and recognized the address as being his newest client.

She remembered the morgue.

Jenny smelled the burned flesh before they entered the room. The acrid scent burrowed into her nostrils and scratched its way down her throat. The metal door to the cold room was foreboding and she felt like an unwelcome guest, as her breath caught in her throat at the reality of it all. The small window in the center of the door was frosted, with crisscrossed wire mesh inside, to protect whom from what she didn't know, and didn't ask. She grabbed the doorknob and froze, wanting to run the other direction.

The officer put a gentle hand on her shoulder and said nothing. She counted her breaths and turned the knob at fifteen. He removed his hand as she pushed the door open with a deep exhaling sigh, and both entryway and girl made the same soft *whoosh* sound.

Small doors lined one whole wall—she'd seen enough television to know what they held and averted her eyes. Another wall held shelf upon shelf of chemicals and books, decorated with jars, which held items she'd rather not ask about. Formaldehyde-bleached flesh bounced lightly in yellowed fluid, some free floating, others pressed tightly to the glass in overcrowded displays. The opposite wall held a massive glass pane she imagined housed an observation room, but the blackness behind the window remained unlit, and the entire thing looked like a polished oil slick stuck on the wall. Her mother lay on a metal gurney in the center of the room.

A white cloth obscured the body, the edges of it alternately wet from the firefighters' efforts or browned by their failure. Ash adhered to the cloth, as if the house and contents were bound to the woman through some strange static cling. Jenny felt her throat tighten.

If either the coroner or officer spoke, she didn't remember it—she didn't even remember the coroner coming with them or being in the room, he just appeared at her side. In a surreal moment, a disembodied hand reached over and pulled the sheet down to expose her mother's head. The brown shoulder-length bob she had expected to see had been completely burned away, leaving a mottled, blackened scalp. She gasped and covered her mouth, willing herself not to vomit in front of them, in front of her mother.

Tears formed and fell from the corners of her clenched eyes, her mouth watered and she swallowed hard. Her hand shot out to grab the table for support without any thought and found purchase on her mother's cloth-covered arm. The tissue below the sheet was crunchy but malleable and gave under the pressure of Jenny's grasp. The damaged skin cracked and what liquids remained burst through the opening to soak the cloth and run onto the floor. Splashing against the cold tile and Jenny's shoes, the viscous liquids filled the room with a new scent altogether.

She felt herself going down when arms came from behind her to hold her up. They asked her something, she replied, and looked to her mother's face again.

The dirtied, blood-soaked head couldn't be her mother. It looked like a china doll someone had tortured and tossed away. The skin was blackened, blistered, and missing in some areas. A cheekbone was exposed, and the tips of her teeth below it peeked out from the ruined flesh around them. Their stark whiteness against the grime of fire and death seemed to shine at her in ironic contrast.

Her eyelids were gone. The melted orbs should have been round and bright but were murky and misshapen. Eyelashes and brows were completely singed away, and left a line of heat-swelled pores marking their existence. The fatty tissue of her nose had melted to the point it no longer looked like her nose at all. It was far too thin and the slight upturn at the end was now missing.

Jenny couldn't believe the husk in front of her was her mother. The pattern of moles on her jawline proved it was, but the roaring flames had even changed them—the skin around them was puckered and red, the brown marks barely perceptible within the leathery brown folds of skin. But they were there. The pattern was evident. The empty shell on the table was Kathy Hayes, her mother.

The rest of the morning, she gave statements, names and addresses for those the cops needed to notify, and doing paperwork she neither understood nor remembered caring about. A female officer brought her back to the house around three o'clock and asked if there were any items in particular she'd want to look for in the structure. The fire had charred much of the outside, but the damage to the inside had included support beams, floorboards, and foundation, and the officer believed the house would be declared condemned and dangerous. They probably wouldn't let her in it again, but the woman took pity and suggested a quick run-through.

She thanked the officer and shut the door of the squad car, expecting to hear it leave. As she turned toward the house, she heard the car turn off and understood the officer was going to wait or watch over her. Which course of action or explanation didn't matter, Jenny appreciated the gesture.

That had been over an hour ago. Jenny was frozen on the front lawn, unable to move, unwilling to walk inside. She hadn't seen Mrs. Sweeney yet and wondered if the woman chose to give Jenny room to react to the tumultuous emotions, or if the widow believed the whispers that had begun before the fire was out.

The joke in town was the fire department had never lost a basement. She didn't find it particularly amusing right now and wished her father were there to help. He wasn't. She was on her own, and she needed to finish this. She forced her right leg forward, and was pleasantly surprised when her left leg automatically followed.

Sifting through the remains of her childhood, Jenny located several charred photographs near the ash-covered caricature of the end table they once rested beneath. The faux wood of the small, single-drawer table had melted away and the beaverboard underneath had been consumed with little more than a whispered rebuttal. It was a cheap table, but it had been handed down from her grandmother when her parents were first together. That alone had meant something. Now, the value of the heirloom was lost, resigned to memory.

Looking around the living room, she could make out the burned carcass of the couch and armchair. Dirtied fluff, wet from the firefighters' hose, surrounded the spring intestines and skeletal frames. The corduroy skins were completely gone.

In the corner, the once overstuffed bookshelf was reduced to a pile. The dry material, eagerly consumed by flame, left nothing but featherlight ash dancing on air currents around the room. Jenny reached up to snatch one of the memories out of the air and it crumbled in her fingertips. She sunk to her knees in despair.

The scene became flashes of destruction. The partially melted remnants of her father's high school baseball trophies lined the soot-covered mantle above her. Her mother hadn't put the laundry away—her conclusion upon seeing melted carpet and splotches of oily pink plastic around a soggy pile of rainbow flecks. Through the doorway to the dining room, she could see the sturdy oak hutch her grandmother had passed down to her mother, promising it would someday go to her. The glass was alternately broken from the intense pressure of the conflagration's heat or melted into long weblike threads of silver that hung from the charred frame. Inside she saw gray, misshapen lumps that could only be the family silver her mother so dearly treasured, and she crossed another heirloom off her mental list.

Jenny stood and walked through the dining room without pausing. She didn't need to inspect the damage she knew the grandfather clock in the corner had sustained. A hand-quilted family tree hung on the wall next to it. In the kitchen, she found the appliances covered in black streaks as the fire-stopping water still dripped down their surfaces and made rivers through the layer of dark ash coating them. The cheap dinette set they had found at a garage sale stood relatively unharmed near the back door, and she felt a wet heat in her eyes at the irony of it. Nothing she cared about had survived. Everything she disliked would remain. Jenny pulled out one of the chairs and thought about sitting on the hard plastic surface but chose to finish what she'd started. Jenny pushed the ruined kitchen chair back and headed toward the door at the other end of the buckled linoleum.

She paused as she entered her mother's room. It was only recognizable by the peeling wallpaper with its maroon scrollwork that now looked like dried blood on the edge of a stained life. Open to the skies, the room smelled less like soot than the rest of the house. The flames had started here. After ravishing everything in the room, the intense flames had crawled up the walls and devoured the ceiling, insulation, and shingles in its hunger for oxygen and freedom.

The open air, however, had not cleansed the scent of burned flesh, and Jenny gagged.

Waterlogged and ransacked for clues, the room was more chaotic than the rest of the house and she wished once again her father had been here to help her deal with it all. In some areas the weight of her steps forced water to rush to the surface of the once light gray carpet, in others standing puddles held tidbits of her life in their ripples.

The oak dresser had burned well, providing excellent fuel for the fire, but was ancient and heavy enough to survive the blaze partially intact. Its blackened frame stood at an odd angle, three of the four legs underneath it were missing—reduced to stains on the carpet where they had once left weight indentions. Water droplets and random piles of sodden ash that were once jewelry boxes, trinkets, and magazines covered the surface of the dresser. At the far end, a patch of black leather with gold glinting from the edge of it marked where the family Bible had sat—the thin paper had burned along with the rest of the room.

A puddle of white plastic dappled with gray swirls was all that remained of the standing fan her mother insisted on running every night. The wall socket next to it was blacker than the rest of the walls and surrounded in a strange foamy substance. Jenny imagined they had used some forensic chemical on it to look for the fire's cause or starting point.

The empty windowpanes were pushed up. She presumed her mother had opened the window before going to bed. The curtains were nothing more than crisp tidbits of cloth, clinging to the splintered wood near the top of the window. The small indoor tree that had stood nearby had been reduced to a pile of black dirt surrounded by broken pottery.

The nightstand's charred remains made it impossible to guess what it had been if you didn't know what it should look like. Jenny couldn't identify any of the items in the pile of broken, shattered, and smoldering refuse. The bed frame next to it was empty.

The once-tall corner posts were now barely two feet high and looked like the scaled remains of a campfire log. Jenny imagined if you touched them, they would crumble and leave nothing but black charcoal residue on your hands, to tell you they had once existed. The mattress was gone, what remained was a skeletal statement of springs, water, and ash. Only the random sparkle from the glitter-filled texturing identified pieces of the ceiling that had broken off and settled into the frame. Most of it had burned there and floated in the currents of the flames, but some smaller waterlogged chunks lay amid the destruction.

Where the floor peeked through the debris, Jenny could see the carpet was gone, and the boards below it were blackened—some areas were completely burned away and exposed the subflooring. Something gleamed at her from next to the frame, lying among the broken and burned pieces of the bed and floor. She bent down to pick it up, but stopped as she got closer. It looked like a tooth.

It looked out of place and Jenny wondered if it was something else, some part of something in the room that wasn't apparent until you destroyed it with heat and water. She reached for it, convincing herself it was something else.

No, it was a tooth. A baby tooth from the size of it.

From what? Whom? There was no one in the house besides her and her mother. Neither babysat in the home. No relatives with children lived in town, had come to visit, or were present during the flames. Whose tooth?

She pushed broken pieces of bed frame, ceiling, and floor out of the way and jumped back in surprise. There were several teeth scattered among the debris. Her heart raced, the sound pounded in her head and felt like it was attempting to jump out of her chest. Her mouth went dry and her hands became slick with sweat. What was going on?

She crouched down to steady herself, covering her face with her hands as she thought. Jenny didn't know how long she remained like that, when her knees began to hurt and she removed her hands. She put a hand to the floor and used the other to brush ash and bits of charcoaled life around.

Near the tooth, she found a heat-bubbled photograph. She could no longer tell what or who had been in the picture and disregarded it. A flimsy misshapen square of ash had two black lines crisscrossing its surface. A curved piece of metal shined from a cooling lump of what was once blue plastic. And it dawned on her. The metal was her old retainer, its case melted but unmoved around it. The square was greeting cards with a thick cord tied around it. The teeth were hers.

Identifying the remains as her baby box made her sigh in relief and instantly cry at the weight of discovery. Tears ran down her face, as she realized the things she'd lost in the fire other than heirlooms. If her baby box was under her mother's bed, so was anything resembling a treasured history of either of her parents. She feared going into her own room to see the loss—the yearbooks would be gone, the photographs of and with friends, the various concert and movie ticket stubs, her life. Her childhood was now nothing more than her own memory, and no proof of its existence remained in the shell that was once her house.

She stood and left her mother's room, retracing her steps through the kitchen and dining room. Jenny didn't want to shuffle through the ash and charcoal of her bedroom. She couldn't do it. She wasn't strong enough. The walls threatened to close in on her, if not fall down around her. The air seemed too weak to sustain her. The death of life and memories surrounded her like a tomb, and she felt the air pressing in on her.

She rushed through the living room and pushed the door out of her way, barely registering the creaking and groaning of the damaged wood behind her. The open air greeted her as she stepped outside, leaving the graveyard of her past behind—unaware she still held her own baby teeth in a tightly clenched fist.

CHAPTER FIVE

Jenny rolled the tooth between her fingers as the smell of her mother's house and her acrid memory of the morgue faded. She subconsciously wiped her nose with the knuckle of her index finger and coughed lightly to clear her head of the ghostly fumes.

Not since the rubble of her mother's house had she felt the need to get out of somewhere so badly. Until now. She rocked absently a few times and wrapped her arms around her gathered legs, the tooth digging into the flesh of her palm, as she curled her hands into tight balls. She swallowed hard as she fought to keep control and took several jagged breaths, feeling the moisture build again behind her closed eyelids. She held the tears at bay and exhaled a final shuttering breath of memory.

The teeth she had found under her mother's bed had turned out to have a logical explanation, and she convinced herself the one in her hand would have one, too. She returned to thoughts of animals dragging remains into the lair—ignoring the jab of logic that reminded her there were no obvious entrances for wildlife. Yet. She pocketed the tooth and returned to the wall. She needed to finish inspecting her prison and find a way out, before animals found their way in—or her captor returned.

The oppression of nothingness and uncertainty allowed her mind to wander too freely, and she reined it in by force. She was afraid the blackness inside would swallow her, if she let herself delve too deeply. The depth of guilt and fear, the scars that bled easily if paid attention to, needed to remain buried. Now was not the time or place for reflection, but she recognized her mind's desire to return there again, and again.

Walking gently, taking care when putting pressure onto the rocky terrain in her stocking feet, she continued tracing the wall. At step thirty-two, she found another corner. The foundation hadn't changed drastically in any manner along the way, but at the corner the stones were far more weatherworn and decayed by age. Her hand found bare earth and she lightened her touch—not wanting a repeat of the bug incident and fearing something worse than insects could fall and add to her growing collection of skeletal remains.

The air in the corner seemed cooler, and she attributed the change to the missing foundation that must have worked as some sort of insulation. Something about this corner smelled different as well, musty. If the aroma of dust and mildew were bottled, that potpourri had been used here.

She felt as if she'd walked into the past, as she had with other scents familiar to her over the years. It always amazed her how you could smell something, and instantly remember an event or place you'd forgotten, like the old car your parents drove. This time it was Grandmother's cellar. It was rarely used, Nana only walking down to the shelf at the bottom of the stairs to either store or retrieve the jars of canned fruits and vegetables she kept there. In exploration, Jenny had gone down with a flashlight once and checked out the farthest regions of the underground lair. The darkness had been different. The smell had been the same.

Nana's basement was both a haven and hell for Jenny. Since no one used it and she had no fear of its deep corners, it became hers and hers alone. There was a forgotten pile of boards and logs in the corner—left over from the old woodburning furnace of her mother's childhood—a small folding card table, a few old trunks of hand-me-down memories, and a long-forgotten workbench. Nana had given her a hammer and nails and a few blankets and smiled when Jenny said she was making a fort in the basement. She nailed one of the threadbare throws to the workbench, creating a curtain she could hide behind—her cubby. She dragged books and toys down and kept them off the floor by using pieces of the abandoned wood as makeshift shelving inside her private space. She hammered larger pieces together and made a stool she used at the card table for drawing. She was never bored at Nana's house. She had her special place and imagination to keep her busy. She was content in the darkness there, happy in the dust-filled den—unless she was behind the woodpile.

Jenny's parents were in a class all to themselves when it came to their fights. She could hear them late at night, starting with low murmuring and exploding into what sounded like nothing short of death threats. Her father was always quick to apologize the next morning if they disturbed her with their *heated conversations,* but her mother never said anything. She'd hide her red-rimmed eyes behind a book on the couch and go silent for a day or two. The few times it got real bad, Jenny had been old enough to understand the existence of danger, but not old enough to comprehend what or why. Her mother swept Jenny from her bed in the middle of the night on those occasions and went to Nana's house. They slipped in the back door without making noise, yet Nana still somehow knew they were coming and was always waiting up for them. She'd tuck Jenny into bed and return to the kitchen where the two women would talk until dawn. Nana was great about not apologizing for anything the next day and making her famous Mickey Mouse pancakes as if nothing had happened.

On more than one of those nights, Jenny's father had shown up at Nana's to *fetch* them. The battle that had started at home would continue as it moved through Nana's little house, shaking the walls and Jenny's heartbeat in tandem with its intensity. Her father never arrived immediately after they did, and from the look on his face and lingering smell of his clothes, he'd stopped by a bar somewhere along the way for confidence. Jenny would listen as they neared the spare room she lay in, tucked back into bed and presumed asleep for the night. One fateful night, Nana had snuck in and told her to run down to the basement and hide. The fear in Nana's eyes scared Jenny far more than the woman's tone.

Once downstairs, she froze. She couldn't hide in her fort. It was too obvious and whoever was going to look for her would search there first, and she didn't want to be found. She didn't want to understand the meaning of that look in Nana's eyes. She looked around and ran from corner to corner, before she finally hid behind the woodpile—hunkered down, knees pulled up tight—and tried to stay awake through the exhaustion of confusion. She didn't remember much about that first night, but hid with the spiders and dust mites in the split wood every subsequent time her father came to retrieve her mother after that first time.

Yes, the darkness here was different, but the smell was the same—confusion, permeated with a fear of the unknown.

Turning to her right, she continued along, expecting the

expanse to be rectangular. Instead, she found another corner almost immediately—or rather a wall—as she stubbed her fingers on it in and avoided walking into it face-first.

Warmer than the earth and stone, the surface in front of her was rough, with steady ridges and small dots of ice. *Wood,* she thought. The cold spots were logically the heads of nails trailing down the stud. More modern than the rock foundation, the fabricated wall jutted back out toward the center of the room. She turned to follow it, excited to have found something new and hoping for stairs to be at the other end of it.

The end turned sharply in only a few steps and she turned with it. Her hands roamed the entire length of it, from the floor to as far as her arms would reach above her head. It was solid—she found no windows, openings, seams, knobs, or hinges. Jenny turned her back to it and kicked it with her heel to check the thickness. The noise resounded in the darkness and sounded thick, but she had felt give in the wood.

The front of the structure was barely wider than her arm span and she followed the next turn, finding open space rather than another length of wood. Excited, she entered the small cubicle and traced the interior of the two sides she had followed. At the end of the second wall, she found rock and earth again and her heart sunk. She leaned against the foundation with her back and slid toward the floor, mimicking her hope. She stopped in a squat rather than sitting completely down and rested, thinking about the small room jutting off the larger one.

There were no shelves inside it for storage. There was no window or doorway, only an open side. The floor felt different and she ran her uninjured foot in a sweeping arc in front of her. No rocks. This was smooth dirt. Poured onto the earthen floor or raked, she couldn't be sure without touching it.

Jenny bent down and picked up a handful of dirt, sifting it through her fingers. It was tiny uniform granules, softer than the other dirt. Sand? It had to be. She absently ran her fingers over the surface of it, doodling designs that meant nothing, as she pondered the meaning. Was there a meaning?

She stopped. Her hand had found nothing new, no more bones or teeth, thank God, but something stopped her. At the edge of her consciousness something was begging her to pay attention.

It was sand, in a cubby tucked into a cellar. An unfinished room perhaps? She dug a little deeper, and found more sand. After further excavation, she found nothing beyond misplaced beach. She looked up into the black of the little room, trying to figure out what the point to the room had been, envisioning the layout she'd mapped so far. Nothing. She rubbed the back of her hand across her nose and stopped, fully aware of what the little voice in her head had recognized before she did.

Ammonia. Urine? Sand and urine made her think of kitty litter, but there were no other signs of a cat anywhere. The scent was faint, old—almost stale—and Jenny wished she had a stick or something to dig around in it. She didn't. Even though she knew the smell, she burrowed in to investigate and confirm her fears. At no place was the ground wet, or even slightly moist. There were no lumps for unpleasant musings. An animal getting into the subterranean room wouldn't be tame enough to use a secluded section for a toilet, but the smell was unmistakable.

She stood and reached above her, hoping for a dropped ceiling or light cord, and found nothing. Jenny kicked at the sand—there were no answers, only more questions. Wiping her hands on the back of her jeans, she continued to follow the stone foundation out of the nook and across the expanse of her prison.

The wall appeared to go on forever. Unlike the first one, this side was missing none of the stones along the way, had no soft spots she could feel, but the floor was uneven. Jenny hadn't noticed it right away, but as the mental exhaustion began to take aggressive control of her physical being, she stumbled a few times until it dawned on her she was going uphill. At fifty-four steps, she felt the decline in the slope of the ground beneath her feet, almost falling when she misjudged where to step because she thought she was continuing uphill.

Jenny stopped, wondering if the mound was a true high point, and decided to rest her injured foot. As long as she actively moved or thought about something else, it didn't hurt, but now she'd stopped. Pain throbbed up her calf, pulsing with each step, and she was convinced her heart was no longer where it belonged.

She turned toward the wall and reached above her head, again feeling for the ceiling. Her hands crawled slowly over the stone and mortar. Her breath bounced back into her face off the hard surface mere inches in front of her.

Nothing.

As far as she could tell, the walls were fifty feet high. Jenny crumpled to the ground, and her breath became punctuated.

"Where am I?" She screamed into the endless air above her. Her arms began to tingle with the heat of anger. She felt it move through her system, running along her veins and muscles until it reached her clenched jaw.

Again, she looked to her watch and rolled her eyes at the stupidity of her actions. She didn't care what time it was. She was more interested in how long she'd been there. Without vision to aid her, her other senses were desperately trying to take over, but the lack of any type of measurement for duration was suddenly driving her crazier than the darkness itself.

She thought about everything she had done so far, tried to guess how long she'd been conscious. Her anger abated, her frustration melted, and she found the adrenaline's absence made her very tired. She was sore, hungry, and scared. *There,* she thought, *I've admitted it. I'm scared.*

Exhaustion took her before she consciously relinquished control. She rested against the wall and pulled her knees up to her chest. Wrapping her arms around her legs, she leaned her head forward.

"I'll rest for a moment. Just a moment."

CHAPTER SIX

Jenny jerked her head upward as footsteps echoed lightly to her left. A small speck of white bounced along in a steady path toward her. A person. A flashlight. She opened her mouth to cry in relief, but felt the restraint against it.

She moved to raise her hand and feel her mouth but found her arms would not move. Tied underneath her still-bent legs, she could feel the rope digging into her wrists. Jenny tested her legs and found her ankles were also bound. Returning her attention to her mouth, she moved her cheeks and lips around in various directions. She could feel the stickiness at the corners of her mouth and tasted the bland material with the tip of her tongue. It had to be tape. As cliché as it was, she was sure it was duct tape.

A new kind of fear crept into her imagination. She watched the dot of light elongate into a clearly visible beam as it approached her. The footsteps grew closer, louder. She could see nothing beyond the flashlight. The person holding it was impossibly darker than the blackness around her. She felt a tear roll down her face.

"Good morning, sunshine." The disembodied voice was gravelly but not deep, a tenor at best. The light, though still aimed at the ground, moved down to her eye level as the man holding it squatted down in front of her. "How'd you sleep?" A hint of sarcasm drifted in the air.

She tried to talk behind the tape. She pleaded with her eyes, hoping they looked inquisitive and complacent rather than terrified and beaten. She nodded toward her hands while she asked to be untied. Her pleas sounded like muffled baby talk and made no sense to her own ears, so she had little hope he would understand.

"Just a little longer and my brother will be back." A dirty hand reached out to touch her face and she turned away from it instinctively. "Hey, I won't hurt you." His voice sounded wounded, and she turned back to plead through the tape some more.

"You want me to untie you, huh? They all do. I can't. Believe me, I wish I could, but Ryan would kill me first and then play with you, and I wouldn't be able to watch."

What? She thought. Did she hear him correctly? Kill? Play? Ryan? She looked between the flashlight and the blackness beyond it. She tried to think of all the people she knew named Ryan, and tried to appear relaxed so he would keep talking. Perhaps she could get a clue as to what was going on if he kept talking.

The only Ryans she could think of were a cousin she hadn't seen since the last family reunion, an old friend from high school she hadn't heard from since graduation, and the two-date fling she'd had in college with a jock who'd adored himself more than he'd ever be capable of loving anyone else. None of them was the type to have tied her up in a cellar. Nor did any of them have reason to.

"Ryan said if I take care of you, he'll reward me." The voice sounded youthful, almost boyish in its delight. "I broke the last one before I could really play and I don't want to do that this time."

A dirty hand shushed her muffled pleas, as he applied pressure to her tape-covered mouth. She winced in disgust and fear.

"Shhh." His tattered, filthy fingernails picked at the edge of the tape. "If I pull the tape off, do you promise not to scream?"

Jenny nodded furiously, assuring him through garbled excitement and hope. He pulled back the tape, tearing skin and fine hairs from her face, and left it to hang off one side. She inhaled deeply.

"Thank you." She breathed in shallow breaths, tasting freedom in tiny bursts. The air smelled different now—rot and body odor mixed with kerosene or gasoline. Jenny feared the new smell was her visitor.

"Now, be a good girl so I can feed you." The hands disappeared and reappeared with a rough-cut bowl and wooden spoon.

Her brows furrowed. "But I'm not hungry," she lied, fearful of what might be in the container.

"No. I have to take care of you. You have to eat. You can't starve like the other one did."

"Other one?" She whispered, more to herself than her jailer.

"Theresa. She wouldn't eat either, but I'm not supposed to talk about that. I'm not supposed to talk about any of them." He lifted the spoon and brought it toward her face in a weaving manner, as if he were playfully feeding an infant in a well-lit kitchen, rather than force-feeding a captured victim. Across the length of spoon, she could barely make out the thick piece of shadow, and moved her head around trying to get a good look at it.

"What is it?" She feared the answer but asked to stall the feeding.

"Ryan says its protein." He moved his arm to the right as his airplane spoon approached the runway of her mouth and the beam of the flashlight lit up the partial finger cradled within the spoon in front of her.

She screamed and jerked her head back, slamming it against the wall behind her and stunning herself out of sleep. Scampering into a tight ball, she looked around her. No flashlight, no person, no body parts being shoveled into her mouth. She'd been dreaming. She released the breath she'd been holding upon waking and a shudder ran through her body as she heard a beep off to the right.

"Thank God," she said softly and listened to the darkness, trying to decide if the sound were left over from the dream or real. Her heart pounded in the resilient silence.

"It was just a dream. A nightmare," Jenny said aloud, as if she needed to hear the words, not just think them. "Nightmares aren't real. There is no madman lurking in the darkness out there somewhere—"

She couldn't finish the sentence. She didn't believe it enough to fool herself.

Instead, she stood straight up and put her hand against the wall, acclimating herself to the direction she was heading before her nap. It was time to get out of here, before dreams became reality.

She traveled to the end of the wall, seventeen steps from where she had rested, and felt cold in front of her. At first, she thought it was just a stone that was colder than the rest, but further exploration with her hands revealed a horizontal bar of metal on the wall.

A little over a foot wide, and as big around as a relay baton, the iron bar curved at both ends toward the wall. There was a three-inch gap between the wall and the bar. The ends of the rod flattened out and she felt the bolt that held it to the wall. It reminded her of a ladder rung and she reached above it optimistically looking for a second one.

"Yes!" Her hands found two more above her head and escape

began to solidify in her mind. She pulled against the bar to test its anchor. The bottom rung held tightly with all her weight on it and she smiled.

Finding a large stone at knee level to use as a step, she pulled herself up over the rung. Jenny pushed her arms straight, locking her elbows, and leaned her waist on the bar. Pulling her knee up to the bar, she climbed up and reached for the next one. With both her knees on the first one, the ascent became easier and she felt her heart race as she climbed.

Reaching above her to the fourth rung she stood on the second, imagining the air was cleaner the closer to freedom she climbed. Jubilation began to run through her. Even the nasty grit on her teeth seemed to vanish in the light of renewed hope.

Jenny felt small bits of dirt hit her face moments before the bar came free in her hands.

Her left hand, wrapped around the third rung, tightened its grip without provocation and her legs tensed, toes gripping the chilled bar beneath them. Her right arm wavered in the air and she looked in the general direction of it, holding the loose bar. Disgust rather than disappointment overwhelmed her and she dropped the useless metal to the ground. She heard the soft thud as it hit the dirt several feet below her.

Jenny reached higher, blindly searching for the next bar. On her tiptoes, she felt the bare edge of it brush her fingertips. Gripping the third rung tightly, she pulled her knees up to the second one and reached again. Balancing precariously, she was not prepared for the bar in her hands to give with the extra weight and she let out a gasp as the bolts came free. Rock and dirt fell into her eyes, and she found herself falling backward.

Landing flat on her back, Jenny felt the air slam out of her chest. She felt the previously tossed metal bar push its way into her shoulder blade. The rough terrain slid against her neck and head. A helpless gasp escaped as she lost consciousness.

CHAPTER SEVEN

Jenny opened her eyes to the bright light, blinked in confusion and closed them again. The sounds of the room swirled together—the soft tread of rubber soles on a tile floor and various machines humming, buzzing, and beeping intermittently—and slowly formed into recognition. Remembering why she was there in the first place, her eyes flew open. Squinting through the haze of drugs and pain, she looked around the room for Dan, or the bassinette.

She found Dan.

Slumped in the chair next to the bed, his chin resting on his chest, he slept. His lack of facial expressions made her believe he wasn't dreaming, and she imagined he had passed out from sheer exhaustion. She looked again for the bassinette and didn't see it. A hand ran absently over her midsection. Her stomach was tender to the touch and she wondered if that was normal. She wanted answers but had no one to ask.

She glanced at the clock. Seven fifteen. Judging by the shadows seeping under the window, she guessed evening rather than morning.

They had arrived at eleven o'clock in the evening and the shock that a whole day was gone showed on her face. She still wanted answers, still wondered where the baby was.

She looked to Dan again, this time noticing the sweat-drenched hair at his temples. She didn't think the room felt warm—perhaps he was dreaming after all. She laid her head back and watched him for a few moments, her hand resting on her empty womb. Her eyelids fluttered briefly and she returned to her drug-induced slumber.

The bright lights greeted Jenny again when she opened her eyes to the sound of a baby crying and snapped to hopeful awareness. Another maternity patient had been moved into her room, and the other woman's newborn wailed for attention and warmth. Jenny thought it was rude to put a new mother with someone who had lost a child. Anger attempted to flare in her mind, but her heart ached in sorrow and extinguished it. She wanted answers and was prepared to wake Dan to get them this time. She turned to jostle him and found him gone.

"I'm sorry, did I wake you?" The other woman's voice sounded tired and betrayed her gleefully energetic expression and behavior.

"Don't worry about it. I'm sure I've slept long enough." She turned over to her right side and stared at the shades blocking the window. The movement hurt her stomach and she winced, refusing to turn back toward the mother and child to find a more comfortable position.

The door to the room opened and Jenny watched over her shoulder as a pale young nurse strode into the room as if making a grand appearance at a social gathering. She smiled and nodded at the other woman, who wished her a good evening, and then looked to Jenny with surprise.

"Oh, you're finally awake. I'll go get the baby."

The simple phrase left Jenny breathless. She had assumed everything had gone wrong. She'd been convinced the worst possible outcome had indeed happened. She was happy to hear it hadn't.

Within moments of the nurse leaving, Dan walked into the room, Styrofoam coffee cup in one hand and a granola bar in the other.

"Jen, you're awake." He rushed to her side, casually tossing the snack on the rolling tray next to her bed. "I was starting to think you'd gone comatose on us." He smiled coyly at his own long-running joke about her hard sleeping habits. She didn't return the smile.

"What happened? How long was I asleep?" She lifted a cheek to meet his kiss, rather than her mouth, as she continued to question. "Where's the baby? Is everything all right?"

"Calm down. Everything's fine." He sat in the chair and scooted it closer to the bed.

"But…"

"Shhh, it's okay." He pushed Jenny's hair away from her face. "Alan is fine. The nurse should be bringing him in any minute."

"Alan?"

"Yes." He furrowed his brows at her. "I thought we had decided on Alan for a boy and Andrea for a girl?" He tilted his head quizzically.

"No. God, no. That was the name I *didn't* want. I said, anything *but* Alan." Her eyes filled with panic and her breathing skipped. "Is it too late to change it?"

"Well, it's been four days. It's on the birth certificate and already been announced in the paper."

"Four days?" Her eyes widened in disbelief and Jenny looked at the clock again as if it were a calendar. "How… how is that possible?"

"Don't you remember?"

"Remember what?" She raised her voice, but Dan silenced her with a hand on her arm and a look toward the other mother in the room. He stood and walked around her bed. He pulled the separating curtain between the beds and mouthed an apology to the other woman, before returning to his chair.

"We came in on Tuesday night. Remember that?"

"Yes. We were watching *Castaway* when the pain started."

"Yes." He nodded and his voice became condescending. "When we arrived, you thought your water had broken, but it was blood. Remember?"

"Yes, yes." Her impatience wasn't going to be quelled with another gentle pat on the arm. Jenny wanted details, and she wanted them faster than he was providing them. "I got into the hospital gown. They put monitors on my stomach and a blood-pressure cuff on my arm. They jabbed me in the top of my hand and began some sort of drip. They called the doctor, and the anesthesiologist gave me an epidural."

"And?" He raised his eyebrows and waited for her response.

Jenny was silent. She remembered the staff rushing around the room getting her ready for labor. She remembered the pain of the needle in her spine. She remembered… waking up.

"What happened? I don't remember anything after that."

"You reacted to the morphine in the drip." His hand returned to her arm. "Your eyes started watering and jumping around. You looked scared, but you didn't speak. I guess you couldn't." He paused, obviously upset as he relayed the information. "You weren't acknowledging anyone or anything. You weren't moving. I thought you passed out, but your eyes never stopped moving."

"Oh God!" She leaned her head against the pillow and closed her eyes for a moment. "I remember that. I could hear you, all of you. I could hear you clearly. And I think… Did you shake my shoulders and yell at me?"

Dan nodded.

"An alarm went off somewhere. I remember wanting to turn my head to the noise. I remember a doctor coming in, but not Dr. Hammond. What happened?"

"The alarm was the baby's heart rate monitor. Seems he was having an allergic reaction to the morphine as well." He stopped and stared at her a moment.

"You died, Jen." He looked away from her. "You died on the table and the medical staff flew into action, pushing me out into the hall."

"But the baby…"

"They had two teams going from what I've been told. They brought you back, but you were completely relying on a respirator for your breathing while they did an emergency C section to get him out."

"Was he..?"

"No. Far as they can tell, his heart rate plummeted but never stopped. His ap-thing test…"

"APGAR," she interjected

"…was a four when they got him to the table. They injected something to counteract the morphine in his system and his ten-minute test was a ten. He seemed fine. He was fine. He's been fine ever since."

Jenny swallowed. Relief closed her throat and questions filled her mind. Dan answered them without her asking.

"The stuff didn't work on you. They kept you hooked up to all kinds of machines for almost forty-eight hours waiting for the stuff to get out of your system. They had two different IV's going, and said very little to me other than they were monitoring you."

"God…" Her brush with death seemed surreal and she shook her head in disbelief.

"Beth sat here with you for hours at a time. She went home for a shower right before you came around on Saturday afternoon, briefly, and they unhooked most of the machines. You woke up again that night and held Alan for a few moments, before passing out again."

"I did? I held him?"

Dan smiled. "Yes, Jen. You held him and smiled and cried. You looked very much like any new mother we've ever seen in the movies."

"I don't remember that." She looked down, saddened at the loss of her first moments with her son. "Is he perfect?"

"Absolutely. Ten fingers, ten toes, and lungs to make a banshee jealous." He grinned. "Jen?" His grin faded.

"Yeah?"

"You can't have more." The matter-of-fact statement took her by surprise.

"What?"

"Due to the emergency situation, they were more concerned with getting him out and getting you breathing again. There was damage to your uterus in the chaos. They don't think you can carry another baby to term."

Jenny felt her heart sink. They had always wanted three children. It had been the first thing they'd agreed upon wholeheartedly, when their relationship had grown serious enough to discuss marriage and family.

"They're not even sure if you can even keep your uterus in its current condition." His voice was barely above a whisper as he broke the news to her, and she wondered why he was telling her instead of letting the doctor do it. "They may have to remove it."

She gasped. Removal meant no chances, ever. A hysterectomy was the extinction of hope. They'd always joked about how lovely twins would be since it ran in both families. They were going to have just one.

Or rather, *she* was.

She squinted one eye, and raised the corner of her mouth in a curious gesture, as she turned to look at Dan. He had said, *you* can't have anymore, not *we*. She felt something break in her heart, as if emotion had a physical location within her chest. Why had he said it like that? Why lay blame or fault by wording it that way?

"I'm sorry, Jen." He reached for her cheek, but she flinched at his touch.

She didn't want to be consoled. She didn't want to be lulled into acceptance. She wanted more children. *They* had wanted more children. *She* would have only one—a boy. A boy that almost died being born, but who in turned killed a piece of her in his effort to escape. A boy whose first moments she couldn't remember. A boy named while she was unconscious.

A boy named after the one man in her life that she wanted dead so badly, she had killed him herself.

CHAPTER EIGHT

She lay with her eyes closed on the dirt floor, awake but thinking. The dream—or memory or whatever it was—had reminded her of her reaction to the morphine. Like now, she'd had a memory lapse then. Could someone have given her enough morphine to lose her memory but not have a physical reaction? Or *had* she gone into full shutdown, and was missing more time than she thought? Pain interrupted her thought, and she realized it was real, not some strange residue.

Jenny moaned softly as she took mental inventory of her body's latest damage. Her back hurt and she twisted, trying to adjust to a more comfortable position. The back of her head felt like she'd been hit with a wet two by four and she reached up, checking for damage. The movement sent an ache through her shoulder blade.

The blood from the previous injury on her scalp had resumed its trickling, and she remembered smacking it against the earth when she fell. Not a lot of blood, but enough to cover her hand in a thin coat and make her wonder how long she'd been out *this time*. To the left of the wound, she found a tender goose egg caused by the fist-sized rock under her head. Her neck was stiff but felt free of actual injuries. She lifted her head and cranked her neck around, trying to get it to crack while she stretched the muscles.

Her left elbow had an abrasion and what felt like the beginning of a large bruise. Her hips were intact but sore. Her knee and foot still hurt, but the pain in her head and back overshadowed it. Her leg felt like a dull, nondescript throbbing in comparison. She pushed herself to a sitting position. Her stomach growled.

Without any type of watch or clock, shadows, sunlight, or other marker to judge by, she had no idea how long she'd been in the dark. More than a grumble, this ache was reminiscent of the crash diet she'd attempted after Christmas the previous year. It felt like the cramping from New Year's Eve—day three and eight skipped meals. She'd looked amazing in the blue sequined dress but was tired, had no energy to dance, and rung in the new year by regurgitating stomach acid through her nose. She was never a fan of vomit, but bitter, foodless nostril juice was worse than any flu or food poisoning.

She checked her saliva. It wasn't running free, but her mouth had more moisture than it had upon her initial waking. Morning-breath slime still coated her teeth, tenfold from the feel of it, and she made a face at the disgusting taste that came with it. Jenny rubbed her finger across her teeth in an attempt to dry-brush them, but her efforts went unrewarded and she only managed to scrape her gums and wipe dust and dirt into the tiny spaces between her front teeth. She licked her teeth the best she could with her parched tongue and spit into the dirt beside her, as her stomach protested its emptiness yet again. She ignored the hunger and concentrated on the thirst that began to supersede pain in her body's alarm system.

She felt around for a small rock and brushed it off on her shirt. She spit on the marble-sized stone and cleaned it off the best she could before popping it in her mouth. It was an old wives' tale, she was sure of it, but her grandmother had always said if you sucked on a pebble, you could satisfy thirst for a while. Of course, it wasn't a five-course meal and did nothing for the hunger, but she figured what the hell, and gave it a try against the dehydrated lump her tongue had started to become.

Beyond the hunger, thirst, and pain, her bladder hinted, with some urgency, it would explode soon. No food or water since her last remembered meal caused her rational mind to wonder if the urge was laced in fear. She felt no wetness in her pants from any subconscious release and relinquished logic for instinct. *She had to pee.* She stood up and thought about the ladder she'd fallen from. If escape was that direction, then she wouldn't have to humiliate herself and urinate in the dirt. She felt the wall for the first rung and resumed her climb.

As she returned to the place she'd been when she fell, she realized the two missing bars made it impossible to go any farther. She couldn't reach high enough to grab the next one, if there was one. Jenny wrapped her arm through the bar she was on and clung there, thinking.

She fought the wail of frustration building in her throat and tried not to think of her cramping bladder. She could get no higher going this route and nothing on the ground had provided any indication of an exit. The smell of the area was musty enough she couldn't imagine it had been opened up to fresh air often, but still believed an escape hatch of sorts was above her—it had to be. An old cellar door set into a floor would have a ladder like this, if not steps. She had to get up there, somehow.

The wall. The foundation was uneven, with larger rocks and holes where damaged mortar had fallen out, and Jenny wondered if she couldn't climb the wall itself.

Feeling around from her vantage point on the ladder, she found no nooks or crannies that would work for her burrowing fingers and grappling toes. She lowered herself to the floor and searched the areas to either side of the ladder.

Without warning, she doubled over in pain. Spasms shot through her stomach and her insides felt like they'd twisted inside out. She moaned as she acknowledged her bladder would not wait until she climbed the wall. She felt a few drops of warm urine soak into her underwear and embarrassment washed through her.

Jenny clicked the rock in her mouth against her teeth and looked around in the dark, contemplating her options and the inevitable decision. She headed back toward the unfinished room, reasoning that it already smelled of urine and, as far as she could tell, the stench seemed to stay in there.

The uneven terrain wasn't as difficult this time, and she grinned. While it was easier to navigate an area she'd already covered in the dark, it nonetheless took longer than she anticipated. It almost seemed to take longer than it should, and her bladder reminded her again of its urgency. The cramping caused her to bend down and she briefly thought of crossing her legs and hopping the rest of the way like a child with no bladder control.

Jenny's arm, dragging along the wall beside her for guidance, did nothing to warn her when she had indeed entered the cubby, and she walked face-first into the plyboard of the other end.

"Damn." She huffed and quickly undid her pants.

As she relieved herself, she rested one hand against the wood for balance. With the other, she rubbed her now-tender nose. "I'm going to look like a battered wife when I get out of here."

Still positive enough to both think and talk of freedom, she smiled but just as quickly shook her head, and wondered if she should worry she'd begun talking to herself. She passed it off as necessary under the circumstances and rationalized it, believing it helped her sanity to hear something. Anything. After all, she'd been talking to Beth for months, and considering her friend was dead, that meant she had been talking to herself for quite a while.

She seemed to urinate for a long time and wished there was toilet paper handy. Jenny had never been a campsy-woodsy kind of girl and preferred porcelain to pine, sheets to sleeping bags. She remembered the few times she'd tried camping. None of them had gone well, and on their last trip to the national forest, Jenny must have seemed ridiculous to Dan.

She had refused to touch the leeches he'd gotten as fishing bait, her phobia ignoring the logic of using the needle-nose pliers from his tackle box. Of course, even with him baiting the hook, she still complained the entire time because of the proximity of the leeches, and didn't understand his constant scolding to be quiet in the boat. On shore, she whined about the stench of the campground outhouse, whether needing to use it, or even looking in the direction of the small bright green shed. She remembered quite well how his voice slowly transformed over the weekend, from calm and instructional to tired and fed up. In hindsight, she didn't blame him one bit for packing up and leaving a day earlier than they had planned. Rain had soaked their tent, the clothes and towels on the line outside, and dampened their already teetering spirits. After hours of her incessant pleading to build the fire bigger because she was cold, he just gave up.

As she urinated, the smell, although not nearly as foul as the fecal-filled pit of the campsite, reminded her of that trip with a strange fondness, rather than the loathing it had actually been.

She couldn't see the stream pooling in the sand below her. She didn't realize she wasn't squatting correctly, or know enough to take into account the cold floor wouldn't absorb the liquid as quickly as it spilled. She jumped when the trickle of piss reached her sock.

"Crap!" She had sidestepped directly into the stream and her foot was now soaking wet with her own warmth. She winced, wiggled her bottom a few times to shake free any droplets, and stood to fasten her jeans. Jenny rubbed her wet sock in the sand behind her, hoping to wipe it off or rub it dry. It did neither, and her foot remained wet, though the urine on it was cooling rapidly in the tepid air.

She reached over to remove her sock and paused, thinking twice about it. She might need that little bit of protection on her feet. She nodded to herself, aware her weight was on her injured foot, and decided to keep the sock. She would just have to try to ignore the smell.

Making her way out of the little room yet again, she found with the urgency of her bladder satisfied, she could limp at a more normal pace. The return trip to the broken ladder took much less time.

Jenny resumed scanning the walls near the metal rungs, ignoring the sand-encrusted sock the best she could. The left side had bigger rocks she could use as steps, while the right had more spaces for handholds. She decided to try the right, relying on the strength in her hands rather than the sturdiness of her feet, taking into consideration the area around the puncture wound had started to throb again and the other was damp and would be slippery.

Finding two large rocks above her head, she grabbed the tops with her fingertips and felt around the base of the wall with her toes, looking for stones to step on. She found an opening her foot fit into perfectly and was ready to go. She took several deep breaths, more for confidence than oxygen, and began her first attempt at rock climbing—promising, if this worked, she would take an actual class when she got out.

With each movement of hand or foot, Jenny reached over toward the ladder to gauge how high she was. She felt where the missing rung was, then the loose rung, and then nothing above it. She wondered if the rungs hadn't been for some other use besides climbing. *But what?*

Twice her hands lost their grip and once her foot slipped off a rock, but the memory of her previous failure and subsequent landing made Jenny scramble to keep her balance and precarious hold.

She was high enough that she rested her foot on the last rung. She slowed her pace, afraid a fall from this height would render her more than unconscious. She reached up, searching for the next handhold, and found a corner. The ceiling. Jenny was stunned it existed at all, guessing she had to be well over ten feet in the air. She'd started to believe she was in a walled cavern of some sort. *What basement had ceilings this high?*

She felt around, her hand roaming from uneven rock foundation to smooth, cool stone. Cement? A poured floor above her? It didn't feel like wood or tile. It didn't feel like anything other than a slab of concrete. Which meant there had to be support beams or other leveling structures somewhere in the darkness. She knocked on it, but it didn't seem to tell her anything. It could be three inches thick—or three feet. The cold slate gave off no resonance and told her nothing, other than you shouldn't rap your knuckles on concrete.

She searched for bigger rocks and sturdier handholds around her, wanting to secure her position before she explored the discovery any further. Digging into the aged mortar above the rocks, she forced her toes into the wall and gripped them to the point of cramping while balancing her heels on the rocks themselves.

Reaching above her again, firmly gripping the uneven rock she clung to with her left hand, she let her right hand explore the edge where foundation met cement. Jenny could feel an uneven line with a rougher texture along the seam and presumed it had some sort of sealant along the top to prevent water and frost from seeping in. Wherever she was, the owner was conscientious about keeping the basement dry.

Feeling outward, toward the center of the room, Jenny closed her eyes and felt every little bump, nick, and crack in the concrete. She reached behind her as far as she could in a straight line out from the wall, then moved her arm a bit over and repeated the process back to the wall in front of her. Following a grid in her mind, Jenny covered what she could reach in both directions from her perch. Nothing. She inched her way across the wall to the left of her, stopping above the useless ladder and repeating the process. The point of the ladder was lost on her and Jenny moved past it, wondering if perhaps it had led up to a drop-down staircase to the side of it. After a thorough search of the area, she gritted her teeth and admitted defeat. Her toes ached. Her fingers had become tender from gripping and scraping across rock, mortar, and cement.

She had hoped to find a hatch. Had thought there would at least be evidence of one—perhaps a seam where a doorway had once been but was now sealed. She found nothing. Escape, if it existed, was back down on the dirt floor somewhere.

CHAPTER NINE

Jenny was surprised at the strength it took to climb back down the wall without falling, and greeted the rocky terrain below her feet with a heavy sigh. She sat on the ground, leaned against the foundation, and closed her eyes. She was feeling physically exhausted and mentally hammered. Of the two, her state of mind worried her more.

Two days, she thought. At a minimum, accounting for her nap and unexpected downtime when she had lost consciousness after her fall, she had been here for at least two days. She was most likely unconscious for the first full day, from whatever drug had been used in the parking lot. Her stomach grumbled, but the hunger pains weren't severe enough to indicate anything more than forty-eight hours, sixty at most. The rock in her mouth had become a foul lump with no taste and less purpose. Her body began to protest muscle by muscle at the exertion and strain she had caused it since waking up.

Her weaknesses welled.

Jenny tried to push them back into the darkness around her. She played mind games with herself—trying to convince her conscious mind she had no fears, no weaknesses. Her memories fought her the entire way, reminding her of all the times when she was weak or afraid. Flashes of memories, tidbits of incidents long forgotten, invaded her thoughts. Unfortunately, there was nothing to look at to stop her thoughts from becoming blooming visuals of things she'd rather forget. The oppression of her situation, the sensory deprivation and lack of a timepiece gave way to her imagination. Her history. Her weaknesses.

Her other senses gone, Jenny's mind seemed to focus on the remaining four. She winced as she recalled the acrid scent of her mother's melted flesh with a clarity that frightened her. Her nostrils burned in protest of the memory and she absently rubbed her nose, pinching it shut as saliva filled her mouth. Was it sadness or the free flowing pre-vomit lubrication she swallowed over the lump in her throat? She didn't know and squeezed her eyes shut, trying to block the memory. Tiny specks of white and orange danced behind her closed lids and she released the pressure to alleviate the hallucination of color.

Somewhere deep inside her mind, the gritty feel of playground dirt mixed with blood, caused Jenny to wring her hands. She brought her fists to her mouth, pressing them against her lips as if to hold back a scream. The taste of blood flowed as she pushed her lips into her teeth and she recalled the horrendous flashes of pain that had accompanied her mouth as it had bounced across the jungle gym.

Abruptly, she stopped and snapped her head to the right, the sound of a baby's cry catching her full attention. She had come from that direction and knew the source of the noise was not in the basement with her. Rather, it was another incident unlocked by her fears, her weaknesses and her surrender to her subconscious thoughts. The noise, urgent and irrational, bounced lightly along the walls before being joined by footsteps that could only belong to Dan.

"No." She shook her head and frantically tried to recall something else—something more positive than the memory that threatened to escape from the cage she'd locked it into years before.

Jenny tried too hard to think of something else, as the nursery door slammed shut in her mind and she jumped at the very real sound of it. The footsteps resumed and grew louder as he pounded down the hall toward her. In her mind, the memory played out, the void around her providing an inviting canvas.

Jenny lay in the bathtub, surrounded by bubbles and the gentle flicker of candlelight. The door that joined the bathroom to the master bedroom flew open and Dan began screaming before he even entered the room.

"What exactly is going on around here? Are you deaf?" She opened her eyes at his voice, her vision swimming before her as it acclimated to the dimness of the room. She opened her mouth to speak, but couldn't find the words.

"Have you gone completely insane?" His voice cracked in anger. "I come home from working my ass off all day and the house is a complete disaster. There's a sink full of cold water and dirty dishes, Alan is screaming his head off. The television is blaring. And you…" The door had slammed against the towel rack behind it and begun its rebound closing. He slapped a palm against it to stop it and stormed into the room.

"You lay in here like a queen with your candles and bubbles and…" His voice trailed off.

She watched as Dan's eyes followed the tiled floor from the sink to the bathtub. In the path of his cursory glance, her clothes sat neatly folded and stacked on the closed toilet seat. Dark towels, their color indistinguishable in the low light, rested against the base of the tub to soak up displaced overflow. Several candles had long burned out or had drowned their wicks in pools of liquid wax. Those that remained flickered against the white walls and barely rolling bubbles in the bathwater. Orange, red, and yellow mirrors of flame danced, growing and shrinking as the flames reacted to tiny air currents in the room.

Jenny's knees poked through the bubbles. Her body lowered into the water far enough for her chin to be coated in fading suds. Behind her head floated an air pillow she'd been resting on before lifting her head slightly to stare at his intrusion. Her hair was gathered high on her head—the bottom edge and loose pieces were soaked from casual contact with the water and the steam that filled the room. Her arms draped across the top of the porcelain. His straight razor sat motionless next to her left hand, lazily dripping thin crimson rivulets down the side of the bath and staining the otherwise pristine scene.

She watched his eyes as he looked closer at the color flickering off the bubbles and exposed water, and knew he had realized the candlelight was not responsible for the dark swirls and tinged bubbles. As his eyes took in the bloodied suds, the droplets on the shower wall, and the blackness of the water, a small gasp whimpered free from his gaping mouth.

"What…" He ran forward, sliding on the steam-dampened tiles and fell onto one knee in front of her. "Why?" He choked out the question as his brows furrowed.

He grabbed both of her hands and turned them over to inspect her wrists. Other than soap running down to drop in globs to the water below, he found nothing. He pushed the drain plug lever behind her neck and reached into the water under her. Holding the crook of her knees and lower back, he pulled her from the tub, swung around, and placed her on the floor in a smooth motion that would have looked rehearsed to any observer.

"Sorry," Jenny whispered, as Dan looked over her wet body. His eyes stopped at her legs and his arm grabbed one of the rolled towels at the base of the tub.

She had deeply cut into her right thigh and merely scratched the left. The pain of the first and fear of the finality on the second had caused her to hesitate long enough to decide one should be enough.

Dan snapped the towel open and placed it over her leg, a dark stain immediately marking the wound beneath it. He put his fist into the dampened material and pushed down as his other hand reached inside his jacket for his cell phone. She winced as numbness was replaced with pain at the pressure of his weight.

After dialing emergency services and giving them the details, he looked back to Jenny. He dropped his phone to the ground and brushed her hair out of her eyes. Concern replaced the anger that had been on his face moments before and he caressed her forehead.

"Why, babe? Why?" He whispered, as she looked past him to the door and the sound of the forgotten baby.

"I'm sorry." Disgust and disappointment rolled through her head as she felt the warmth of guilt flow through her system and temporarily replace the coolness the blood loss had caused. He would never understand. He couldn't. And Jenny would never bother to explain it to him.

The postpartum depression had mixed with the hatred harbored for her child. She loathed that Alan was named after, and therefore a constant reminder of, a man she had despised. She blamed the baby, rather than the medication or doctors, for her inability to have more children. And for whatever reason, it gave birth to guilt for the abortion Dan didn't know about—the abortion Jenny had convinced herself was a necessity and hadn't thought of for years. Something happened that morning and her emotions piqued.

She stood in the doorway to the nursery as Alan wailed for her affection. She wanted to shake him, smother him—do something not only to shut him up, but to be rid of him and the pain he caused. For whatever reason, she couldn't do it.

Guilt and hatred made an intoxicating combination and her reason caved in on itself. The guilt led her to the bathtub, and her irrational mood twisted her vision of reality. The hatred turned inward and she punished herself. As the blood spread through the soapy water, she thought of the babies she would never have.

And the one that she threw away.

Jenny and Dan had only been seeing each other for about five months when she found out she was pregnant. She had never been promiscuous, but Dan had wooed her with all the right words, actions, and intentions right after she'd come out of the worst relationship she'd had with a man since her father. Dan hadn't pushed sex, hadn't made any grand promises, and had been very open and honest about his intentions.

They were in school at the state college just outside Black River. Dan Schultz had a full ride on a scholarship. Jenny was attending classes part-time on what her income and mother's insurance would allow. He'd told her after watching his older sister drop out of college for family life and never finish her degree, he would *not* settle down until he graduated. Dan said he looked at college as the place to find someone with similar interests, education, and background.

Someone to help pass the time that may or may not be the one he graduated with into the real world. They'd found each other by accident outside the library.

Jenny was an avid reader, always had been, and because long distance was too expensive to talk to Beth at her private college as much as Jenny wanted, she spent her spare time reading. While she appreciated the idea of the library, Jenny had never enjoyed the dust-scented solitude it shelved. She preferred to perch in the sunlight on the wide ledges outside, or on the steps themselves, as she lost herself to worlds other than her own.

Engrossed in her latest phase of Patricia Cornwell novels, she greedily scanned the pages, witnessing autopsies and police protocol as she tried to beat the author to the killer. She could block out anything when she read—her friends claimed a tornado could scream by and she'd never notice—and was sprawled across the far edge of the library steps on her stomach, solving the current mystery. Her legs kicked at the air behind her, while she remained oblivious to the world around her.

Dan had his face buried in a thick book on Teddy Roosevelt, as he researched for his upcoming thesis paper. "Politicians Versus Business Owners" had been approved by his advisor, and he roamed in and out of the library daily, feeding his findings to index cards, notebooks and memory. He'd walked the library's marble steps enough times he didn't need to look up from his book to navigate them. But he wasn't expecting to trip over the slight blonde girl lying on them.

In a tumble of arms, legs and pages, the two of them rolled down the steps. At the bottom, they separated. Dan's face trying to hide annoyance, hers openly showing hostility. She opened her mouth to speak and stopped when she looked up at him. He towered over her, and in his shadow, Jenny took in his eyes and mouth and build before the sarcasm ever left her mouth. Instead she laughed. His lips slid slowly into a smirk and he joined her. They brushed themselves down and he invited her to coffee. They hit it off immediately.

They spent every available waking minute together—talking, laughing, or quietly doing their own studies. Neither of them feared silence and could sit for hours next to each other, fingertips touching or legs brushing each other, without a word. They discussed politics or cartoons, childhood television shows or theology with the same intense grace and lighthearted tone. They laughed, a lot, and both admitted it felt good to be content. It was casual, almost a friendship more than a relationship, and they were very comfortable with it that way. The night they lay talking of philosophy in the dark led naturally to their first truly physical contact and neither of them regretted it afterward.

Then she missed her period.

She passed it off as stress between school and work. She'd been late before. Hell, she'd missed a whole summer once when she was younger. She didn't feel different and therefore didn't act different.

Then she missed another one and panic set in.

She'd gone to the twenty-four-hour convenience store and sheepishly bought a home pregnancy test. Jenny had to wander the store for almost forty-five minutes, waiting for other straggling late-night shoppers to vacate the premises and offer her the semiprivacy of the lone night clerk. She never planned to visit the store again at night, as she refused to risk letting the young attendant recognize her for her purchase.

The instructions said to use it right away in the morning, when the hormones would be most concentrated. She laid it on the counter in her small bathroom and crawled into bed, hoping to fall asleep and wake up, ready to go—just like she had as a child on Christmas Eve. It didn't work and she lay in the dark staring at the ceiling for most of the night.

Jenny recalled how her mother had raised her. She thought of Dan and his plans for the future. She absently rubbed her tummy, and pondered what she would do if the little stick in the package turned blue.

Adoption was just not doable. She loved kids and could never carry one to full term only to never see it again. Abortion scared the crap out of her. She'd known girls who'd had one and been changed forever. She began to come up with relatively safe *accidents* she could have to dislodge the embryo from her uterus and *naturally* rid her of the problem. The campus and her apartment building both offered a variety of staircases she could fall down. The college's pool area could easily provide a life-threatening slip under the right circumstances. The…

She couldn't do it. She couldn't risk hurting herself, or worse yet, knocking herself unconscious and having a doctor inform Dan she'd been pregnant.

She thought of keeping it—of telling him she was pregnant and just living with whatever action he took. Being a single mother scared her, but she'd watched her mother do it and was fairly certain she could do a better job without much effort. But then she thought about her eating habits between school and work, or rather, her habit of not eating. Jenny hadn't been taking care of her own body, hadn't been getting much exercise, and the stress of school would surely take its toll on a pregnancy. But she had another year and a half of college and knew a child would put a stop to her graduation.

Dan only had a semester left. Perhaps he was close enough to graduation to change his plans for settling down. Just maybe, she could keep both the baby and the father. Maybe.

As first light peaked through her curtains to change the lines and shadows along the ceiling she stared at, Jenny convinced herself she didn't know what she would do.

It was officially morning but she continued to stare at the ceiling. The stress of the options and opportunities she had to choose from made her tired and she couldn't get up the strength to take the test for almost two more hours. She almost called Beth, twice, but instead nodded off out of sheer exhaustion. She woke to the regularly set alarm clock announcing the beginning of her day.

She gathered her clothes and entered the bathroom. She reread the instructions on the test before following them to a T. She climbed into a scalding hot shower, hoping to wash away the filth she imagined the test itself had stained her with. As Jenny turned the water off and reached out for a towel, her eyes glanced at the stick lying on the back of the sink.

Even in the steam-filled room, she could see the blue and her heart sank.

Resignation flowed through her veins and chilled her skin. Jenny wrapped a towel around her body, without doing any precursory drying, and left the bathroom. Walking to the kitchen, she opened the far right drawer and pulled out the phone book. Her appointment was made before the water had soaked through the towel.

She had lied to Dan and told him she'd gone to see Beth. When she got back, she claimed an earlier Pap smear had tested positive for cysts and they'd done a biopsy, which caused her to bleed. She'd blamed the procedure on the pain that doubled her over occasionally, and said the prolonged bleeding was causing her mood swings.

She apologized over and over, whether he said something about her behavior or not, and believed he never had a clue of what she was truly attempting to make amends for.

⁌

Jenny had never told him and he had never suspected, as far as she knew. The sincere worry in his eyes—as he talked to her, and tried to keep her awake, waiting for the paramedics to show up—snapped her out of whatever depression she'd been in for the last few months. She made a promise to her dying self. If he managed to save her, her demons would remain her own. She would blame postpartum for this episode and suffer whatever therapy they prescribed. She would learn to love her child and make sure he never knew how she'd felt for his first few months. She would turn a corner, be a better person, live a better life.

The last thing she heard as she lost consciousness on the bathroom floor was the parallel sounds of the approaching sirens and the squealing of her only child, crying from his crib—wondering why no one was paying attention to him.

CHAPTER TEN

Jenny shuddered at the memory of her attempted suicide. It was never the weeks of observation or months of therapy she hated remembering. It was the pitied look Dan began giving her. The sense of distance, similar to a parent and child as the younger approaches their teen years, that echoed from his expressions and negated the words he swore were true.

She did give him credit for stepping up to the plate, though. As she lay in the hospital, and later spent several hours a week speaking to various counselors, Dan took good care of their son without so much as a hint of protest.

Jenny always assumed he must have had long talks with his mother on the specifics of child rearing. Or his maternal instincts were just stronger than hers, as he never asked how or why to do anything with Alan. He just seemed to know when he should do something, what he should do, and why he should call the doctor when the other two failed.

The initial thoughts she'd tried so desperately to avoid had run their course and naturally blended into thoughts of Dan. He'd been a trooper for two years, out of some twisted sense of true love or for the sake of their child, she didn't know which, but they survived her brush with death and all the healing it required. In a sense, it strengthened their relationship, and things improved, almost to perfection. Until it fell apart eight years later.

She hated thinking of him, though, and tried to take her mind off Dan. Sure, they'd been very civil after the divorce, and she still loved him in many ways, but it was a lost cause. Their history was just that, *history,* and as the saying goes, if we don't learn from it, we're doomed to repeat it. Jenny was not going to repeat any of it. She was determined to move forward.

She tried to focus her memories, and her subconscious wanderings, on her son.

She thought of the backyard, and the sandbox that had once been filled with small cars and trucks. The dunes and miniature valleys disturbed by the ruts of her son's roadways. She recalled the garage and its wasteland of forgotten youth, from the tricycle he outgrew to the flat basketball that no longer caught air to fall through the bent hoop hanging off the garage.

The phantom smell of his clean hair as a small boy invaded her nostrils. It transformed into the distinctive tang of his dirty clothes as a child, and the odor from his preteen taste in grooming products that wafted from his room now. The smell of popcorn always reminded her of him. Every night, for as long as she could remember, he made a bag of microwave popcorn as his bedtime snack. When he was younger, she'd convinced him he made the best popcorn and she would only eat it if he made it. It became a game, a ritual, and one she still visited on occasion. Jenny wondered if he'd made any since her disappearance. She realized she was more afraid for him than she was for herself, and found relief in her automatic priorities.

Just as she'd promised herself, Jenny had changed after her suicide attempt. She read to Alan, took him on walks, played on the floor and immersed herself in her son's view of the world. She put aside her issues with faith and had Alan christened under Dan's Lutheran beliefs—Beth and Dan's brother-in-law acting as godparents. She joined the PTA, only to be kicked out for her supposedly obtrusive views on liberal teachings and political games that interrupted classroom protocol. However, through it all, she had always been concerned she didn't really love him, couldn't love him—because of his name—and had spent the years deliberately trying to use it on a regular basis. In the end, Jenny was ashamed, as she habitually referred to him as squirt, munchkin, honey, or any number of other terms of endearment—not only to his face, but also in her mind.

Even as she was changing, in the aftermath of her suicide attempt, she continued to push the subject of his name. Dan wouldn't allow her to change it, saying it was a silly reason to go through the time and money. She told him they had twelve months after the birth to change it legally, free of charge and red tape. He didn't care, and they fought for the better part of ten of those. Twelve years later, she still remembered those fights.

She remembered the fights her parents had when she was young, and often wondered if it was a *guy thing* to start fights at midnight, in the dark, after you'd gone to bed. She would bring up the name change, casually, pleasantly during the day. She tried not to show how upset she was about it, but he always saw through her charades and turned it around on her. Dan would claim her anxiety was depressing him and blame her for his temper, because she wouldn't let it go. Jenny didn't buy it and tried to ignore those comments, but couldn't ignore the hurt they left behind. She would drop the idea and finish out the evening without another word. Not acting upset, or being snide or curt with him, but just giving him space because, while she begged for action, he boiled over quicker each time she broached the subject.

They would brush their teeth, check the doors, crawl into bed and turn out the lights. On those nights, there were no thoughts of romance and she would roll away and snuggle down into the blankets. She'd fight to fall asleep while thinking of other things. She'd ask both a God she didn't believe in and the *other* Alan for forgiveness. She'd pretend to be asleep already when he inevitably spoke up.

Fighting at midnight seemed to be the only time Dan could truly say what he wanted, what she feared he believed. Even if he always apologized for it the following morning, he'd get it off his chest and into her mind. Horrible things passed for conversation in the glow of the hallway nightlight. Words burrowed into her soul and no amount of coffee-cup remorse could take them away. He had thrown her suicide attempt in her face numerous times, calling her everything from a coward to an unfit mother. He accused Jenny of getting pregnant on purpose with less than a year left, because she "didn't have the guts to finish college and enter the real world." He claimed Jenny didn't love their son—that she never would and only pretended. His words sunk in, made themselves at home, and burrowed into her enough to make her wonder if they were true. With effort, Jenny could forgive the anger. She could never forget the deliberate hurt that surfaced with it.

During those fights, she had alternated between defensive and aggressive. She tried to explain she knew someone named Alan who had hurt her, but Dan wouldn't hear of it without the details. She wouldn't divulge those—couldn't divulge those without exposing her own guilt. He said it didn't matter if someone from her past had the name. Her son wasn't *that* person. And she should love him no matter what his name was. She forced the tears she hated and considered weak, in hopes that playing the estrogen card would work and he would cave to her whims. She tried every angle. He never wavered.

They argued on occasion about the bills or other unimportant things, like his habit of leaving his dirty clothes next to the hamper rather than in it, but the only thing they ever raised voices over, bordered on domestic violence with, was Alan's name—usually ending in how she wasn't maternal enough and held the name against the baby. Jenny knew she did, but couldn't admit it, so she denied it and claimed Dan was just being spiteful. She would eventually scream that she would love her child no matter what his name was—and he won the argument just like that, every time. He would roll over and calmly declare they didn't need to change his name, and they didn't need to discuss it anymore, and promptly fall asleep. She would lie awake for hours.

It was generally the only thing they fought about and over time the fight became a silent one. When Alan was old enough to start babbling incoherently, she became worried he would know what they were fighting about and stopped bringing it up.

If she'd known better, Jenny would have thought Dan purposely named him Alan to upset her. She almost believed that Dan knew about Alan and was punishing her, since no one else seemed to think they should. But she knew better. She knew there was no way Dan could know about Alan. She'd never used his name when discussing the nightmares that woke her in a cold sweat. She'd never mentioned him when conscious, unless they were watching a movie or something on television and someone reminded her of him. Then she would just cringe and say she once knew someone like that.

But that was the other Alan, she reminded herself, not her son. Not the boy who daydreamed his way through school yet made the honor roll every time. Not the child conscientious enough to take on chores without being asked. Not the kid with more friends as a child than she had had during her lifetime. He was different, different from his namesake, and different from his parents, and she fully believed he would succeed in everything she had failed.

And if she didn't get out of this blackness, she would fail again.

Jenny pulled herself together, stood up, and resumed her mental mapping of her prison. There had to be a way out, and she was determined to find it. She was strong, *just ask Dan.*

The ladder had provided no escape, the unfinished room no answers, and she began to plot what she would do if she finished following the wall around to her bone marked corner and found no way out.

Could it be in the middle? God, she hoped not. The room was at least… She paused, thinking of the expanse she'd covered. Thirty-two steps on the first wall, seventy-one on the second. It sounded huge and her memory of it seemed to make it bigger, but a fine thread of logic remained in her conscious and she figured her feet were not twelve inches long. At most they were eight inches. She hadn't been doing a long stride, but a short shuffle. Quick estimation dried her mouth and her throat tighten with anxiety. The room had to be twenty by sixty, or better—the middle would be impossible to search thoroughly in the dark.

Without any light source, or being able to feel the wall, she'd have no way of keeping a straight line in the center of the room. There'd be no way to do an effective grid and be satisfied she'd covered it all. Perhaps she could attempt a corner-to-corner route in the hopes of locating the middle.

The chances of there being a light source were slim. On the one hand, the partitioned walls meant someone had worked down here, on the other the defunct ladder made her think the location had been abandoned. If the light switch, which may or may not exist, was located outside the room, she would never know. If it were inside, she would find it on the wall. Unless it was a pull cord, she thought. If there was a string hanging from somewhere in the expanse, she knew she'd never pinpoint it and her hopes sunk again just as the arm in front of her made contact with the remaining wall.

After running face-first into the wooden partition, she'd learned to use one hand to trace the wall and keep herself in a straight light, the other in front of her. While her right arm felt nothing but air in front of her, her left ran up and down continually on the foundation, looking for blemishes, changes, anything. She'd run the entire length of this wall, from the ladder to the corner, without finding anything else useful or even thought provoking. The disappointment was only masked by the confusion in her count.

From the ladder, she'd counted twenty-three steps. The ladder was only four paces from the corner. That meant this wall was only twenty-seven steps where the opposite wall had been thirty-two. Why would a foundation not be an equal rectangle?

An addition? No, that didn't make sense. They wouldn't dig a partial below the surface. They wouldn't need to, and she'd never heard of anyone doing that. Then again, construction wasn't something Jenny knew a whole lot about, thinking she'd never heard a rule saying you couldn't do that either.

She turned the corner to continue on, but when she raised her arms out, feeling the darkness at ninety-degree angles, she realized her shoulders were getting tired and put them back down. She rubbed each of them for a few moments and rolled them a few times.

Her spine popped and cracked in protest. Her muscles begged for mercy, and Jenny noticed the soreness was traveling down her arms toward her elbows.

The mental and physical requirements were taking their toll on her, and Jenny slumped her shoulders in resignation. Her foot was throbbing and most likely infected. Her knee was tender to the touch, the air cool against the sticky abrasion. The back of her head was heavy with crusted blood and dirt. Her elbow was free of blood but soreness echoed lightly in the bones. She was a wreck.

She needed to rest. She needed to eat. But her need to escape overpowered them both and she sighed heavily before forcing her arms up and out and stepping forward.

CHAPTER ELEVEN

Jenny's fingers traced the rocks and mortar with a feather touch, her autopilot monitoring variations in texture and temperature while her mind wandered through the corridors of knowledge and experience. She thought of every movie or book she'd ever run across that featured a trapped woman. They never ended well, and she'd always believed it had everything to do with the choices they made along the way. When they should scream, they whimpered. When they should run, they froze. When they should attack, they cowered. Whether it was for dramatics or storyline, they always seemed to do the wrong thing. Occasionally, even the men she had seen in similar situations fell victim to "wrong place, wrong time." Jenny promised herself she wouldn't make those mistakes.

But it wasn't necessarily the fatal errors that crept from her subconscious and reminded her of those storylines. It was the people who put the victims in those situations. The monsters often thought of as the simple boy next door, or the quiet guy at the office. The monsters who stacked the odds, created the labyrinths, and by some odd twist of accidental fate, were caught. Not always, but more often than not, and that gave her hope.

Forgetting the question of *where,* Jenny let the more pertinent question of *why* roll around unchecked. Why would someone have put her in here? Why would they not have come back to check on her yet?

Obviously, whoever had seized her outside the pharmacy hadn't been seen in the parking lot. Nor had they been spied carrying or dragging her unconscious form into whatever building sat above her. The only noises she'd heard were her own swallowed echoes and the soft mechanical hum that periodically bounced lightly from somewhere within the walls.

Was there someone above her? Were there people going about their lives while she panicked below? Should she scream? Would they hear her? Would it make a difference? Jenny supposed it all depended on their involvement, if they existed at all. Did they know she crawled around below them, banging into walls, tripping on rocks, bruising and battering herself in the name of escape? Or were they not part of the plot? Was she being held somewhere below the public, in a residential neighborhood, or perhaps business district? How ironic would it be if she were within blocks of work, hidden below the city with school buses rumbling overhead, neighbors and visitors traveling back and forth? Was that the sound she kept hearing? They didn't have a subway of any type and most of the railroad tracks were exempt. If it was the drone of vehicles, it would be more frequent, unless— Could her prison be some forgotten foundation in the country somewhere, with only the occasional traffic or traveler?

She didn't know any of the answers and a pinprick of pain began to pulse behind her left ear. The stress headache would cripple her in the light, but down here, in here, whichever the case may be, it was simply an annoyance. In a strange sense, the new noise was a welcome change from her heartbeat and breathing, painful as the throbbing might be, and she listened to the staccato of her blood as it pushed its way through a pinched vein in her temple. Jenny blinked as she became aware of her aching jaw, and caught herself grinding her teeth in rhythm to the headache. She had to stop or she would induce a migraine for which there was no medication handy and the pain would be far more intense than any of her injuries—stalling her progress, making her a victim. Instead, she tried to focus on the thoughts at hand. The question of *who* seemed to hold the most relevance, as it may explain both the *why* and *where* of the situation.

Who did Jenny know that would do this? That was the question she'd been quietly tossing around ever since she woke up. She'd been skipping around the direct question, playing with the possibilities both consciously and not. But now, as she concentrated, it aggravated her that she didn't have a solid, obvious answer. You'd think an enemy of this magnitude would jump to mind. A suspect and well-founded motive would be apparent if she knew who'd grabbed her and thrown her away, to be forgotten. Maybe she was forgetting someone—or something.

The unambiguous first choice for consideration would be Dan, but even at their worst, he wouldn't do something like this. There had been a few things that made her think of him, the foundation, the clay and rocks, but it was too—well, to be honest with herself, it was beneath him. With an unwavering belief she could handle herself, he would never do this to her just to test the notion. He would never jeopardize her life and risk hurting Alan. He would never stoop to this level. Not Dan. Maybe someone else in her past, but not the man that always talked over the television volume during the news to explain why criminals should be dealt with harshly and how he was willing to dole out punishment out if they ever called for volunteers. No, he abhorred the type of person that would do this far too much to become one. But who then?

Enemies in her life, much like friends, had come and gone but never really left imprints beyond their initial confrontation and the sting of short-lived anger. There just wasn't anyone she could think of who would do this.

But what exactly was this? Perhaps if she could figure out the motive or the desired results she could backtrack to figuring out who.

She exhaled a frustrated grunt. She was just going in circles. *Okay then,* Jenny thought, *motive. What are we looking at?*

She was in an unfinished, unlit hole in the world. There were no signs she'd been visited while sleeping and no one had peeked in on her while she was awake. There didn't appear to be a door—*yet,* she reminded herself—for easy access.

She hadn't been bound or gagged in any fashion, so she had to believe her captor was secure in her inability to escape. Or perhaps they weren't planning on keeping her long enough for her to try. She shook her head and moved past the finality of that outcome.

So, was she being kept for a definitive amount of time, kidnapped perhaps? Left in this cave while the ransom was delivered? But who would be asked for ransom? She had no family left and Dan didn't care. Even if he did, he didn't have any money to speak of in terms of wealth for ransom demands. Ransom couldn't be an option—it just wasn't logical.

The victims from countless movies screamed in Jenny's mind. The failed heroes of an endless stream of suspense books begged for her attention. The lack of visits, no food, and the absence of supplies or amenities forced her to look at the situation for the bleak truth it might be. If she was not in here to eventually be freed, then why?

A twinge of fear crawled up her spine and gave her shoulders a subtle shutter. Left to die just because? Like some sort of psychotic experiment on how fear may affect how long a person can go without food and water? Or how long they can be trapped in the darkness before they break down and crack? And why pick her? Was she just lucky enough to be in the parking lot when they decided they needed a victim and no one was around to stop them? The indecisive randomness of those choices forced them to the bottom of the list. Only as a last resort could she succumb to believing she'd been casually selected on a whim to wither away.

Would there be visits? Jenny remembered her nightmare from earlier that day—or was it yesterday? Time was becoming more of a blur as it passed. Would the visits be as she had dreamed, brutal and playful for the torturer? Or was there a point to the torture? Could she possibly have information someone wanted?

Sure, Jenny worked at Harding News Harold, but she wasn't a journalist, she was an advertising liaison. She'd never had a taste for gossip and in no way involved herself in the business of snooping and scooping. She didn't interview politicians or businessmen. She didn't even bother discussing the editorials or analysis that went into the "We the People" section of the paper. Jenny simply took their ad copy and graphics, designed layouts, and handed them the final products with copies from billing for their co-op programs. She didn't even do the billing for the ads she put together. With further thought, she could not even think of anyone in her small town who may have something to hide that could possibly require such excessive measures to protect. She felt confident she was not here to be silenced.

The extreme fiction and entertainment she'd watched over the years poked its question out of her subconscious again and hung like the smell of burned food in the air around her. She could fan it all she wanted with other thoughts, open the windows to let in fresh air with concentrated efforts elsewhere, but she couldn't escape the possibility screaming for attention, gagging her senses with its brutality. Could she really be nothing more than someone's idea of fun? Was she going to be running for her life, chased by a chainsaw-wielding maniac? Would they cut her up into little pieces and feed her to their watchdogs, or worse, themselves. Could it be a madman—or God forbid, an entire family—who thought they were above her on the food chain? Were there really people out there, as portrayed in the movies, who took human life without any concern or thought of the consequences?

She swallowed hard at the idea that sport killing and cannibalism had made its way into an almost accepted commonplace in society, and balked at the idea of it rolling far too easily around her thoughts. She couldn't bring herself to believe there were a large number of individuals in civilized areas breaking laws unspoken or deemed unnecessary to put to paper for their obviously heinous nature. Those lunatics were the exception, not the rule. Harding was a small town—no exceptions would go unnoticed.

If not the extreme edges of sanity in a closed society, then perhaps she was the victim of a highly functional serial killer personality. Not all were sloppy, nor were all stupid—she'd read and watched enough to understand the basic mechanisms that made them tick. A shudder traveled up her spine and spread through her shoulders. Visions of the very polite, well-educated, and prosperously employed Hannibal Lecter from Harris's books offered another shiver to her already crawling skin.

The hair on the back of her neck stood up as she imagined herself the target of a normal, almost mundane citizen with a dark side who never failed to surprise friends and relatives when the truth came out.

No one ever expected that behavior from Bundy, Gacy, or Dahmer, and killers like that were usually caught after several murders.

Which victim was she?

Would she be the lucky survivor saved in the nick of time, when the authorities finally put it all together? She wouldn't wait around and hope for that. She couldn't. She believed survival in any extreme situation required proactive behavior, and she was determined to do just that.

But what other options could there be?

Jenny moved past the extreme imaginings brought on by late night horror movies, best-selling books, and shocking headlines, wondering once again about revenge. While she couldn't come up with anyone who would do this to her, she was unnerved by the fact she kept returning to that scenario. She paused, rested her weight against her left palm on the wall, and let herself really think.

She'd been avoiding looking inward, but now jumped with both feet—honestly delving into her memories for an enemy worthy of this. She searched for an adversary that clung to the past and dared risk the repercussions this type of retribution could produce. Was there anyone who would risk their own life just to take hers?

Maybe.

CHAPTER TWELVE

Jenny had never thought of it at the time, only realizing it as an adult and looking back on that day, but the postapocalyptic gray sky had been fitting for the somber occasion. Instead, at the time, she'd concentrated on staring at the ground, the dirt-specked shine of her black patent leather shoes, and the ripple of white lace around the ankle of her short socks. She'd thought it ridiculous they had dressed her in such childish attire, and still did, but at the time, she hadn't spoken for four days and didn't feel the need to break silence to protest her outfit.

She remembered how the tears felt as they rolled down her face, cooling her skin in the autumn air. She'd watched as they fell from her chin and became lost in the drying brown grass of the cemetery.

She'd never been to a funeral until that day. Her parents had always said she was "too young to understand." They believed she wouldn't comprehend the need for communal grief and the black humor dotting the event to prevent random breakdowns.

Her parents didn't realize those things, and death itself, were much easier to explain than the hope people carry on after mortality slapped them in the face and reminded them they were not immune.

When she was seven, she'd helped her dad bury her cat, Samson, in the backyard and cried for days afterward. She'd been five when her mother flushed Jenny's first goldfish—won at the fair—and sniffled alone in her room as her mother returned to the household chores as if nothing tragic had just happened. Both times her tears had been for the pet. Both times she had worried her beloved critters would be alone or afraid, wondered where they had gone and if they would have friends and sunshine there. Both times she had recovered, eventually, in part due to the playfulness and company of a new pet her parents provided in their attempt to explain the circle of life.

But in the graveyard, she grieved for herself and the difference was profound. Her parents couldn't console her with insulting presents and ignorant rhetoric, designed to appease rather than assist. Her mood matched the weather and the forecast wasn't promising.

She did not see the crowd gathered in shades of black, blue, and brown at the edges of her waterlogged vision. She did not hear the words of sympathy and strength whispered by the pastor at the front of the group. She did not feel her mother's arm draped over her shoulder for support and reassurance.

The only sense that seemed to be working was smell. And the scent of death surrounded her. The tang of nature's mid-October demise assaulted her senses with the conflicting moisture of moldy leaves and crisp air. The reek of freshly churned soil escaped from under the Astroturf cloth, hiding the reality of the mound in plain view. She sensed the earthworms and grubs that writhed in the dirt. Jenny knew clumps of red clay, the same mud she had played with in her backyard, leaked its watery blood through the pile waiting next to the gaping hole in the ground.

She frowned at the elaborately stitched mats covering the area around the open grave, glowered at the golden frame outlining the inevitable doorway. The flowers transported from the funeral home encircled the dark casket with their futile color and vitality. The entire scene was decorated to make it seem peaceful, serene, and acceptable—anything other than what it truly was.

Jenny found it strange the adults were even marginally soothed by the masquerade. She thought it was odd a thirteen-year-old could see through the fanciful attempt to hide the truth, while the adults welcomed the fantasy. How could these people continue to breathe knowing they would someday be the one surrounded by false beauty and forced enchantment?

The pastor reached down, slipped his hand under the out-of-place green that hid the graveyard dirt, and withdrew a fistful of dark, wet soil. As he spoke the words, familiar enough to those around him that several whispered them along with him, she returned her gaze to the ground in front of her. Jenny shifted her weight, pulling free from her mother's shaking hand on her shoulder. She crossed her arms in front of her, blocking out the chill in the air and the shudder that tried to pass through her limbs.

She swallowed back the remainder of her tears. They did nothing to reduce her sorrow and only made it difficult to breathe through the gasping sobs and pounding heartbeat. There was no point crying for the man in the coffin in front of her.

Her father was dead.

He wasn't there to buy her a new puppy or hold her while she sobbed. Daddy wasn't going to tell her pretty lies about God and angels and the reunion of all loved ones in heaven. He wasn't going to have anything to do with her future grief. Jenny turned her turmoil inward.

Gravity emptied the remaining moisture from her eyes. The tears followed the trails of their predecessors down her face and dropped to join them on the hard ground. They fell not for the man in the casket, but for the girl standing beside it.

A hollow swelled in her chest and new grief entered her core. Her life would be changed forever, and she was angry all these people were more concerned with an empty body that no longer cared if they paid it attention or not. They should be concerned for her, for her mother, for their future—rather than the nonexistent future of her father and the stories he left behind.

Jenny didn't remember leaving the grave site and returning to the church. She was only aware she'd put a rose on her father's coffin because several people later commented on how touching it was. She nodded at memories and warm wishes she barely heard. Someone put a paper cup of punch in her hand and she drank—it had no taste. Somewhere between the cemetery and the reception, she had gone from bitter to numb.

Other children and teenagers had already forgotten the mandatory grieving for an uncle or friend of their parents. They ran about, playing games and giggling in the corners of the large church basement. Occasionally one of them would look her direction or stop in front of her and beckon her with their eyes to join them, but none of them spoke directly to her.

The busybodies of the family, neighborhood, and church surrounded Jenny's mother. They hugged her, held her, patted her shoulder, and offered empty words of redemption and reassurance. Kathy continued to dab at her eyes as her shoulders shuddered, careful not to ruin her makeup.

The pastor sat at one of the long tables set up for the bereft buffet, hands folded in front of him as if in prayer. His downcast eyes glanced about the room under his brows as if he were taking notes. He followed the stream of women stopped to talk to Jenny's mom, some of them keeping his attention as they walked away, and Jenny wondered why—but welcomed the distraction.

Jenny followed the pastor's eyes. It was perhaps the most interactive thing she'd done since her father's death. She found it fascinating to see which women he watched and which he gave nothing more than a cursory glance to. After a few moments she noted a pattern forming.

He hardly noticed the elderly women from the church and other social grounds. The family members were more carefully tracked as they gathered in small groups, each cluster then ranked their own value on his interest meter. Some circles were never given another thought, while others were the target of his occasional second glances and hard stares.

But the neighbors were the ones he truly watched.

Pastor Thomas Henderson had come to their small town almost five years beforehand. He'd been here long enough to know everyone by name, almost long enough to know the individual history of each member of his parish, but not quite long enough to have developed truly informed opinions on everyone in town. Today he seemed to be filling in some of those blanks, and he scrutinized their every movement with his hooded eyes and folded hands.

Jenny watched as Pastor Tom's eyes held her neighbors in prolonged contemplation. His head tilted ever so slightly as he listened in on various conversations. She followed his gaze and tried to listen to what he found so interesting. The tidbits she caught made her stomach turn. It seemed she was the subject of today's gossip.

"Elise said they found her next to the body." Lisa Marshall from across the street leaned past old man Sims at one of the made-up tables, aiming her gossip at the other women there. Jenny immediately knew they were speaking of her and was amazed they would do so at such close proximity. "She hasn't spoken a word since they found her, you know."

Ruth Sweeney piped up, "Poor child. Some form of catatonia, I'm sure."

"Just shock." Sandy's raspy voice suggested too many cigarettes, late nights, or both. Jenny's mother had been unable to hide the shock on her face when Sandy and Joe showed up at the church. They were best known for sitting on their couch, drinking, while their twin boys, Dean and Glenn, roamed the neighborhood causing havoc. Jenny wondered if they were out of character enough to actually be sober.

"Well, what do you expect?" Mrs. Sweeney glanced at Jenny and quickly looked away when Jenny met her eyes. Her voice lowered, but not enough "She's just a child."

"It's guilt," Mr. Sims spat, interrupting the women. New to the neighborhood, he had made the polite lap around the block and introduced himself the previous month. Today he sat, stoic, quietly drinking his coffee. A retired fireman and ex-army, he'd fought both the declared enemy and nature's enemies. He had grown bitter with age, weary of life, and it showed in the way he glowered at the next generation while making nice with the adults in the small community. Everyone in attendance knew he was there more for appearances than concern.

"Edward..." Mrs. Sweeney hushed him with her long-unused teacher's voice. "How could you?"

"Look at her." He met Jenny's eye with no shame and glared at the girl. "She doesn't seem very upset. She hasn't cried since the funeral."

"You don't think she's cried enough this week?" Sandy furrowed her brows at him.

"Every time I've been there she's been curled up under a blanket on the couch or hiding behind her closed bedroom door," Ruth interjected. "I'm telling you, the child has been damaged. She's going to need therapy."

Damaged? That's what they thought of her? Whatever happened to being allowed to grieve, turning your emotions inside, or just being stunned by something? Her father was dead. She'd been there. Jenny had watched the paramedics cover his head with their standard white sheet—forfeiting the fight, surrendering his life for him. She watched her mother make preparations and answer the door numerous times to flowers and food. Jenny sat numbly on the bed while her mother chose a suit and gave it to the funeral parlor assistant, to dress her father properly for his closed casket. She watched them lower his coffin into the ground.

And yet, none of it seemed real. Her vision had been swimming all week, her ears betraying her with whispers and nothingness. Food had no taste, waking up each day had seemed pointless. Yes, she was in shock. But damaged? Hardly.

Curious, she focused her attention on other groups of whispering relatives and neighbors. Part of her didn't want to know what they speculated over in hushed tones. Part of her wanted to know the truth behind their facetious smiles and polite conversation.

Her aunt Karen and much older cousin Julie spoke of holiday memories. They recalled Christmases both before and after her birth. They wondered aloud if someone should stay with Kathy and Jenny, to make sure they were okay, and help around the house, while they adjusted to life without John. Jenny smiled, happy they weren't speaking of her in a negative way, but dreading the inevitable mother hens that would flow in and out of their house.

Near the buffet table, Karen's husband, Uncle Charlie, spoke with a tall man in a three piece suit. Jenny presumed from his stature he must have been one of her father's co workers. They spoke of boring things like life insurance and policy addendums for death benefits. She soon lost interest.

Dr. Hammond, who had been the family doctor for two generations, sat solemnly near the bookshelf filled with Christian literature and a colorful collection of the Holy Bible in various versions, languages, and print runs. He had been consulting her mother all week and Jenny was convinced there were prescriptions involved to help the woman sleep.

Next to him was the much younger Mr. Peters from the corner house on their street. She didn't even know his first name, only that he managed one of the local banks and all the women in the neighborhood gossiped about him being very young for such a position, and how he truly earned it. They were a dirty bunch of women when they wanted to be and a half smile broke Jenny's statuesque expression briefly at the thought of it.

They spoke in whispers and glanced at her mother several times. They never looked in Jenny's direction. Their faces grew stern as they adjusted their position, their backs fully facing Kathy and the dwindling line of well-wishers. She only made out the words *mortgage* and *medical* before their hushed tones were silenced by their direction.

She noticed the kids had all gone quiet and looked around the room. Two younger cousins were once again filling plates at the buffet table, the rest were absent and she presumed they had gone outside to get away from the stench of religion and death that floated in the stagnant air of the basement.

Glancing at the pastor, she saw his gaze was locked, and she too returned her attention to the foursome at the far table.

"What was she doing in there anyway?" Mr. Sims questioned, raising an eyebrow and waiting patiently for them to see things his way.

"She'd come home from school to an empty, quiet house. Of course she was going to check all the rooms to find Kathy." Sandy's raspy voice was incapable of truly whispering and carried to Jenny's ears as if she were at the table itself.

"And where *was* her mother?" His eyes traveled over to the table he had recently been giving truthful condolences at. As he watched the bereaved gather, their sobs waxing and waning according to the audience they had, you could see his contempt. Jenny realized for the first time Mr. Sims's talks with her father in the garage and on the sidewalks were more than polite. John Hayes had been the only member of the family Edward Sims thought worthy of his time and attention.

"Honestly." Ruth covered her mouth in either mock shock or genuine misunderstanding.

Lisa leaned forward and cocked her head, like she was scolding a pet that had chewed up a shoe. "What exactly are you insinuating?"

"You know damned well," he spat, shaking his head at their obvious blindness. "Was he really dead *before* she got home?"

The trio of women sat upright, leaving the huddle of secrecy and removing themselves from his circle of conspiracy.

"Honestly, Edward. Retirement has made you boorish and your imagination overactive." Ruth sighed and stood, coffee cup in hand.

Lisa and Sandy looked from Mr. Sims to each other and back again, before each leaned outward, peering over his shoulder at Jenny. Their eyes had changed. They were summing her up. Jenny could see them contemplating what he'd said. The paper cup in her hands bent inward at the pressure she applied to the sides of it.

She remembered those accusations, the looks that followed it. They couldn't, could they? Did they believe his wild notions? Could one of them still believe it today—here in the dark? Was it possible for them to accidentally know the truth—and act on it?

CHAPTER THIRTEEN

Jenny shook her head and stood up straight, letting her hand drop to her side. She'd moved from that neighborhood long ago and hadn't seen any of those people for over a decade. Yet, when she thought of enemies or grudges, she relived her teen years in Black River without provocation.

After her father's death, Jenny was treated more like an adult. Not out of respect, but out of need. Her mother needed to discuss finances with someone. She needed to vent her frustration on someone that wouldn't share her worries with others. She needed an adult to help her through the insanity and she was stuck with a thirteen-year-old girl. She made due.

Jenny started babysitting to raise extra cash for the family. Her mother needed the extra support, no matter how little, as there was something about her father's life insurance not paying until the investigation was complete. The problem was no one in her neighborhood would hire her to watch their children.

Old man Sims became more and more hostile toward her and her mother. Often shaking his fist in the air as they drove by and screaming things they never quite heard. He would sit on his porch swing without rocking it, and stare at their home. Jenny started shutting curtains at night and pulling shades at bedtime. The old man was starting to make her nervous, and her mother showed twinges of fear on more than one occasion.

Mrs. Marshall stopped dropping by with invitations to various home merchandising parties and rarely called her mother for those customary weekend barbecues. Jenny noticed she never waved or spoke to them when they ran into each other and often kept her head down, as if trying to avoid recognition. At least she was polite enough to wave back or offer a cursory greeting when Kathy or Jenny spoke or motioned first.

Sandy Turner returned to her couch with husband Joe. Seldom seen before the funeral, the pair was seen less afterward—even missing neighborhood get-togethers offering free drinks and promises of all-night entertainment. Their boys ran the neighborhood as they always had. But if Jenny let herself believe it, the twins were attacking her property and belongings less often than before—and she felt an unspoken gratitude for that among the rest of the slanderous attitudes—but that didn't mean they talked to her any more than normal, or even asked if she was okay.

Only Mr. Peters from the corner, the new guy on the block who wasn't privy to the backward glances and hushed gossip, treated them like neighbors. He had helped Jenny fix the chain on her bicycle more than once, and had offered to help her mother with odd jobs around the house.

Any one of them from the neighborhood could be cruel when they wanted to—they'd shown her and her mother plenty of times. But *this* type of cruelty? Tossing her into a dark basement with only fear to color it. She couldn't believe they would hold a grudge that long, and then bother to hunt her down in another town. Hell, she didn't even know if any of them were still alive.

Of course, there was always Alan's family.

If the darkness could get blacker, it did, as her thoughts drifted to the man that had ruined her life. She replaced sentimentality with anger. She repeatedly clenched her fists and released them, trying to pump the emotions from her system physically.

It wasn't that she had flat-out murdered him, so much as she just hadn't saved him. That distinction had been the driving force to her recovery and still clung to her memory of the incident like a clutched teddy bear. Ironically, she hadn't given up the comfort of stuffed animals for very long when it had happened.

Barely fifteen when school let out for the summer, Jenny had been ecstatic when Alan Taylor had asked her out. She'd floated about the house in a daze all week waiting for Saturday night to arrive and thanking her mother repeatedly for not saying no.

At fourteen, her mother allowed her to go on what she referred to as *group dates.* Safety in numbers she always said and Jenny enjoyed many Friday night pizza parlor gatherings and going to the movies with several friends, current heartthrobs in tow. At sixteen, she would be allowed to date one-on-one. *Alone* with a boy. She couldn't wait. When Alan asked, Jenny was hesitant, convinced her mother would never say yes early. But her mother was in a good mood and Jenny was pleasantly surprised with her mother's approval.

Saturday she spent the day on the phone with Beth. They alternated between giggling at the dirty thoughts their teen minds danced around and serious discussion on the social changes dating a junior would bring. Especially in light of Beth's recent fascination with Dean, who was a year younger than the two of them, and was in no way helping their social stature. Perhaps, once the twins were in high school, the stigma wouldn't be bad enough to keep Beth from dating Dean. And Jenny's date this summer may finally prove to her classmates she wasn't a waste of their time. Maybe they'd even look up to her like they had after the incident with Heidi. She didn't crave the attention or popularity, but acceptance was a tasty morsel she'd missed horribly since her father's death.

Pampering herself as if it were the prom, she began getting ready hours before Alan actually arrived. She'd chosen a pair of low-rider jeans Beth referred to as Jenny's "butt pants" because they gave her flat behind more curve than it actually had. Untucked was a simple white button-up shirt, unbuttoned to reveal the rhinestone-decorated blue tank top underneath and the gold chain her mother had loaned her. Small gold balls pierced her ears and showed when she habitually pushed her long hair behind her ears.

Glancing in the mirror when she heard the car door slam outside her bedroom window, she still wasn't quite happy with her appearance. Regardless, she flew down the stairs intent on not making him wait like she was one of those high-maintenance cheerleader types. Mother stood at the bottom of the stairs holding her hand out.

"Calm down, Jen."

"He's here though."

"Yes, but let him come up to the door. Let him knock. Make him meet me." She spoke as if going down a checklist. "There's a reason for these traditions, you know. I'm not just being mean." She smiled.

"Okay." Jenny sighed and slumped her shoulders in resignation.

"Today's boys have different ideas of respect." She lowered her voice as if it were a secret to be shared in confidence. "My father always said there were signs before the date to let you know if it would be worth your time. You never want a boy that sits in his car and honks. If they whistle at you or command you like property, it's an indication of what they'll be like once they're truly relaxed around you."

"Oh, he wouldn't—"

"The true tests, though," her mother continued as if she hadn't been interrupted, "are your parents and theirs." Her voice changed again, true seriousness coming through, as if the entire meaning of life was about to be revealed. Jenny raised an eyebrow, somewhere between intrigued and confused.

"If they show fear or disrespect when meeting your parents it tells you many things. And how their parents treat each other is how you can expect to be treated."

"Okay." Jenny simply listened and wondered how harsh her grandparents had been on her mother growing up. Then again, a different era with unique social issues often had vastly diverse beliefs and practices.

The sharp knock on the door turned both their heads. He'd arrived and the moment of truth was behind the painted oak door.

The smile on her mother's face, as Jenny looked back from the Dodge Charger's window, let Jenny know he'd won her approval. He'd been polite and charming to her mother, answering her questions without hesitation, and opened the car door for Jenny when they got outside. Mother's guidelines seemed to indicate a perfect gentleman. Of course, she'd never met his parents or seen how they interacted, but that would come with time. Jenny smiled to herself, impressed she was actually listening to her mother's advice without any of the normal teenage resistance.

Much to her delight, Alan took her to the local theater and chose

Harrison Ford's latest movie for their evening entertainment. Ford had been her favorite actor since his role as Han Solo, and Indiana Jones cemented his place in her list of top three actors. She had declined an invitation to watch the film the previous weekend with her friends and had been hoping he'd choose this one so she wouldn't have to force Beth to see it again—although she knew, her best friend would jump at the chance. He bought popcorn and soda, leaned in close for occasional comments, and didn't complain when she asked him to sit and watch the credits with her. He didn't put his arm around her until after she'd giggled at the odd jobs listed at the end of the film, and then he only did so to squeeze her briefly before helping her out of her chair. He was a perfect gentleman—her mother could have snuck in, sat a few rows back, and been impressed.

Afterward they enjoyed a simple meal at one of the local mom-and-pop diners popular with the high school crowd for the inexpensive deserts. These little diners came and went as fast as the graduating classes cycled through and she wondered if it had anything to do with the kids that adopted the establishments as their own. An ex-waitress owned and operated the current hotspot. Her face was pleasant and she welcomed the kids every afternoon, but something in her eyes told Jenny that years of experience with unruly customers just might be enough to keep this diner open longer than the others. A decade worth of waitressing in truck stops and dealing with after-bar locals explained the woman's toughness, but Jenny could never figure out how she had so much patience with the rowdy youth cycling through her doors. She was forever smiling and instructing people, both young and old, to call her Jean whenever they attempted madam or ma'am or miss.

No one was hanging out tonight to see her with him, but she enjoyed the meal anyway, and they chatted as they ate. His parents both worked long hours and had for as long as he remembered, leaving him to his own devices. She nodded quietly, pleased he took up sports to occupy his time rather than take advantage of the empty house and to raise hell. Another reason her mother would approve and be less likely to decline another invitation—should Jenny be lucky enough to get one.

After the best chocolate sundae Jenny had ever eaten, she pointed out Jean had started to clean around them. They still had an hour before her curfew and she didn't want the evening to end at all, let alone early, so she agreed to a walk after dinner and they left. He parked at the high school football field, but rather than leading her to the stands as she expected, he crossed the street to the elementary school playground. He sat on the swing and kicked himself into gentle motion. She sat facing opposite and they talked of school, friends, parents, and their plans for after high school in a jumpy, quid pro quo style.

The *perfect gentleman* was an act, though, and as they got up to leave, he led her over to the small fenced-in area that housed the outside electrical boxes for the school. At first, she thought the moment was romantic, as he put a hand on the fence beside her head and Jenny swallowed back her nervousness, awaiting the kiss she'd hoped for all night. What followed happened in a blur of slow motion that felt like forever but took less than five minutes.

His kiss came, but not as the gentle, almost hesitant peck she had expected. It was not her imagined moment stolen directly from an unrealistic romance movie or novel. It wasn't what she had fantasized about all week long.

Alan's lips brushed hers roughly, his tongue pushing against them and forcing its way into her mouth. It was abrasive, almost abusive, and a part of her was excited, while another part of her was afraid.

Jenny hadn't prepared for this, but she wasn't sure she didn't want it either. Her body didn't melt into his as she'd imagined, but neither did it go rigid in open protest. Jenny's knees buckled from the rush of emotion but she caught herself and stood upright, unintentionally pushing up against him in her surge upward to keep her footing. In response, his free hand grabbed her breast, kneading it until he located the nipple and pinched it. It hurt, it wasn't a turn-on, and she winced beneath his kiss.

He didn't seem to notice and dragged his fingers down the front of her. Alan grabbed her waistband and pulled her closer as his tongue dove deeper. He focused on what he wanted and she didn't think he noticed or paid any attention to signals or signs. He didn't allow her to come up for air to voice approval or grievances.

He pushed her back against the wall again, and pulled her tank top from her jeans. His hand slipped under her shirt and the feel of his fingers on her flesh was an odd mixture of adrenaline-rushing fear and exhilaration. His palm pushed upward with enough force to pull at her skin and she thought it would tear. Jenny gasped beneath the pressure of Alan's lips, accidentally opening her mouth wider as if in acceptance and he eagerly continued his exploration, pushing his tongue deeper into her mouth and nearly gagging her. He grabbed the fabric at the top of her bra and pulled it down, releasing her breast. He cupped her almost gently for a moment before the force returned and she felt his fingers close around her tight enough Jenny thought he'd made a fist with her flesh squeezed into the center of it.

Alarms went off and she worried she was in danger, but somewhere inside a small voice told her to relax, don't jump to conclusions and wait it out for a moment—maybe he thought this was mutual, maybe he didn't know she was in shock. Confusion overwhelmed her until his hand traveled back to the waistband of her jeans and she tasted the change in the air between them. Alan expertly pulled the material at an angle and she felt the button release. She snapped out of her inner moral battle and her hands shot to his chest and pushed on him, trying to force him to back up, to end the kiss, so she could verbally protest. Alan didn't budge.

She squeezed her eyes tight. Stars danced beneath their clenched lids. Jenny raised a leg and calculated where his foot was, then stomped hard to get his attention. His focus was rapt and he didn't seem to notice, making her wonder if she'd stepped on a rock rather than pound on his toes. Jenny raised her leg again, this time with upward force, and connected with his groin.

He bucked backward, but didn't back up. He gasped as he released her mouth, but not before biting down on her lip out of surprise. His hand on the fence worked through the holes in the wire and his knuckles turned white as he squeezed mesh. Alan's other hand slid slowly from her waistline, past her breast, and stopped in midair at shoulder height.

Her eyes flicked from his hand to his face—something had changed in his eyes. It wasn't pain or shock looking back at her. The hand swung forward with lightning speed and connected with the side of Jenny's head. Her vision shook, her mind spun, and on some level she tasted the blood trickling from the corner of her mouth. Her eyes swam back into focus in time to catch his hand on the back swing as he finished his one two technique.

Her lip started swelling immediately and she thought of the Novocain-induced puff of the dentist office. Her face ached with a throbbing rhythm, like an offbeat drummer trying to keep time, and she realized the beat was her own pulse. Blood filled her mouth as fast as she could swallow it. She tried to spit it out but it dribbled instead and ran down her chin.

The next swing wasn't meant to connect with her face, but she didn't realize it right away. Instead, the force behind his arm was funneled into his fist as he wrapped his grip around her arm and twisted. She spun away from the fence forcibly and lost her balance, going down to one knee.

"What the hell?" Spittle flew from his lips. "Who do you think you are?" He pushed her down onto the ground, slamming his foot into the small of her back to add insult to injury.

She could feel his breath on her neck and knew he'd knelt down. Jenny held her breath waiting for the sexual part of the attack to resume—waited for her rape to be over. It didn't come. She heard him scuff the gravel in the yard as he stood up.

"You're not worth it." He almost whimpered the comment, grabbing her shirt by the collar and hoisting her back onto her feet. "Time to go."

The car ride was the second longest ten minutes of her life. They didn't speak and Alan drove recklessly. Jenny was glad the date was almost over and hoped he wouldn't tell everyone what had happened—or worse, lie about it completely—in some sort of macho locker room brag session. She would have been content if they lived their lives and never mentioned tonight and never spoke again. Hell, she'd be okay if they never even had eye contact again and wasn't even sure if she wanted to tell Beth about what had happened. For now, she concentrated on not crying in front of him as she gingerly felt her face, poking experimentally at her cheek and checking all her teeth.

Her left eye felt puffy and she thought her vision was a bit blurred. The cheek below it felt like it had been broken into several pieces and superglued back together like a school project. On the right, the lightest touch on her jawbone sent shivers through her and she worried it really was broken. Her split lips continued to leak blood into her mouth. She'd swallowed enough for her stomach to begin protesting, and she began to feel nauseated.

Jenny was looking out the window, subtly checking for broken teeth with the tip of her finger, when she saw the movement. A flash of brown came out of the deep ravine.

Alan saw the deer as well, but a fraction too late.

He hit the brakes and turned away from the animal. At normal speeds it might have been the right amount of steering, but his anger had been focused on the pedal and they were traveling too fast to begin with. Alan oversteered and the car began to slide. He turned the steering wheel into the skid and tried to pull out of it, but the car had already moved enough to grab the loose gravel of the shoulder and, instead of straightening, it slid farther off the pavement. The rear of the car went over the edge of the road and tipped them into the ravine.

Jenny lost count of rotations after the second flip. She banged her head on the side window several times, causing a small spiderweb of broken glass to form next to her. The vehicle was filled with a cacophony of screaming metal and small explosions of glass. She only realized the car had stopped rolling when she noticed the silence. She lay on her side, as the sound of metal squealing somewhere behind her ground to a slow torturous stop. She was amazed they had landed upright.

Her seat belt had prevented her from flopping around the car as it flipped, but her chest and waist were burning with pain from the pinched force of the strap against her. Jenny pushed on the button to release it and cried out in pain. Her left hand was bleeding and busted, nerve endings dancing to a silent staccato beat. She used her right hand and reached across to undo the belt.

She looked over to Alan's empty seat. The windshield was shattered but still in place. The side window was broken and several large pieces were missing. The door on his side hung on its hinges at an awkward angle. Had she been unconscious? Did he already go get help?

She pushed her bruised shoulder against the door and pulled the handle. It wouldn't budge. She tried ramming into it and frantically flipped the handle back and forth. Frustrated, she crawled across the seat, dragging her hands across broken glass, and climbed out Alan's door.

In the moonlight, the car looked horrible. She wondered how they had survived it. The crash-test dummy commercials never had vehicles this smashed up. The roof was partially caved in. The trunk lid had popped open, torn off, and was lying in the ditch somewhere out of her line of sight. The two tires Jenny could see on this side of the vehicle were both flat.

She looked up to the road and noticed the deer standing there. It stood motionless for a moment, its peaceful night shattered by man and metal, before running off across the road. She reached in to find her purse on the floor of the car, but it wasn't where she'd left it. She stood back up and decided she'd find it later as she turned to follow the deer up the embankment.

Halfway to the incline of the ditch, she found Alan. He'd been thrown free of the wreckage—she wasn't shocked he didn't have a seat belt on—and lay in a crumpled mess on the wet grass. She found it ironic the skid marks the tires had burned through the grass framed his body, and then she wondered exactly how he'd ended up between them. She wiped blood from her lip and bent down to see if he was okay.

"Alan?" Jenny whispered and shook his shoulder slightly. His left leg was bent out at the knee, hyperextended with a bit of bright white bone sticking out just above his kneecap. He murmured something inaudible and she tried again.

"Alan." Jenny spoke a little louder and leaned closer to his face. His eyes fluttered. His hand brushed hers as he reached up, but his hand fell back to the ground and Jenny assumed he didn't have the strength to complete the movement.

"Help me." The hoarse words were faint, and she watched the battle for survival wage within his eyes.

"I'll go get help." She jumped up and headed up the side of the embankment, remembering the house they'd passed around the bend, only a couple of blocks away. Maybe they'd even heard the crash and had already called help.

"Hurr—" His voice faltered again, and the end of the word died in the air.

She scrambled up the slick grass and gravel and reached the road. There were no signs of any other vehicles, and Jenny could see no lights in the direction of the house. She began walking that direction and got almost ten steps before she realized she was limping.

She managed five more and stopped.

The night was silent. The houses had been mostly dark along the road—children would be in bed at this hour and their parents, if awake, would be watching television or reading in low lights. The animals were silent, crickets and night birds holding their collective breath in the wake of the screaming metal and shredding rubber. She looked around.

No one was in sight. Nobody knew they had crashed. *And no one knew about the incident in the schoolyard,* whispered from the back of Jenny's mind, reminding her of her anger. Her fists clenched at her sides, her teeth ground against each other, and she took in a deep breath of the night air.

She turned and walked back to the wreckage, and Alan's body.

"They're coming," she lied to him as she knelt down. Reaching for his hand, Jenny watched hope spark in his eyes while the brightness dimmed. She didn't tell him to fight, or stay with her, or any of those other phrases you so often see people doing on television. She just held his hand and watched him. His breathing was quiet, quieter than the silence around them, and she had to concentrate to hear it and judge his condition by its rhythm.

The battery to his body was a conglomeration of banging around the vehicle and then being thrown free. Jenny imagined the broken leg was caused by landing, but beyond that wasn't sure. Her fingertips explored the wound on her own temple, as she traced his matching marks with her eyes and thought of the missing side window on his side of the vehicle. Without a seat belt, she figured the cuts across the front of his face included some glass marks. Even in the dim moonlight, she could see the purples and yellows as they began to flow across the surface of his face in the haphazard patterns of bruising. Blood trickled from his left ear, both nostrils, and the various slashes. The swelling on his lip had closed off the split there and stopped the bleeding, but not before it leaked down his chin and across his neck in a wide smear. She felt the tiniest pressure in his grip a moment before his breathing began to skip erratically.

"Jen—" He attempted to spit to the side but it dribbled down his cheek instead.

"Shhh." Not that he should save his energy, but Jenny just didn't want to hear it. Her anger coursed through her bruises, pausing on the ones caused by him and not the accident. Her back ached, her jaw was sore and her head throbbed in unison with both points of pulsating pain.

"But Jen, I'm—" She put a finger to his lip to hush him and looked up toward the road. She wasn't sure she could watch as he died, but she sure wished he'd hurry up and do it already.

He turned his head to the side and twisted free of her fingertips. "I'm sorry." Alan looked at her with a bloodshot eye. Jenny let go of his hand and sat back. She pulled her knees up and wrapped her arms around them, gripping her muddied legs and considering the weight behind his words.

Did he mean the accident or the incident before it? Did he mean anything at all or was it just fear of death talking? How was this going to play in her relationships with other boys? What was going to scar her more—the rape attempt, the accident, or the decision to let him die? It wasn't the first time she'd let someone die in front of her, but it was the first time the decision was conscious. As far as the accident, Alan had attacked her sexually, lashed out physically when she'd denied him, and then put *her* life in danger with his angry driving. He put them here, not her. She repeated the rationale until she believed it.

Alan reached for her, his fingers flexing in the empty space between them. She looked back to his face but didn't offer her hand.

"Sorry—" His eyelids fluttered before closing. His chest continued to rise and fall.

She sat, immobilized by the battle inside her. She was still angry, but fear and sympathy started to burn away at the edges of it. Jenny worried about which of them was the monster, and raised her hand to unconsciously chew at a fingernail. Opening her mouth sent a jolt of pain through her jaw where he had struck her earlier, and she whimpered as she withdrew her hand. She looked back at Alan.

She knew who the monster was. She had felt his wrath.

Jenny stared at his chest, refusing to make eye contact again. She ignored his incoherent rambling and attempts to talk, with nothing more than a blink for acknowledgement.

It took him ten minutes to die, the longest ten minutes of her life.

Help finally arrived. A car she hadn't even heard go by had reported headlights in the ditch. They found her next to the body, rocking back and forth on the grass, and assumed she was in shock. Jenny would later claim she'd been unconscious and he was already gone when she came to in the car.

There were rumors about her bruises not looking right for a car accident, but she pretended not to hear them. It was easier to ignore those whispers than it was to shut out the claims she was somehow responsible. Suggestions were more opinion than anything, and based on nothing more than his popularity and her relative unimportance. The date had not helped her social life. In a sense, it had scarred it.

CHAPTER FOURTEEN

Jenny pushed that final thought out into the darkness around her and pretended she hadn't remembered it in the first place. The rest could not be disregarded, not after she'd dug it from the depths of her locked memories. Death had surrounded her throughout her life. Like a guardian angel, it hovered, and the whispers that followed were not unreasonable. After all, she always seemed to be present when accidents happened.

She swallowed hard, pushing Alan out of her mind. Reminiscing was getting her nowhere other than paranoid, and melting her resolve into guilty resignation. The night was far enough removed to be nothing more than a blur with a smattering of details, but the aftermath carried on long enough to be easier to recall and harder to forget. The rumors, the looks, the quiet that seemed to shadow her when she entered a room—it all worked at the edges of her anger now, just as much as it had then. Jenny still hated him, would always hate Alan, but she'd stopped blaming herself long ago, while sitting on a mud-slicked stretch of grass—and a dirt floor in the dark wasn't going to change that. The past was the past and led nowhere. The present was the preamble of the future, and she wanted a future. A future outside of this prison.

Putting her hand back on the wall for guidance, she got no farther than three steps when her fingers ran across a change on the wall. Her mind registered the subtle difference and stopped her dead in her tracks.

This was not age and erosion. This was purposeful. The marks had been carved into the wall for a reason. And the message was not one she was ready to accept.

A little below shoulder height, carved into one of the softer rocks in the foundation, five rough lines ran in a crooked row on the wall, mostly parallel to one another. A sixth line crossed the first four at an uneven angle. No wider than a pen tip and about as long as her index finger, the meaning of the calendar glowed in the darkness like a lighthouse beacon on a starless night.

Someone had been marking time. Someone had been there before her. The safe assumption of the bones belonging to an animal was gone. They were now open for debate and her logical side was losing the battle the fear inside her began to wage.

Jenny felt herself sliding down the length of the wall. She found the ground and curled up, hugging her knees close to her and ignoring the pain flaring in her leg as she brushed across the wound. She began rocking, just barely at first and then building to a frantic rhythm. Her physical balance teetered as much as her mental state.

She closed her eyes as warm tears ran down her face unchecked, without guilt or shame. They followed the curve of her nose and pooled at the corners of her mouth. The salty excretion leaked between her quivering lips and she subconsciously licked it away. Some of it continued down her chin and fell off into the dirt below her. Her eyes burned, her breathing became shallow, and she lost control.

She cried like never before, releasing everything she had ever bottled up, ignored, or forgotten. Gentle sobs became bleak wails, the crescendo rising and falling as her throat closed and opened, her mouth alternated between dry and moist, and her mind worked around everything that had happened, everything she'd found.

Six days.

Someone had been down here for six days. Maybe more. Then what? Where did they go? What happened to them? Did they make it out? Did they die here? Were they killed and left here, or buried among the sand and rocks she was sitting on? The questions bombarded her conscious, but it wasn't answering. It had gone inward. Jenny had become the little girl she never was and let the emotions run their course. She had no choice. It was just too much.

Six days.

That thought started and ended every string of questions her brain could throw at her. How long had she been unconscious? What day was she truly on? Why wasn't there a seventh hash mark?

Jenny slowly tipped onto her side, curling into the fetal position.

Six days.

Her senses were fried. Her mind was a Ping-Pong match of concern and ideas. Her body hurt down to the very bones, muscles pinched and ached, and wounds throbbed. She eventually cried herself to sleep, pure exhaustion taking over.

Fitful dreams full of an endless string of negative possibilities didn't give her any rest. Once again, the man in the shadows visited Jenny, but this time he tried to convince her to cut herself while he watched. He provided her with a rusty X-acto knife and made the first cut for her, taking a chunk of flesh from her thigh and holding it in front of her to see. His disembodied voice asked if she'd like him to save the pieces, letting them dry, preserving them. In another version, he slowly used a rusted piece of twisted metal to shave off her skin—peeling it like a ripe banana and then feeding it to her like a baby. In another version, she pulled her own skin off and fed it to him in some twisted game of lunatic foreplay. She moaned and jerked in her sleep.

At one point, Alan Taylor came out of the darkness, eyes blazing with accusation. His mouth moved in exaggerated anger. His face was a twisted expression of rage and guilt, revenge come to call. She turned away from him but he moved like a shadow and was instantly in front of her again. Jenny withdrew into herself. He loomed closer, and his words were still undecipherable breaths. With a finger extended, he vanished mere inches before reaching her.

Her father and mother visited her and reminded her of all the things she'd done wrong in her life. Her mother silently held up report cards and the police report from when she'd been caught shoplifting candy at the corner store. She wept as her mother shook her head in disappointment. Her father raised his eyebrow accusingly—the movement caused the gunshot wound to open like a third eye. He pointed to a woodpile, lit up by a bare bulb, in the corner of her dungeon, and grinned. He reached out to caress her with the expression she spent three years avoiding—the raw emotion of his desire written plainly instead of reserved for her eyes only. She fought back at both of them with instances of perfection and happiness in her life. Jenny tried to tell them about her college degree, steady job, wonderful son—they were having none of that. They offered no praise and continued to remind her of the things she'd spent a lifetime trying to forget.

Dan was there, too. In the darkness, he offered her razor blades and pill bottles. Filled bubble baths with bloody water and calmly folded bloodstained towels while discussing custody arrangements for their son. He suggested changing his own name to Alan and said hers could be Alana. He smiled and never raised his voice—his calm frightened Jenny more than any anger he'd ever shown her. He vanished into a doorway that opened in the darkness—beyond it she could see the abortion clinic waiting room and heard them calling her name.

Familiar voices floated without faces and recounted any insecurity she'd ever had. Childhood memories walked in and out, horrific caricature cameos. Co-workers and ex-bosses invited themselves in to explain to her the things she hadn't considered in a sick game of "if you think that's bad, how about this?"

Jenny woke with a start. At first, the beeping sound made her think she was back at the car crash and the keys in the ignition were reacting to the open door, but soon remembered the puffed eyes were not caused by some jock's idea of foreplay and let the sound fade with the nightmares. She'd gotten too close to the edge of her sanity, as if it were a physical location, and her balance on it was precarious at best. It had torn her down, attempted to rip her apart, and reduced her to what she strived her entire life to hide—a victim. She remembered where she was and what had taken her to that edge.

Six days.

Somewhere in the darkness that thought created a pinpoint of light, motivation to get out. At best guess, she'd been there two, maybe three days—four was possible but not probable. Jenny now believed she had to get out in the next two, because there was no seventh hash mark.

If there had been others, then she could have been a random victim. If there had been others, the crime could be considered serial. There would have been something on the news. She never watched the news anymore, or read the paper. She just didn't have time, and regretted it.

Jenny sat up, leaned against the wall, and tried to ignore the grumbling in her stomach. She was hungry. She was thirsty. She was sore and tired. But above all, she was a survivor and if she didn't have as much time as she thought, she'd better at least get back to the corner where the bone was. Perhaps she could use it to fend off whoever took the seventh day away.

It had somehow become a symbol of her strength, a tangible motivation. She needed to get out. She needed the bone.

CHAPTER FIFTEEN

Jenny carefully searched the ground for whatever instrument had carved the marks and found only a broken watch and further proof she had not been the first to wake up here. She could feel the crack in the timepiece's crystal, but the edges didn't seem to have any worn or sharp places to suggest it had been the tool used on the stone. Jenny pocketed the broken watch with the tooth and used what she started thinking of as "survivor's braille" to check the wall for more messages, more clues—any details that could lead to her escape.

After brushing her hand up and down and following the path of the foundation for several steps, she found yet another change in her prison's circumference. She stood still for a moment, anticipation catching her breath and holding it. She'd found another corner. Her hand wrapped around a turn in the wall that went *out*, not *in* like the makeshift latrine.

The air smelled different suddenly. It stank of fresh dirt and cool water, rather than the mustiness she'd grown accustomed to. She wasn't sure if she would have noticed it if she hadn't been there as long as she had, didn't think her nose would have registered the difference.

Goosebumps ran up her arms, her flesh reacting to the temperature difference, slight as it was. She smiled.

Escape.

She rounded the corner and immediately noticed the rock and mortar give way to wooden planks. Her hand pulled back as if burned, but her mind lit up with hope. In a moment of excitement, she thrust her hands out to her sides at the victory she knew was just ahead.

Her right hand smacked against another wall, jamming her index and middle fingers and shooting sparks of pain through her arm. Jenny cried out and hugged her injured hand. A string of profanity raced through her mind but never slipped from her mouth—a well-ingrained habit of having young ears around her. She released her fist and shook her fingers, hoping the sharp tingling would abate. It didn't, and Jenny bit her lip as she reached out for the opposite wall more carefully.

No more than four feet separated the two walls. Both were made of wood and by running her hands up and down, she could feel the individual planks. They ran horizontal, each about a foot high. She couldn't tell the length of the planks without moving, and found no nails or stud dents. A hallway? She was convinced it was a walkway, or a doorway. A way out.

Keeping both hands out, feeling for nails or seams in the wood, she walked into the cooler air and breathed deeply through her nose. Elation guided her and she was careless.

Jenny pushed slightly on both sides, hard enough to give herself small splinters that dug into the tips of her fingers. She ignored the pain and figured she'd deal with it when she got to the door. After all, in the light, she'd be able to see the shredded wood in her flesh and remove it easier. Jenny's hands were by her sides, so she had no way of knowing where the hallway ended, and she would have smacked her face, yet again, had her foot not hit something first.

Effectively kicking the end of the hallway, she stopped with her foot still raised and almost lost her balance—she teetered for a moment and then put it down, steadying herself.

The end, she thought and squinted, looking for cracks of light in the door. Jenny had felt no seams, no breaks in the wood. She traced the walls forward until she found both corners and discovered the wall in front of her was also made of wood. She pulled her hands back, flexed her fingers for a few moments, and then hesitantly put both hands straight out in front of her. Jenny felt around the area for the doorknob. She found nothing.

Frowning, she traced the wood with her fingertips, looking for a hinge or handle of some sort, believing it could be an unconventional door. She had no idea how right she was when her fingers brushed across a cold metal lump above her head.

It wasn't a hinge. It wasn't long enough and lacked a barrel shape. It wasn't a lock. It felt like a key had been pushed flat with intense heat. The small nub that stuck out was big enough for her index finger and thumb to grip. Below, the metal butterflied out about a quarter inch on both sides.

"Oh." Her own voice startled her, as audio punctuation of the shape dawned on her. It was a wing nut. Flaring out from the center, it held something in place.

"A door," she breathed in relief.

She felt the seam in the wood just below the center of the clip, as it ran horizontal to the vertical metal, and smiled as she turned the nut parallel to the wood grain. She ran a hand along the edge of the panel to the right, looking for a complementary screw to turn. She found it and twisted. Nothing happened.

Jenny slammed her fist against the door out of frustration and felt it move, ever so slightly. Reaching up, she could feel the gap at the top, the ledge more promising than any ladder rung had been. She squatted and felt around the bottom edges, looking for lower clips to twist. She could not contain her grin as she located and turned them, holding her palm against the center of the panel to keep it from landing on her head.

The Larsons' basement had one of these doors in it and she knew it would fall straight open. When she'd babysat for them, the kids had shown her the little room that once led to a storm door in the backyard. They'd locked the doors outside with a chain and it was no longer usable, but the kids still thought it was a fun little cubby.

She hoped there were no chains barring her way at the other end of this doorway.

Slowly releasing the pressure on the door, she felt it tilt toward her and straight armed the wood to stop it from falling. Jenny stood and found the right edge, now loosened from its moorings, and curled her fingers around it. She slid her left hand from the center to the opposite edge and gripped it firmly. She pulled toward her and heard the wood break free from its housing.

It was heavier than she expected, but managed to keep from dropping it on her feet. Lifting the heavy board to the side, she leaned it against the wall next to her and turned to the doorway. Jenny placed her hand out in front of her to feel her way through. The mummy-mimicking motion was becoming second nature and she smiled—until she heard what she believed was her heart actually breaking. Her smile was replaced with the unbelieving open mouth of soundless shock.

Her hand had found a wall of dirt.

An eternal breath ended with a brutal, inhuman cry as she screamed until her voice cracked. The sound filled the small space of the short hallway and fled into the larger room beyond, echoing far louder and longer than any of her previous noises had proved possible. She kicked the dirt, her hand curled into a fist, and she pounded it on the blocked doorway several times, forcing bits of sand to kick back at her face. She opened her fingers and released the dirt inside them, splayed her hand and leaned against the wall of dirt.

She would not cry. She would not quit.

The dirt was compacted with only a few spots of loose soil, which trickled down over her hand like fine sand filtering through fingertips at the beach. It was slightly damp and much cooler than the ground or other areas of open earth she'd found. Her head dropped to her chest and she drew a raspy breath.

The bastard had filled in the cellar doorway and yet another escape route vanished into the abyss. Jenny felt defeat rising in her chest, desperation keeping it at bay with a fleeting thought of her son. It was all she could do to keep her inner voice from convincing her she was going to die in here.

No. She wasn't. She couldn't.

She closed her eyes and thought of Alan. She remembered his first day of kindergarten and how their school supply list had included hair gel and cologne because he wanted to impress his teacher. She thought of his love of all things popcorn and the many gag gifts they'd bought for each other over the years—everything from popcorn still on the cob to apple-flavored popcorn, which made them both gag and laugh. Jenny remembered his first tooth and the tragedy of explaining why he should put it under his pillow for the tooth fairy rather than shoving it through the fabric of his teddy bear because *he* didn't have any teeth and Alan wanted to share. She touched the pocket that held the tooth she'd found in the dark, but refused to let the evidence interrupt her memories.

She remembered their Sunday matinees—and how they would purposely find the worst movie in the video store, just so they could laugh hysterically at it. Dan never understood their connection, he never understood their twisted sense of humor, but he never once tried to intervene or stop them. Dan didn't understand why Jenny tried so very hard to let Alan be *her* Alan, rather than a reminder of another—why she strove to have a relationship that would make up for the shock and hate she'd initially greeted her son with. She gave Dan his time as well, watching from the window as they played catch, or took apart the car engine in a failed attempt to fix it before calling a mechanic. They allowed each other their own relationships with their son. They carried their own memories of him. She wasn't willing to give up either of those things. After her breakdown regarding his name, after finally letting herself move on and accepting her son for the beauty he was, she couldn't imagine life without him. Jenny needed to find a way out. She needed to see him. She needed—

Maybe Jenny wasn't as self-reliant as Dan thought. Maybe Jenny wasn't as hard as she pretended to be—as hard as life had tried to make her. She thought of Dan and a lump rose in her throat, threatening her airway. She swallowed it down. Jenny missed her boys, both of them.

Jenny spun her back around toward the open room. *Keep going,* she thought as she bit on her lip. *Just keep going.* She thought of that annoying fish in the Disney movie Alan had watched and rewatched, over and over. Its singsong "just keep swimming, just keep swimming" became stuck in her head as she moved forward. She smiled, her mood briefly rejuvenated by the silliness.

Returning to the main room she turned left. She still needed to locate the bone she'd used to mark her starting point. She forgot about counting her steps. If she couldn't get out, she'd at least make a stand. She'd retrieve the bone and return to the dead-end hallway. Then she'd only have one side to defend.

Her subconscious prodded her forward and she moved faster, not caring to explore anymore. She was no longer feeling the wall. She was no longer walking with a carefully placed step. She no longer cared about what was awaiting her in the dark. Jenny had a new plan for survival, and slow and steady were no longer a concern.

Until the floor moved beneath her.

She barely registered the different surface under her sock before her foot slipped out from under her and she dropped onto her tailbone. Like falling on ice, she was walking one moment, and the next, was sprawled on the ground wondering what had happened. If there'd been lights overhead, she'd be staring at them right now. Instead she saw tiny specks of yellow and white peripherally, landing hard enough to daze herself.

Jenny sat up and felt the ground around her. It felt like everything else in here and she was tired of playing Helen Keller with her surroundings. She was ready to accept it must have been a wet spot when her fingertip touched cold metal. She pulled it toward her and it came without force.

It was definitely metallic, but very light for its size. As big around as her head, the flat, disc-shaped object had a raised ridge and a slight circular indention running around the center of it. Small, hard bumps alternately flaked off when she touched them, or stayed right where they were as if glued in place. Curious, she picked at a few of them. Some could be chipped off with pressure, others were almost part of the dish.

Dish? Plate. *Oh God,* she thought.

First the hash marks, now she found what looked to be the remains of someone's last supper. Six days. But on one of those days, they'd been fed. Which day?

She lifted the metal plate to her nose. There was no smell to give her a hint of what it had been or how old it was. It was old enough that any mold or mildew had come and gone. It was old enough that it was hard and odorless. Jenny tried to recall if she'd ever seen food left out long enough to get to this stage. She thought of the crime shows she loved and couldn't remember them ever drawing conclusions based on the state of food at the scene. She drew a blank.

She tried to bend it and found, for its lightweight appearance, it was tougher than she expected. She couldn't tell without light, but she didn't think she had even slightly bent it, not even a kink in the rim. Jenny didn't debate for even a moment before she decided it could definitely come in handy and hung on to it.

Putting one hand out to help return her to her feet, she made a startling discovery. Her hand touched the edge of what felt like another plate. In a squatting position, she reached for the plate and miscalculated, putting her hand in the center of it, and found something even more horrifying. She didn't know whether to rejoice or scream. The second plate still had food on it.

After a cursory, featherlight feel of the surface, she found the plate held three items. Something solid and spongy, possibly meat, was cold to the touch. What could have been a roll, or bun, had turned hard as a rock. What she'd put her hand in had an outer shell. Inside was malleable, almost sticky, and felt like instant potatoes looked. She hated fake flakes.

Jenny picked up the second plate to test the scents and freshness, a bug of some sort skittering across her hand as it moved out of her way. Her stomach churned in disgust, but grumbled in anticipation it might be edible. She licked her lips and swallowed, noticing the saliva was running free in her mouth again at the thought of food within her grasp, but her stomach cramped tightly, reminding her of its size and emptiness.

The potatoes were real. They still smelled like potatoes and when she poked them, she found they were still semisoft at the center. The tougher substance had barely any smell at all, but did have the texture of a slice of beef, or maybe pork. She could feel the tissue on the edge of it where it had dried, and when she picked at it, it peeled away in strings. The rock bun smelled overly starchy and she guessed it to be bakery, not homemade. She attempted to break it in half, but the solid chunk crumbled at the edges from the force.

She sighed.

There were so many questions.

How long had it been here? She didn't detect any immediate mold or mildew. If she was home and this was on her counter, Jenny would guess she hadn't done dishes for a few days. But at home it would have had some signs of decay on it and she felt the items again, with a softer touch, trying to find dots of fuzz or patches of slime. How long did it take for mold to develop? The bugs would have found it immediately, but mold required a bit of time, and in the right conditions. She thought back to science class and couldn't recall.

Was it put down here the same time she had been? Was it even for her, or was there someone else? Someone else here now, or someone else here right before she had arrived? Jenny hadn't heard any noises to indicate another person and she'd even spoken out loud and shouted a tentative hello or two—and screamed a few times. No, she decided, she was alone down here. Any company would have made themselves known by now.

The big question, however, was *should* she eat it? Should she risk food poisoning? If there *was* mold, what kind of sickness would that cause? Would it debilitate her or kill her? Regardless, it would likely stop her progress. There was also the possibility the food was intentionally poisoned, and there'd be no way to find out until it was too late. Her stomach rumbled again, gently prodding her to make up her mind. She did.

Jenny knew her strength was waning. She knew her injuries were slowing her down. She knew in order to get out, she would have to survive being here. She'd have to eat the proffered meal. She reasoned she could peel away the outside, and any mold or insect feces on the outer layer.

She raised the meat, smelled it again, and peeled the tougher strands off the top, exposing the core. Jenny opened her mouth. She tried not to think of all the insects, worms, and whatnot that might have been crawling over it or licking it with their vile little mouths. She plugged her nose with one hand and took a bite, chewing only a few times and then swallowing it down as hard as she could.

Bits stuck in her teeth. The dry beef wadded in a ball in her throat and threatened to suffocate her. She longed for a glass of water, anything, and tears formed in her eyes as she choked the food back up and spit it out.

This was not going to work if she behaved like a starving child. She wiped her mouth, ran a finger under her eye to smear away the lone tear gagging had deposited there, and tore off a smaller piece. Again, Jenny pinched her nose as she popped the morsel in her mouth and chewed. It didn't taste bad and she thought either it didn't have much flavor, or the nose trick really worked. She'd never tried it before and felt like a little kid suffering through Mom's unwanted meal. A vision of Alan suffering through her mother-in-law's rendition of meatloaf made her genuinely smile

She swallowed the meat after chewing it long enough for her saliva to kick in and make it mushy, but before it dried her mouth like bad Thanksgiving turkey would wedge itself in her throat again. It slid down easy enough. She imagined if she opened her mouth, she would hear the food hit bottom. Relief flowed through her as she pushed a finger into the pile next to the meat, to dig out some of the softer potatoes. Food. She smiled.

Her smile faded. Her ears perked up. She could hear the faint sound of the motor again as it echoed through the walls like a whisper. It was never a constant. She couldn't pinpoint the source. But something about its rhythm and cycle gnawed at her. *What is that?*

CHAPTER SIXTEEN

An elevator? No. Jenny continued to chew. Her jaw sped up as primal hunger became automated and taste stopped being an issue, or even a thought. She listened to the fleeting sound and tried again to identify it. Without a doubt, she knew it was a motor. The light whirring noise hummed like metal in motion. Jenny knew she recognized it and grew frustrated at her inability to place it. Elevator had been close, she thought. She knew it had to be a subtle noise—one you don't think of when you hear it. She figured it was a natural noise in everyday modern life and racked her brain trying to pinpoint it as she ate.

Jenny gagged on the meat twice, and again wished she had something to drink. She didn't know if the pebble trick would work after a meal. As she finished the last of the potatoes, scraping it off the plate like a kid wiping out a cake mix bowl, she forgot her decision to leave the shell in case of contamination from fungus, insect or worse. She felt better with something in her stomach—a touch tired maybe, but not like the tryptophan-induced exhaustion of Thanksgiving. She ran her tongue over her teeth and licked her lips. Bits of food between her teeth were nothing compared to the fuzz she was convinced coated them. She needed a toothbrush in the worst way—

A refrigerator!

That's what that damn noise was. She heard it at home every morning while brushing her teeth, as it echoed from the kitchen like breath—never thought of but always there. The motor on a refrigerator had kicked in somewhere. A fridge in someone's house? Was she under someone's kitchen? She closed her eyes and listened for the noise again to try to judge the distance now that she knew the source. It had stopped.

If she was underneath someone, she was in imminent danger—they could decide to come down anytime. She wouldn't have time to run, hide, or defend herself appropriately. She stood up to continue forward, an empty plate in each hand.

She thought of all the places a fridge could be, as she walked along the wall, dragging the edge of the metal dish along the rocks in the foundation. The plate felt the bumps and changes in the stone her fingers were no longer paying attention to, as it bounced in her light touch and made gentle, almost rhythmic sounds. A kitchen, a basement, a garage, a barn—where else had she seen a fridge? And did it matter as much as the fact that it was plugged in and therefore being used? She was concentrating on the fridge—the meaning of it and the hint to her location she was certain was right there, just beyond her grasp—and almost tripped when her leg bumped into the bone indicating her starting corner.

"What?" she questioned rhetorically. She hadn't gone very far from where she'd dined on cold meat and sticky lukewarm potatoes. Jenny grunted under her breath in disgust. The food had been right next to her if she'd have gone to the right instead of the left. But her belly was full and she wasn't going to dwell on it now. Now was the time to fight her way out of here.

She stacked the plates together in one hand, reached down to retrieve the bone, and an odd thought dawned on her. If she'd walked the circumference and the ladder was defunct, and the cellar entrance filled in, then how did she get in here? There had be a way in through the ceiling somewhere. Maybe a rope ladder. No, that didn't sound right. How would they climb a rope ladder with her in tow? Unless they dropped her—but with the height of the ceiling, she would have been more battered, if not broken. Could it be one of those folding types, the kind that slide down when you pull a cord? Maybe, just maybe, Jenny could use the bone as a prodding stick and check the ceiling. She raised it up high over her head and waved it around. She didn't feel it connect with anything. Her idea to crisscross the room repeating the motion died on the first attempt when her diagonal bearing veered off and she had to waste time using the wall to go back to her corner. She squatted down. She needed to rest, needed to think.

If there were overhead lights in here, then the room would be lit up and she'd be seen right away. If she hid in the unfinished room, she'd be hidden from view if he came in at the right angle. But she'd also be blind to his approach. No, she liked the hallway idea better.

Jenny yawned. She could no longer tell if it was regular fatigue that wore at her, or exertion. She stood again, grabbed the plates and bone, and headed back to the hallway. Perhaps she could use the door as a shield of some sort if she could get it to stand on its edge in the middle. If she could—

The doorway!

She stopped and held up the plates in front of her as if looking at them. She adjusted her grip on the bone in her other hand. Jenny had removed the door from its shell. The cellar entrance behind it was blocked by dirt. The dirt was put there, it wasn't raw earth. It didn't have root systems growing through it—not necessarily anyway. It wouldn't have rocks and blockages. It was *just dirt,* right? Some of it had been loose, falling through her fingers like sand. If he filled it in after dumping her in here, it would be fresh, unpacked by weather and time.

She could dig her way out. Even if the outer doors had been removed, and the area seeded with grass, the outside world was *right there.* At most, it was only seven or eight steps up to the surface when the stairs had been there. Cellar doorways were never very deep. She could dig. She had tools.

It was time to leave.

CHAPTER SEVENTEEN

Standing at the wall of dirt, Jenny paused and thought about what the best possible route would be. If she dug high, she'd be working over her head, and she was already sore. If she dug low and it caved in, she'd have that much more above her, on her, and would suffocate before she had a chance to back out. She chewed on her lip and tried to recall any knowledge she may have—any situation that might have been similar—anything that would help her out. From snow forts to sand castles, she kept returning to the same conclusion. You dug where it was softest and left the packed material for support.

She put the bone and one of the plates down on the ground to the left of the door. Lifting the other above her head, Jenny felt for the top of the dirt. Finding it, Jenny put the plate against it and pulled down toward the ground. Plenty of dirt came away freely, falling onto her and landing in her eyes and mouth. She spit out the bits of earth, blinking her eyes to keep them free of debris. It seemed the whole doorway was soft and she worried it was too soft to allow digging without a collapse and suffocation, but repeated the action to see what happened.

This time only a little dirt came away, mostly from the right side right at about waist level. That was her spot. She put the tray down and dug in with both hands, figuring it would be quicker to burrow hand over hand and use the dishes when it got more compact.

She felt the soil push its way under her nails as she forced her fingers into it. Small pebbles, sand and softer, almost silky pottery-style dirt surrounded her hands. Fistfuls of damp ground came out in a gritty cascade, covering the ground below her and burying her feet. She felt proactive, rejuvenated by the action itself.

On some level, Jenny felt like a little kid playing in the dirt, and fondly thought back to her days of backyard burrows and shoreline castles. Something about digging for discovery and building for creativity, when given nothing but the dirt in front of you, made you feel free as a kid. As a preteen, she'd taken a pottery class at the local college and felt that same freedom as the warm, wet clay ran through her fingers. Her imagination spun into reality on a wheel between them.

Of all the things she'd thought of since waking up here, this felt like the first truly pure moment. It came without guilt or worry for Alan or Dan, or even Jenny herself. It came from that secret place you hide those treasured memories, often forgetting about them for long periods of time, only to remember them because of the strangest triggers. The dirt was triggering younger, carefree days, and as much as Jenny wanted to stay there, she acknowledged the innocence of the moment fleeing, as she switched to memories of Alan playing with his cars in their sandbox.

She recalled his extravagant highways and overpasses made of twigs and leaves. His Matchbox cars crashed with a frequency that would alarm the D.O.T. His buildings often toppled mysteriously and buried the travelers. Sudden floods caused by the hose, or *sue-*

mommies would wipe out everything and he would gleefully begin building his little disposable streets anew.

When he got older, he traded in the sandbox for an old pickax he'd found in the garage, but still continued to dig into the earth and come away covered head to toe, like any other boy his age when left with no other form of entertainment. She'd asked him several times not to dig in certain parts of the yard. After many rounds of her stern looks and his stomping feet, he'd agreed and begun excavating the ditches behind their house. A particularly deep ditch became The Mine, as he reported his daily findings to her. Old magazines, discarded soda bottles that *must* be antiques, and the odd piece of metal—bottle caps, twisted bits of hubcaps and the occasional coin.

The day he came dragging the skull into the house didn't go over as well.

Enjoying a cup of coffee with an older neighbor, Jenny didn't see him come along the side of the garage or enter the back door, but Anna saw him round the corner of the kitchen. The middle-aged woman shrieked like she'd been pinched and dropped her coffee cup. Jenny jumped up and stared at her, wondering what was wrong, fearing something as serious as a heart attack had surprised the woman. It wasn't until Anna started stammering about germs and filthy bugs that Jenny's expression twisted from fear into confusion. She looked behind her, at what Anna was directing her hysterical lecturing.

There stood Alan, a smile beaming from ear to ear, covered head to toe in dirt and grime and wet mud. In one hand, his pick dangled. The other hand rested on top of the antler branching off the giant skull on her kitchen floor. He stood tall and proud—an African hunter home with the kill. She gasped at the scuffed head at his feet. Then smirked. And finally broke into laughter, eventually doubling over with side cramps.

Anna didn't see the humor in it. The woman spat something about bleach and left the house, giving Alan and his prize a wide berth. Jenny laughed until her breath threatened to stop all together and tears ran down her face. She straightened herself up and asked him about his day. He continued to smile, the glint in his eyes a combination of pride and relief that she hadn't reacted like the neighbor.

He explained the skull had been half-buried at the bottom of the ravine, and he'd freed it because it was cool, but also because he didn't know what it was. She thought it looked like a moose from the antlers and suggested they give it a proper burial. He balked at the idea and asked if he could clean it off and keep it. She saw no harm in it and told him to use dish soap and the hose, and maybe, just for everyone's safety, dump some bleach over it. They chuckled at the mention of disinfectant, reminded of Anna's reaction, and dragged it outside. That damn moose skull was still hanging in her garage.

Jenny smiled as she pulled dirt toward her. She missed Alan horribly. She had no idea how long she'd been gone, but the inability to see him or hear his voice made her chest ache. She could picture him easily and remembered the sound of him sleeping, but needed more. She needed to get out of this hole in the ground and get back to her son, her life.

She realized the moose skull had been out of place in the city ditch and again thought maybe the bones she'd found were as well. Animals were tenacious when it came to dragging their food off for privacy while eating, or storing for later. It was still a possibility, wasn't it? She remembered the plates of food and her optimism was swallowed like the tepid potatoes, forcibly, over the lump in her throat. The only animal that had dragged any bones in here had deposited them with flesh still on them, and food to sustain them—

for a while. Instead of heightening her fear as the fleeting thought had in the past—enough that she never let herself fully let the idea percolate to the surface and become reality—it angered her. How dare they, whoever they or he were.

Her hands dove back into the two-foot hole she'd created while daydreaming and hit resistance, hard. She yelped as she pulled her fingers back to her mouth on instinct. Jenny removed them with a grimace and spit dirt out, scraping her tongue on her teeth and trying to rid her mouth of the earthy taste impulse had deposited. She rubbed the tips of her fingers and felt the jagged edge of the nail she'd smashed. Softened by the moist dirt, it had torn low along her cuticle and stung to the lightest touch. She shook her head, amused she'd almost thought *I broke a nail,* like some pampered suburban wife who didn't have to garden or cook or clean for herself and could bother with perfect fingernails.

She wiped her finger off on her shirt, determined to ignore the pain and continue forward. She stopped and thought about it. She didn't have to put her fingers back in the hole to know it would hurt like hell for longer than she cared, before it went numb. It wasn't like there was any Neosporin handy, or bandages. She didn't have work gloves. She didn't have a choice. Jenny chewed on her lip as she thought about her options.

She lifted her shirt, bit into the edge of it, and tore a small strip from the bottom. Jenny wrapped it around her finger and tied it. She knew digging in the dirt wouldn't keep it in place for long, but it only had to stay until the pain of pressure against it—even protected she knew she would feel it—numbed it enough to stop caring. A broken nail was *not* going to be her downfall.

Bending down to retrieve a dish to dig into the harder earth that had torn her nail, she was shocked to realize how much dirt already lay at her feet. In her absentminded digging, she'd just pulled the dirt out and let it fall as it might, not thinking about what it might bury other than her feet. She rooted around in the pile and located the bone and plates. Jenny shoved the bone into the wall of dirt to the left of where she was digging, for safekeeping, and gripped both plates with intentions of using them rather than her hands to break through the packed soil.

As she leaned into the opening, her shoulders caught on the sides and prevented her from reaching all the way in. She was going to have to widen the hole if she planned to crawl through it. Beginning at the entrance again, she knocked dirt from the edges until the hole was almost three feet wide. She then worked her way inward.

Her mind turned inward again as well, and she thought of the darkness she kept finding there, as she struggled with the darkness surrounding her.

She'd never been afraid of the dark, once she'd passed the initial childhood fears of the unknown under your bed or in your closet. She'd given up monsters long ago, replacing them with the men that came through her life, the tragedy that seemed to cling to her, and the reality of the world around her. Yet here she was, in a darkness she should probably fear, and she feared the void of her own blackness more.

She tunneled, widening the escape route as she went, and wondered when exactly life would stop beating her up. She thought of talking to God and asking for assistance, but that would make her a hypocrite and she knew it. She and God were not on speaking terms—they hadn't been for years. They'd had their first fight when her father died, their last when Beth died. She promised herself she'd never speak to him again.

But that didn't mean she couldn't talk to Beth. Logic told her it would be like speaking to dead air, talking out her issues, getting through this insanity by holding onto a thread of hope. The rest of her told logic to shut the hell up. Maybe, just as she had been all through school and college, Beth would be there for her. Maybe she could get through this if she *believed* Beth was there helping her. And maybe, just maybe, Beth could reach from beyond the grave and offer some assistance, advice, encouragement—forgiveness.

CHAPTER EIGHTEEN

Jenny knew many adults had a certain age in their minds they believed marked them as old. For some it was thirty, for others forty—the optimists held out for fifty or higher. Sometimes, people believed if they acted young enough—or foolish enough—they could recapture youth, postpone old age, put off the inevitable. Midlife crises had been named such because of its propensity to strike, because it wasn't a myth or rumor. But ask any kid on the planet how old is old and, nine out of ten times, they'll tell you the same age. Thirty. To anyone under thirteen, thirty was the beginning of the end.

There was no age that truly bothered Jenny. For the most part, she was just happy to be alive and have those she loved around her. Generally content with what she had, she wasn't one for having wish lists or working overtime to afford the next new toy she didn't need. Age was age. It was just a marking of time. It was how you spent that time, and what you remembered of times past, that counted. And sometimes what you'd forgotten.

Jenny's thirtieth birthday came and went with a small bakery cake decorated with Batman—Alan's idea—a homemade birdhouse made of twigs and mud, and a card with a handwritten coupon for dinner and a movie. She was happy with that. Beth joined Jenny and Alan for cake and television, helped tuck Alan into bed and went home shortly after, like any other night. And Jenny was fine with that.

Beth was a different story.

Beth called one evening in a complete panic.

"Thirty-one? How did that happen?" Beth's voice cracked and Jenny wondered if she'd been crying or drinking. "Weren't we twelve just last summer? Didn't you just give birth to Alan? Where have our lives gone?"

Nope, not crying or drinking, just cracking. Jenny thought surviving last year would be the end of Beth's doomsday mantra of how old she was and how much of her life was gone. It wasn't.

"Bethie." Jenny's tone was something akin to what she'd use on Alan when he was injured and didn't want to go to the doctor's office. "We're not old, hon. We're just getting good."

"Yeah, good. Like on *Logan's Run*. Remember that show, Jen? Life was over at thirty."

"Beth!" Jenny would have spit if she'd had anything in her mouth. She hadn't thought of that particular television program for decades and here was Beth believing in an outdated prime-time notion of entertainment. "We thought that because we were young, not because we would never get old. We're going to get old, hon. It's what people do. And someday we'll live together in a nice little cottage with a ton of cats—just the two of us in our bad hats that cover our blue hair." She expected Beth to laugh at their shared vision of their future with no men. Instead, Beth started crying.

"How can you say that? Dean's *dead,* Jen. Dead. Apparently, we're old enough to just *die.*"

The cause of the hysteria reared its head, without Jenny having to dance around it for an hour before forcing Beth to fess up to what triggered this attack. "It was an accident. He didn't die of old age."

"No, but he died." Beth's voice became a scared whisper. "The first boy I dated. My first real boyfriend, first make-out session, first dance. So many things with him or because of him—and now he's just… gone. I can't call him. I can't reminisce. I can't—"

"Beth." Jenny didn't want to come across as harsh or uncaring, but couldn't hold her tongue.

"What?"

"When was the last time you called Dean? Seriously?" Jenny tried to keep her sarcasm to a minimum and continued to tiptoe around Beth's feelings, as out of control as her emotions were at the moment. "I haven't seen either of the twins since I moved away. You ran into Glenn only because you were back in Black River for the weekend."

"But I saw him. I *could* see him. I *could* call Dean…" Her reasoning trailed off and Jenny worried for a moment Beth had hung up.

"Beth?"

"I'm here."

The silence allowed Jenny to hear the crackling in their connection, the little clicks and ticks always present, but they usually talked right over and ignored. She couldn't push Beth. She could only nudge when the moment offered itself—it wasn't now, not when Beth had gone quiet. Her strengths at calming Beth had always been when her friend was at the height of hysteria, not in the dungeons of depression.

"Jen?"

"Yeah, hon."

"Why didn't we go to the funeral?"

"I didn't have a babysitter. Dan was out of town. You had

meetings." Jenny thought for a minute. "Or rather, meetings you used to keep from facing death and age. So why now?"

"I don't know."

"So how do we fix it? Do we need to road-trip and visit his grave? Would calling Glenn help?"

"No. I don't know." Beth's voice faltered. "I don't even know why it struck me so hard today. Christ, he died almost three months ago."

"Three months? Already?" Jenny hadn't realized it had been so long. "Wow. So, okay. Now what? Should we go out? Girls' night out? We'll drink, and you can talk about Dean, and I'll bring up that party you made me promise to never bring up, and we'll laugh and cry and heal."

"I'm still old. Another birthday coming."

"So, how about a birthday party? We didn't do one last year."

"No, I was avoiding it last year. I think." Beth paused and Jenny heard the distinct snap of a soda can being opened. "Yeah, a party. Can we?"

"Sure, why not?"

"Excellent! Let's make it big, really big. Let's do what I should have done last year. I'm not going down the road of old age without a fight, damn it. I want it to be something memorable."

It was.

For someone who had never liked to be the center of attention, and begged each year for everyone to just let her birthday come and go, Beth went all out that year. She helped Jenny plan what would be a *surprise* party—one Beth fully planned to pretend to be surprised by. From the color of the streamers to paying for the banquet room at their favorite tavern, Beth was more than involved—she was obsessed.

The theme was the islands. Fresh fruit served on wooden skewers, leis for everyone—with extras to take home or hang in their cars to remember the event—and even a fire permit to allow for tiki lights inside the bar. Beth had gone so far as to suggest they cover the floor in sand, but Tony didn't like the idea much and shook his head. That was a full sentence from Tony, the short Italian bartender and owner of The Spot. Tony had a big, bad attitude and an even bigger chip on his shoulder—being Italian by blood, but taking after his grandmother and living with that impossible power trip in a five-foot-four frame. He'd let them do just about anything else they'd wanted, but sand in his bar was out of the question.

He did agree to the lawn chairs instead of the regular folding chairs and hard-backs currently in the room, and helped them haul the furniture to the basement. He actually thought it sounded like a hell of a good idea for a party in the middle of winter. Tony asked if he could pay for some of the supplies so he could carry the theme for a few weeks or so, and see what it would do for business. Beth laughed and said he could have anything left when she was done. Jenny beamed—the party was making Beth happy and turning Tony into a social butterfly, or at least a minor-league conversationalist.

When they finished, the backroom had been beautifully transformed into an oasis, and the girls didn't want to wait until the next day to start the celebration.

"Hey, Tony!" Beth called to the front of the bar. "We need a practice run—would you set us up?"

He grunted and leaned over the counter so he could see through the doorway to them. Tony tossed a curt nod and questioning eyebrow to the girls.

"Margarita, please." Jenny smiled and gave him her "like you didn't know" expression.

"Mai tai! *With* umbrellas, please."

Tony acknowledged them with another grunt and vanished from sight.

"So," Jenny leaned back in the chair and lifted her legs, crossed them, and plopped her feet on the chair next to her. "What do we have left to do?" She looked around at their hard work and could almost believe they were in the islands. The ambiance was definitely layered everywhere she looked. A newcomer wouldn't question why the invitation had said, DRESS FOR VACATION! DOOR PRIZE FOR BEST HAWAIIAN SHIRT.

"Pick up the pineapple upside-down cake in the morning." Beth held her thumb up to represent the first thing on their checklist. She'd had fun planning and decorating, but Jenny could see the anxiety still hanging behind her eyes. Jenny had noticed the occasional silence throughout the day as well, but hadn't said anything. She just had to get Beth through the next twenty-four hours and then she hoped her friend's spirits would be lifted and Dean forgotten, or at least put in his proper place of sadness, rather than depression and a cold reminder of their mortality.

"Put oil in the tikis, 'cuz Tony said not to fill them and leave them overnight tonight." Jenny added and Beth flicked her index finger out with her thumb. As if on cue, Tony walked in and put the umbrella drinks in front of the girls. He looked around and said nothing, his way of approving, and left without a word.

"Oh—" Beth dropped her feet off the chair and sat up, reaching for her drink and widening her eyes at Jenny. "We have to find that CD. You said you had an idea where?"

"Seriously? You really want Tiny Tim at your party?" Jenny stirred her frozen strawberries with the thin straw and removed the umbrella, placing it on a napkin next to her.

"Yes, I'm serious. Look at this place—Tiny Bubbles is an absolute must." Beth grinned with more sheer happiness and honesty than Jenny had seen since the phone call that had sparked all of this.

"All right. I'll pick you up in the morning and we'll hunt it down."

"And we don't stop until we find it, right?"

Jenny nodded.

"Even if it means hitting the cities?"

Jenny lifted her margarita. "If we must."

"Yah! Thank you, thank you, thank you, Jen." Beth leaned over and hugged Jenny, almost spilling their drinks. They gulped down what remained in their glasses, looked around one more time, and bid Tony farewell.

The next night, the scene was immaculate. Music played quietly enough that people didn't have to shout over it to talk. The flicker of the lamps caused dancing shadows against the tropical posters covering every inch of wall. And the gathering of Beth's twenty friends waited. Invitations went out to those chosen for a number of reasons, ranging from actual friendships to acquaintances, from those that would get a kick out of the décor to those older than she, that would make her feel younger, even on her birthday. The crowd waited, poised to jump up and shout.

Beth entered in front of Jenny, who had "dragged her out for a night on the town," and the voices blended as one, shouting their welcome to the birthday girl. She acted surprised—she did better than she'd ever done in any of their high school plays or college drama productions, and Jenny wondered briefly if Beth had missed her calling. She grinned, giggled, and even squeezed out a tear of overwhelming happiness. The partygoers ate it up. No one ever had a clue she'd planned the whole thing, down to the decision to cut the pineapple chunks into circles rather than squares for the stick-fruit display.

The night went without a hitch and Jenny found herself standing back and watching, happy to observe her friend and assign it to memory. Even the absence of her new boyfriend, Jack—on an unavoidable business trip in Chicago—didn't affect her.

Then again, planning it with the queen of paranoia had been draining. When exhaustion hit Jenny, it was only ten thirty. It was as if someone had slipped a roofie in her punch and then slammed her into a wall. She felt it throughout her body and knew although it was worth it, it would take days to recuperate and she wasn't even drinking. Jenny didn't think it right to bail, so she snuck coffee from Tony up front and stayed with the group as long as she could. She made it through a spur-of-the-moment limbo contest with a push broom, the drunken hula dancing that put karaoke embarrassment to shame, and then the presents and cake. Finally, there was no fighting it. Either she was going to fall asleep in her lawn chair, or they were going to have to think about calling it a night.

Beth protested. She was having fun being the center of attention and enjoying the best birthday bash she could have imagined. She didn't bring up the reason for the party, but was genuinely having the time of her life and didn't want it to stop. She gave Jenny the look. The same look they'd been giving each other since second grade. The look that meant, *please don't ruin my fun.*

Jenny could do nothing but respond with the *you're on your own* shrug. She was dog-tired and didn't know if she'd be able to drive safely if she didn't leave soon. Jenny had been the designated driver for the birthday girl and with that safety net, Beth had had more than enough alcohol and not enough food. She was already past happy drunk, and closing in on bombed. They spoke without words and Beth finally asked Cheryl if she could give her a ride home because Jenny had to work in the morning—ever the friend, she tossed the little white lie to protect Jenny from becoming a "party pooper." Cheryl agreed and Jenny made two rounds through the stragglers saying her good-byes before dragging herself out of the back room. She left the coffee cup on the bar up front and nodded good night to Tony.

Jenny had been so tired, the next morning she couldn't even remember the ride home. As she leaned against the wall in the kitchen with one eye open and both ears listening for the gurgle at the end of the percolating cycle on the coffeepot, she barely remembered crawling into bed. Somewhere in the house, a phone rang. The small portion of her mind functioning on pre-caffeine automation heard Dan's voice and panicked for a moment. Dan? *Oh yeah,* Jenny thought. He'd agreed to watch Alan at her house and crash on the couch. He must have grabbed the phone in the living room. Who calls at six o'clock in the morning? God, why was she even up? *Damn her internal clock,* she thought, but forgot her own questions as they were overruled by the double popping sound she'd waited for—coffee was done.

Stirring her creamer-lightened coffee with both eyes closed, Jenny slumped over the table and tried to convince herself she wasn't old because she'd stayed out until two o'clock and felt like it had been five in the morning. She never heard Dan enter the kitchen, part of her conscious had already decided he'd gone back to sleep. His voice startled her—his words would echo until her final days.

"Jen." He pulled out a chair and sat down, putting his hand on her shoulder.

It was all she could muster to answer with a grunt and sip more coffee.

"Jen." The urgency in his voice was a bit louder, clearer. "Hon, there's been an accident."

"Mmmm." The words barely registered, but the term of endearment and his tone woke her up. She furrowed her brows at him, her pre-coffee fog turning to confusion and anxiety. "What?"

"Honey, Beth was in an accident."

Her chair shot backward underneath her, as Jenny jumped to her feet and grabbed her purse. She moved on pure instinct and didn't even stop to realize she still had her pajamas on. Jenny was halfway to the back door when Dan stepped in front of her.

"No." He took her keys from her. "Go change, I'll drive."

On the way to the hospital, Dan told her what Cheryl's husband had explained on the phone. The girls had stayed until almost three in the morning before Tony finally called it a night and kicked everyone out. They shouldn't have been driving, but he tried to rationalize it by saying it had been the other driver who'd caused the accident. The early morning milk truck driver had fallen asleep at the wheel and ran through a red light. The girls had been giggling and not paying attention. The truck pulverized the passenger side of the Pontiac Sunfire—Beth's side.

Cheryl had sustained cuts and bruises, some minor and others that required attention. She was currently listed as stable, with a total of seventeen stitches and a prescription for pain medication. They said she could go home later that day if her condition remained the same.

Beth had been in surgery since arriving. They'd fixed several issues and stopped her internal bleeding. But the damage to her kidneys was going to require more surgery, and they'd stopped midway through when her stats dipped below safe operating levels. They packed her, stitched her up, covered the area and said they'd go back in and try again in a few hours, after her body had recouped a bit from the previous surgeries and she stabilized a bit more. She was sheltered away in the intensive care unit until then.

She hadn't regained consciousness since the accident.

Jenny didn't remember the car ride, not even the stop at her in-laws' to drop off Alan on the way. She couldn't recall parking the car. But she remembered the smell upon walking through the automatic doors. If she'd ever been curious about what the smell of desperation was, all she'd have to do is walk into any hospital and take a deep breath. Whether waiting to be treated or currently getting treatment, whether the victim or the loved one, everyone in that building knew desperation, and she hated it. The loneliness, sorrow and anxiety the sterile white walls and antiseptic air provided seeped into her skin and burrowed toward her soul.

Dan spoke to the woman at the front desk and ushered Jenny into the elevator. She had no idea how many floors they traveled before the doors opened again, only that the ride seemed to be in slow motion, while her mind ran in light-speed circles. The doors opened soundlessly and the odors of this particular floor hit her before the sound of the machines registered—the intensive care unit. Four doors down the hall to the left, in a room marked only by the number 1208 and a clipboard on the wall, lay Beth. Jenny stopped at the doorway, her rush to get to her friend's side belayed by the reality of what faced her.

Through the doorway, Beth lay on the bed. Her flesh was gray—not white, not translucent, and far worse than any imagining of the term "pale" could bring to mind gray. The color around her came from tubes, surgical tape, iodine stains, and blood that had yet to be completely cleaned from her skin. The montage of color mixed and ran, the liquids drying in blotches, and the equipment creating stark lines of contrast against them.

Jenny could hear the wheezing sounds of Beth's assisted breathing. She saw the machine, with its accordion pump inside, visually mimicking the rhythm she heard. Her friend's chest barely moved with the forced air, and Jenny gasped, afraid she'd seen Beth's chest rise, fall, and fail to rise again. The shallow sounds were also relayed to the monitor stationed above the bed. Four lines of color ran across the screen. Each line represented a different vital sign. Each track moved at a separate erratic rate across the dark monitor.

Dan nudged her gently from behind. She didn't budge. She couldn't. She couldn't enter the room and think of Beth as anything other than the battered lump of broken flesh that obstructed her view. Jenny needed to find a happy thought, a wishful memory, something to give her a better vision of Beth so she could go in there and be brave for a friend that most likely wouldn't notice she'd even bothered to show up. The best she could do was recall the previous night and the elation Beth had expressed during her party, the utter glee she wore on her face. Jenny told herself the genuinely wide smile and almost obnoxious laugh that had echoed through The Spot was Beth on a good day. This was simply Beth on a bad day—a very bad day.

Jenny swallowed and stepped into the room.

The seven steps to the bed seemed to take an hour, but Jenny finally reached the iron rail and put her hands on it for support. The clinical smell vanished. The colors of Beth's appearance were forgotten. All she saw was her best friend—the girl that sat by Jenny in kindergarten because she wanted to share the crayons, ran for help that day on the playground with Heidi, and had been there with her through the good and bad ever since.

She remembered cooing a few "oh honeys," and pushing Beth's dirty, bloodied hair to the side. She got a washcloth from the bathroom and did what the nurses hadn't had time to do yet. Jenny cleaned the stains from Beth's skin the best she could with warm water and hospital soap. She couldn't let Beth's mother see her like this. When the initial shock and nervous need to do something wore off, and both patient and room were as clean as Jenny could muster, she dropped into the chair next to the bed. She reached through the bars and stroked Beth's hand, interlocking her fingers and squeezing softly. She didn't let go of it. She didn't speak for the next several hours outside of asking Dan if he'd get her a cup of coffee.

People came and went—co-workers and friends, acquaintances, and last night's partygoers—but in the end, none of them could handle the oppression of the situation and left after little more than a good thought and cursory sentiment. Tony's stoic behavior blended in with the rest of the visitors, and Jenny didn't notice he'd sat in the chair next to her for as long as he did until Dan pointed it out later. Jack called and expressed his concern and sympathy, telling her he was changing plans and catching the next flight home. Jenny didn't remember the conversation but apparently told Dan, who later reminded her of this when he asked if he should leave. She had answered with only an expression and he stuck around, loitering at the vending machine and roaming the halls—he gave her space, but stayed close enough to be support if needed.

Jenny alternately harassed and helped the nurses when they came in, wanting to be proactive in Beth's recovery and trying to learn more about what was going on and what they were doing. She asked question upon question and was disappointed the nurses, schooled as they were, played dumb and told her she'd have to ask the doctor.

When the doctor finally came around, he ignored Jenny. Dan had gone to get something to eat in the cafeteria and she was keeping silent vigil in the dim room. Maybe the doctor didn't see her. No, he did. He just wanted to avoid the hurt that came from talking to the patient's family, and with Beth's mom stuck on a layover in

Minneapolis, Jenny was all Beth had for family at the time. Jenny finally spoke up as he made little noises while going over the charts hanging at the foot of the bed.

The prognosis wasn't bad, but it wasn't all good. Beth's stability wasn't what they'd hoped to see by now. They had removed the damaged kidney, and were concerned about the stability of the other. A renal vein thrombosis was being watched and something about a possible embolism—which scared Jenny. A lot of multisyllable words and medical definitions were whispered, and all Jenny understood was they'd fixed plenty but still wanted to go in and explore the surroundings of her surviving kidney and remove some clot if feasible. They wouldn't be able to do the surgery tonight because of some confusing medical term Jenny promised to look up when this was done—perhaps in the morning—but the doctor hadn't sounded too awfully confident about that either. An offhand comment led her to believe they may life-flight her to another facility for care if she stabilized, but in the next breath he said she was out of danger for now and they were doing everything they could for her. He politely suggested Jenny go home and get some sleep, eat a decent meal, and call to check on the patient as often as she wanted. Jenny couldn't do it. Hard as it might have been to enter the room, leaving it would be downright impossible until Beth opened her eyes and let her know it was okay.

Beth didn't. Beth didn't flinch, moan, or even snore in her drug-induced sleep. The shock of the accident had yet to work its way out of her system and the lasting effect of emergency narcotics and anesthesia didn't help. Beth remained unconscious. Jenny remained alert at her side.

At some point in the middle of the night, Jenny nodded off in the chair—still holding Beth's hand—and woke to the shrill wailing of an alarm and scuttling of several bodies that filed into the room as if they'd been waiting just outside the door. A large woman pulled Jenny and her chair out of the way as one unit, and gave her a halfhearted look of apology for the rudeness. Jenny jumped from the chair and pressed her back against the wall, as she watched the flurry of activity.

A gurgling noise came from the bed and Jenny bobbed and weaved around the staff trying to get a look. Blood had filled the tube in Beth's throat. More of the bright crimson liquid frothed at the corner of her mouth and spilled down her chin. Something was wrong. Jenny winced when they pulled the tube free and blood sprayed across several of them. Orders were barked, trays were uncovered, and instruments flew from white sheet to gloved hand and back again.

Scared-looking interns rolled two machines into the room. One looked like the portable ultrasound machine Jenny remembered from her pregnancy; bags and tubes lay on top of the other cart and Jenny couldn't make out the box below them. A blur of activity blocked her view, and Jenny tried to imagine what they could be using the machine for, waiting for its purpose to rear its ugly head. Jenny wondered what a dialysis machine looked like and then questioned why she would think of that particular item.

Time slowed and her mind not only wandered but also made mental note of every strange little detail she *could* see in the chaos around her. The nurses were mostly brunette, except for the pale-haired girl with no makeup who tore open a small silver package from the cart tray. She had a Band-Aid on her left index finger, no wedding ring, and short but manicured fingernails. To her right, a darker beauty, whose hair was shorter and therefore not required to be pulled back like the other girl's had been, had frayed nails that struggled with the tape she was attempting to tear off and drape on the edge of the cart for future use. Both worked without speaking—the others made up for it.

A husky-voiced female and a lone male nurse in the room busied themselves with the tubes from the other cart. They spoke in curt commentary rather than questions or requests, stating what they were doing out loud as they went. She hooked a tack tube while he clamped a vacuum hose. Tack tube? Vacuum hose?

Jenny turned back to the other pair of nurses, willing herself not to look at the remaining girl whose hand was shoved inside Beth's mouth, fingers pulling blood and spit out as fast as she could scoop it.

The blonde nurse smeared Beth's belly with lubricating jelly while her partner turned on the ultrasound equipment. Just as the nurse began to rub the wand across Beth's belly, the other pair barked something Jenny didn't quite understand. The girl sweeping Beth's mouth pulled free and grabbed the tube handed to her. She forced it down Beth's throat. After what seemed like four feet worth of half-inch tube had vanished into Beth's gullet, the nurse announced she was in.

The machine in question was clarified as it came to life, humming and whining at the same time. After a few moments, blood came up through the tube. Jenny followed its path to a bag on the cart and realized they were pumping Beth's stomach. She glanced at the other two and understood they were watching the process on the screen. The room swam as she watched them fight for Beth's breath, Beth's life. Jenny lost focus, as she heard them barking about clots and blockages.

She sat back down in the chair, guided by a hand she hadn't seen coming but that must have been aware of her sudden desire to lie down. The volume in the room remained steady. Orders were given.

Findings were shared. Jenny understood there was a perforation in Beth's stomach somewhere and they were trying to locate it. She heard them discuss more emergency surgery. She was vaguely aware one of them called someone else on the wall phone. They spoke of blood volume lost and displaced something. Their frantic words lost all meaning as she sat, stunned by their activity, and inactivity. She'd expected them to take Beth to emergency surgery like the television doctors did, but they continued to work where they were, throwing used items, discarding the wrappings from new ones on the floor, and literally bathing Beth in liquids Jenny could only assume were meant to clean or sterilize. They worked fervently but the monitor above Beth's head never stopped beeping.

Until they backed away from her and the honey-haired nurse reached up and pushed a button to silence the alarm. Jenny fixated on the fingertip that had quieted the room. She didn't know which of the others said it, but someone said the time out loud. It was two forty-seven.

They quietly filed out of the room, leaving equipment and supplies where they lay—scattered about the bed and floor. They left Jenny in there with Beth, forgotten in her silent shock.

Something small and quiet inside Jenny told her what it meant. Something else ignored that voice. She felt a rush of heat wash across her body, through her face, and escape in tears that fell without effort. She pulled the chair back over to the bed and took Beth's hand once again. With her other hand, she picked up the discarded wrappers and disposable instruments left on the bed, and tossed them in the trash can next to her. She pulled the sheet back up across Beth, tucking it over her shoulders and making it look like she might simply be sleeping.

The interns and nurses had left the railing on the bed down

when they walked away and now Jenny had no barrier between her and Beth. She leaned forward and lay on Beth's chest, holding her best friend's hand to her cheek. Jenny drifted into a fitful sleep, tears continuing to warm her face even as Beth's body slowly cooled.

When Jack woke her the next morning, she had curled into the fetal position in the chair. Beth's mom was still not there. And the bed was empty.

CHAPTER NINETEEN

The claustrophobic smell of the dirt Jenny dug through reminded her of funerals—at the moment, Beth's. It had been hard to lose the one friend she'd known all her life, even harder when she'd needed her over the months since then. Jenny wanted Beth back in her life, and if she couldn't have her back, then it was just as easy to talk to her as if she were still capable of hearing. It wasn't the first time. It wouldn't be the last. Jenny was surrounded by death and destruction, but it wasn't the death she spoke to, it was the life that had preceded it.

"I'm sorry. I should have stayed and drove you home." She repeated the apology that opened every visit to Beth's grave. "Or forced you to leave when I did. I let you down. I failed you." Jenny continued to pull dirt out as she spoke. "I wasn't there when I should have been. I wasn't there for you." She paused, swallowed a dusty wad of spit, and squeezed her eyes shut. "I need you. Bethie, help me out here, hon."

Jenny had dug several yards into the dirt. She was far past her standing reach and had climbed in a while ago. She scooped the earth behind her as she went, conscious not to block her way and kicking whatever she could free of the hole she'd created. Comfortable with the depth, she started digging above her head at a slight angle. She turned toward the sky and the hope of freedom.

"Who?" she whispered to the shadows that her mind had equated with Beth. "That's the thing that's really starting to bug me." In the shallow tunnel, there was no room for echoes and nothing answered her questions. "If I could figure out who, I might have an idea about the why, or the where."

She thought for a moment as she pushed dirt with her feet and let her tired arms rest. She'd gone over her life—there were no enemies, no *living* enemies. There was nothing that would warrant this type of punishment, or sentence, from someone she knew. Maybe temporary anger over the years, but not revenge-worthy hatred. She worked, went home, did the family thing. Jenny didn't do much outside of that, and certainly nothing to invite anyone to treat her like this. She started thinking of every single person she knew in her life. A list of sorts started forming in her mind and she recanted it aloud to Beth's imaginary ghost.

"Dan?" She could almost hear the tsk noise Beth would make at such a suggestion. "Okay, you're right. That's just ridiculous. He got out of the marriage. We're not bitter or mean about it anymore.

"If this were Hollywood, or some other alternate universe, it would be Alan, but the kid isn't capable of this." She spit a bit of dirt that fell onto her lip. "He's got some friends that could be capable, but I've never done anything to them either." She thought of the boys that Alan hung with, particularly his old friend Steve.

That little shit, she thought. Steve had done everything a boy could do to get into trouble. She pitied his teachers, worried for his parents, and wondered exactly how many things he'd done that warranted calls to the principal's office or police station. She knew of a half a dozen or so—she bet there were plenty more that weren't common knowledge. The kid had been horrible since kindergarten and she'd been biding her time, waiting for Alan to grow tired of Steve's friendship.

Jenny remembered the first time Steve had gotten into trouble and dragged Alan along for the ride. The neighbor on the corner at the time was a timid little bleached-blonde woman. She seemed to always have a glass of something amber in her hands, and even though Jenny wasn't a huge drinker and didn't know what it was, she was pretty damned sure it wasn't iced tea. The woman, Stacy, had a habit of shaking her drink just enough to make the ice cubes tinkle—you could hear her coming most evenings, as she crossed the yards to talk to Jenny and Dan while they sat out back. Her equally but naturally blonde daughter in tow, she'd lean against the fence and gossip while Jenny and Dan smiled politely and feigned interest, rolling their eyes at each other after she left.

That evening, however, she had neither the drink nor little Kaitlyn. And she wasn't sauntering or coming to gossip.

"Where's that boy of yours!" she shouted from the yard between their houses, too angry and impatient to wait until she was close enough to talk in a civilized tone. "Where is he?"

Dan and Jenny looked at each other with raised eyebrows and he answered, "In the woods out back."

"Well, either you go get him, or I'll do it myself—"

"Whoa. Wait. What happened?" Jenny interrupted her.

"That little punk and his friend tried to kill Kaitlyn's cat."

"Wha—?" They spoke in unison, neither of them finishing the question.

"Dennis saw it, and told me all about it." She cocked her hip when she reached the fence and planted a hand on it. "Those little bastards tried to drown Snowball in a bucket of gasoline."

Jenny was horrified. Alan? She couldn't speak and just stared at the accusation on Stacy's face. She was sure her mouth hung open in visible disbelief. Dan was not struck speechless.

"Bullshit." He stood up, the lawn chair he'd been sitting in slid backward and screeched on the concrete patio. "Alan wouldn't do that. Christ, I don't think any kid would actually do that. Why would you believe that?"

"Why wouldn't I?" Stacy shrugged. "Kaitlyn found the kitten lying on the back steps, soaking wet. Came in and told me there was something wrong with him, he smelled funny. When I went outside, Dennis yelled from his garage he'd seen your boy and his redheaded friend put the cat in the bucket by the chain saw. That bucket was full of drained gas, the cat smelled like gas. Two plus two equals—"

"But—"

"I just got back from the vet." Stacy cut him off—she wasn't listening, she was lecturing. "The cat has to stay overnight and be specially cleaned and medicated. Its eyes are puffed shut and it may be blind. My daughter is screaming and crying."

"We'll—"

"You're damn right you will. And you'll punish that kid of yours and pay for the vet bill, too." She spun around to leave, shouting over her shoulder, "You'd better hope that cat doesn't die or I'll bring this to the cops."

Dan and Jenny stared at each other. Could Alan have done this? Could Steve? They were just little kids, both just barely seven years old. Were they dangerous or didn't they know any better? No, they knew better. There *had* to be another side to this story. Without a word, the thoughts passed between them and Dan walked off the porch toward the ditch and trees beyond their house. Jenny went inside to call Steve's mother. Dan and a very upset-looking Alan walked in just as she hung up.

"No answer at Steve's house."

"Yeah well, Stacy just got in her car and took off—she's probably heading over there."

"So?" Jenny nodded at Alan, as Dan pulled out a chair at the kitchen table and gestured to the boy. Alan sat, eyes wide, lip quivering.

"I didn't do nothin'." He looked up at Jenny, his baby blues glued, refusing to meet Dan's eyes.

"Start at the beginning, hon. What were you guys doing over there in the first place?"

Dan placed a hand at the back of Alan's neck. Jenny knew it was meant to be supportive, but it looked for a moment like he was going to strangle the boy, and she knit her eyebrows together, questioning him. Dan moved his hand to Alan's shoulder and stared back at her, compliant but looking confused as he spoke. "Alan, just tell us what happened. You know the rules."

"Yep. Burn down your house, but don't lie about it."

Jenny smiled as he repeated the mantra she'd been saying all his life. A lie only gets you into more trouble and you can't apologize for a lie without it permanently tarnishing others' trust in you. You can apologize and make amends for just about anything else.

"But I didn't do anything. And I told Steve not to, too." The last part came out in a half whisper.

"From the beginning, kiddo." Jenny pulled a chair out and sat in front of him, straddling the chair and leaning on the backrest.

Turned out they hadn't dipped the cat into anything. He admitted they'd been chasing the cat. Steve had heard they always land on their feet and wanted to test that theory. When they caught the cat that morning, Steve threw it up into the air as high as he could and watched it land—sure enough, on its feet. They did this several times, the cat getting more and more agitated. It began hissing at them and tried clawing Steve when he picked it up. On the last toss, Steve spun it as he let go, wondering if he could make it dizzy. That time it didn't land on all four legs, maybe two. It didn't run away from them either.

When Steve leaned down and picked it up it "*really* hissed at him, almost growled like a lion," and lunged forward, biting the soft tissue between his thumb and index finger. Steve screamed and threw the cat at the ground. He grabbed the bucket sitting there, not knowing what was in it, just seeing liquid and knowing cats hate water. He swung the bucket toward the cat, flinging the liquid out in a massive wave onto the animal. It mewled and *then* they smelled the gas.

Alan had never lied about anything and to this day Jenny believed his version of what happened. She confronted both Dennis, regarding his fabrication, and Stacy. Dennis stuck to his story. She didn't know him well enough to figure out why he would lie about what the boys did. Stacy was still upset, maybe more so because it wasn't just a dip in the bucket but an ongoing torture of sorts. Steve's mom believed none of it and blamed Alan; no big surprise—she never did take responsibility for anything Steve did. Jenny quietly paid her half of the vet bill and let the matter sweep itself under the neighborhood rug.

Stacy and Kaitlyn moved away a year later when Stacy remarried. Alan wasn't allowed to play with Steve for a while, not that he was told not to, but he was advised he would probably stay out of trouble that way. He listened. They didn't hang out again until the cat moved away.

Then they set fire to an old well foundation—or rather, the weeds growing inside it. The fire was out before anyone could even get alarmed. The stone walls contained it, and it burned itself out when it ran out of dry grass. But still, it was a fire and they had been there when it started.

Jenny knew that wasn't Alan. Steve was always getting in trouble for playing with matches or lighters, and when neither was available, he had the patience to create fire with a magnifying glass on hot days. He was trouble. She didn't know then about the McDonald triad. She knew now. She had watched a special on court television, which explained the commonplace of bedwetting, cruelty to animals, and fire starting in the developmental years of many serial killers. Now when she thought about it, she wondered if Steve wet the bed. Fire starter, cruelty to animals, a mother who didn't care—when Alan had finally grown tired of Steve a few years ago, Jenny had breathed a sigh of relief. She wondered where Steve was now. What kind of trouble was he getting into with his new friends?

Could it be him? No. He was still a kid. And she'd never done anything to him, even when she had reason to kick him out of the yard or say no to sleepovers. It just couldn't be him. Beth would agree with her, even if she never agreed with Jenny's putting up with him only because he was Alan's friend. A little part of Jenny felt uneasy she could even entertain the thought a child could or would do this for as long as she had. This had to be an adult.

None of her co-workers seemed right, none of her neighbors—sure, there were some in the past that may have toyed with the idea of doing something to her, but this wasn't just her. There was evidence here of someone else, she had to remember that. Maybe it wasn't personal, maybe it was random. It would be awfully odd if someone had a grudge against her, and a history of grudges that end with missing persons—

Missing persons?

Jack.

"My God." She stopped digging, a tingle worming through her body. "Beth. My God— How could I be so dumb?"

She had thought of Jack when recalling her last memories—their lunch, and briefly when she thought of Beth, but she hadn't really thought of him since, mostly Alan and Dan. That in itself was weird—not Alan, so much as Dan. Why would Jenny concentrate on her ex, rather than on the man she was currently seeing? She'd worry about the implications of that later. Right now, she needed to think long and hard about Jack. She needed to purposely concentrate on him—especially since his last girlfriend vanished without a trace.

CHAPTER TWENTY

Jenny had met Jack for lunch the day she had ended up here. She remembered that, though it was still a bit foggy. They'd made plans to meet up again Thursday. Jenny was pretty sure Thursday had come, and maybe gone. Was he worried about her? Did she want him to be? He could very well be the person who put her here. She thought she knew him well enough and trusted him, but did she really—on either account?

She'd heard the rumors about the girlfriend right after she started seeing Jack. Jenny's friends described a fiend, but she didn't see it when she looked at him. Her friends claimed he was abusive, yet he seemed gentle as a kitten around her. For the first time in her life, she didn't believe her friends. Even Beth warned her he had a *history*. Normally that would have been all it took for her to walk away without a word, without even the common courtesy of telling him. But she didn't. Beth didn't give up, snuck it into every conversation they had, told her it was rebound from Dan, and pointed out any domestic violence rolling across the television. Especially if it ended in death. Because that's what it boiled down to. Murder—or the assumption of it.

When Jenny got sick of listening to it, she asked Jack. He said Ashley just walked out on her life, leaving during one of their fights one night. According to the rumor mill, she didn't go anywhere—certainly not farther than the flower bed in the backyard. Without trepidation they declared Jack a killer, and Beth agreed. In the end, Jenny agreed to talk to the detective in charge of the case and Beth set up the meeting through a friend of hers who was a neighborhood acquaintance of the cop.

Jenny sat in the local Denny's by herself for over an hour waiting for Detective Johnstone to show up, and was just getting her check from the waitress to pay for her coffee when he walked through the door. He smiled apologetically. "Ms. Schultz?" She nodded as he took the bill from the girl's hands with the smoothness of a con artist. "I'll take that. The lady isn't quite finished yet." He flashed a perfect smile at the server and slipped into the booth opposite Jenny. The same smile still on his face, he parted his teeth just enough to let his words slip through. "Sorry, duty called for a change."

"For a change?" She put her purse back down, not about to hold a grudge against an officer for being late while on duty, but intrigued by his comment.

"Yeah." He spoke to her while making eye contact with someone behind Jenny, pointed to his coffee cup and nodded. "It's awfully damn quiet around these parts, Ms. Schultz. Don't get me wrong—it's good that it's safe and relatively crime free. Good for raising kids and retiring. But for a cop, it can become rather monotonous."

"Understandable. So what was today's emergency?"

"Nothing exciting if that's what you're asking, but it detained me nonetheless." The waitress arrived and poured him a cup of coffee. He thanked her with a nod while dabbing a napkin at the drops that had missed his cup and landed on the table.

"Ahh." Jenny took the hint—keep to business, his remarks had been rhetorical and she wasn't here to pry into his life, but rather her boyfriend's. "Well then, how about Jack?"

"Well, contrary to the excitement level around here, the evidence indicates Mr. Hill hasn't done anything wrong. He and his fiancée had an argument and she left. He agreed to a lie detector test and allowed us to go through his home with a fine-toothed comb. We found nothing. No signs of anything that would indicate otherwise. He even volunteered his computer to our department, in case Ms. Cass had left some sort of clue as to where she went. We found nothing. Even after the tech geeks used their magic powers and rescued previously erased information—there was nothing. Well, other than his affectionate emails to other women—probably what caused the fight."

"Oh." She filed the random email information and pushed him for a solid answer. "So you don't think she's missing?" Jenny soundlessly tapped the pad of her index finger against the side of her coffee cup. This was going to be a quick meeting. They could have done this over the phone and saved her an hour of sitting and waiting.

"Well, I didn't say that. I said Mr. Hill didn't appear to have anything to do with her disappearance. She could still be missing, and her family still has her listed as such, but he wasn't involved as far as we can tell."

Jenny stared into her coffee for a moment before looking back up to him. As her expression twisted into confusion, his softened, making him look less official.

"Disappearances do happen, Ms. Schultz." He reached across the table and put a hand across the top of hers. "That Spencer girl went missing last year two towns over. They never did find her. They're rare around these parts, and almost always a misunderstanding or lovers' spat such as this, but there's nothing saying she didn't leave the house and run into trouble elsewhere. We haven't had a missing person in over thirty years in Harding, but the surrounding communities seem to have troubles on a more regular basis."

"Thus the mundane," Jenny interrupted.

He smiled. "Yes. We're apparently the safest neighborhood in the county. But that said, she could very well have left this town and been nabbed in the next. Or, as her family is unwilling to believe, she may have just left town, abandoning everyone and everything. Is there any behavior with Mr. Hill that makes you question his innocence?"

"No. Oh no. Nothing of the sort." Jenny shook her head and almost laughed, noting his hazel eyes did not blink as he waited for her answer. "Just precaution really, and satisfying my friends that are against me dating him."

"Well, people like to think the worst of others when there are doubts. If you go back through history, Ms. Schultz, plenty of people were tried and found innocent but were still persecuted their entire lives as if they were guilty. Mr. Hill will likely be persecuted for this until the next big thing hits town, but he shouldn't be."

"You really think that? You *personally* believe Jack didn't do this, or is there just not enough evidence? What about that police instinct you hear about?" Her fingers fidgeted under the pressure of his hand as she watched his eyes. "Detective Johnstone, am I safe with this guy? I live alone with my son."

"Ben. Please." He withdrew his hand and took a drink of his coffee. "Like I said, at this point, there's no reason not to. But no, I really don't think he did it."

Her shoulders relaxed and her jaw unclenched. He went on to recap the public information she had missed and those around her had recapped. How their seemingly perfect relationship turned sour right in front of friends, and they began to argue enough for the neighbors to notice. How she didn't show up for work, or take any personal items with her, or even let her family know where she was going. It was an open missing-persons case, but one the authorities believed had nothing to do with foul play on Jack's part. He even added the previously unheard information that Ashley had contacted the police to report a domestic dispute next door, and asked Jenny if she really believed she wouldn't have reported Jack if she'd felt she was in danger. As an afterthought, he added Ashley was a consenting adult, and if she wanted, she could disappear without anyone's permission.

Detective Johnstone felt Jack was innocent because of his genuine worry and absolute cooperation. He explained there is usually hesitancy when the significant other is involved, like telling them to come back tomorrow when they arrive to ask questions or search premises. Jack did nothing of the sort and called often to see if there was anything he could give them that would help. Detective Johnstone—Ben as he repeatedly reminded her while insisting on referring to her as Ms. Schultz—truly believed him to be innocent and suffering in her absence.

She felt bad for doubting Jack and after over an hour of reiteration from the officer, Jenny was confident Jack was innocent. She apologized to Ben for keeping him so long, and flagged the waitress for the check Jenny insisted she take care of as a thank-you for his patience and explanation.

Jenny couldn't help but notice he kept touching her—her hand on the table for the most part, but also her shoulder and back as they stood to leave—and wondered if that was a calming technique they were taught in the academy, like using her name a lot, or if he was flirting. As he handed over his card and wished her luck in her relationship, her fleeting worry evaporated completely. He smiled and told her she probably wouldn't need the card, since he didn't think she'd need to call him about Jack anymore.

Even after the long talk and explanation, by the time she got home that evening she couldn't decide if her doubts had returned, or if it was guilt for doubting him in the first place, and Jenny told Jack about her conversation with the officer. He smiled and sat her down. He wasn't upset and gave her intimate details, in hopes of soothing her fears.

According to Jack, he and Ashley had been fighting all summer because she was insecure. As he told Jenny about it, he used the word *paranoid* on numerous occasions—but looked away whenever he did.

He'd been spending more time than usual online, as he'd found a group on an Internet chat that also enjoyed camping and fishing. Jack quickly became attached to them as a whole and checked the website several times a day. Ashley complained he spent more time on there than with her, and didn't understand what these people provided she didn't. Ashley and Jack camped together several times each summer and fished whenever the weekends were free to do so. They didn't have friends go along very often, but still, they went together and she didn't understand why he needed to talk to other people about it, when he could go with her and actually do it.

Jack had laughed it off as jealousy and continued chatting with his new friends.

Ashley's subtle comments became bitter, her pleas turned into arguments, and the relationship started going downhill. They'd have a fight about his online friends and he would tell her he'd stop, if that was what she really needed. She would back off and say that was unnecessary, because she didn't want to tell him what he could and couldn't do. He'd follow up by sarcastically asking *what exactly she wanted from him* and it would escalate all over again. It was a yo-yo of emotions, from anger to contempt—they would declare they didn't care anymore at the height of their pain, ironically caring too much and attempting to cover it. Eventually she would break down and cry. He would promise to cut back. They'd go to sleep thinking the problem solved.

But Jack admitted to Jenny he never really cut back. He would put on a good show and stop for a few days, but then something would be happening, something he considered important because these were his friends. Ashley called it drama. She deemed it unnecessary. And she belittled the friendships because he'd never met any of them and didn't know how they were in real life.

So Jack fixed that.

He met up with one of the girls from the message board one night at a local tavern. She was traveling through the state on her way to visit family, and thought it would be great to stop and have a drink with him. He agreed. They met and had a wonderful time talking about the others in the group, jobs, family—the gamut. He returned home and slipped into bed, Ashley's sleeping body never stirred. He wouldn't find out she knew about his rendezvous until several months later.

Then the conversations online started getting a bit more personal, and not just with that girl. Rather than talking to the group in a massive chat room, like he always had, Jack began joining the group only to open smaller, private windows with specific members. Members he continually told Ashley were just friends. She disagreed.

Ashley told him she didn't understand why he only talked to the women. She felt threatened by them, and wasn't ashamed to say so—repeatedly, at the top of her lungs. Jack told her it was just friends, he wasn't interested in any of them—it wasn't like they were talking on the phone every night. Then he threw her *own* male friends at her as an example of what he was doing. She maintained it was different and continued to disapprove. He made a point to show her when he was talking to the men in the private chats to prove it wasn't just the women.

The air between them grew thick with tension. He spent more time online. He spent even less time with her.

Jack told Jenny all this with sadness in his eyes, like he could see now what he was doing then, and felt sorry for the whole thing. He admitted he didn't want to go out with Ashley as often as they used to. He didn't want to watch movies anymore. Ashley seemed to get very quiet about the whole thing. Then he went secretive, thinking he was keeping the peace.

Jack started closing the windows whenever she walked past the computer. He opened a new email account with a different password than the one she knew. He stopped talking about his "friends." Jack and Ashley's history of interesting discussions about every part of life turned into strained small talk about politics and society, nothing personal. Ashley seemed sad but content.

Late that July, he came home from work later than usual and found her standing at the door waiting for him. Her eyes were swollen and rimmed with red. She said nothing as he walked past her and put his briefcase down. She waited for him to get his shoes off, go to the bathroom, change his shirt and get a beer from the fridge. When he got to the living room to sit down and relax, he saw Ashley still standing by the door. Her face was a statue of anger and pain so evident it didn't need words.

When she finally spoke, her voice sounded broken. Apparently, while digging for an old email from her mother, Ashley had stumbled upon an email from one of his "friends." The wording was ambiguous, the image attached was not. While no nipples were showing, the lacy bra in the picture showed plenty of cleavage and was clearly an open invitation to something other than a medical examination. The "friend" alluded to a meeting at the bar down the street from them.

A quick mental check and he realized which email she'd found. It wasn't from the girl who'd stopped for a polite drink on her way through town. She'd found the one from the other girl. The one he'd snuck off to meet with every intention of doing whatever he wanted when he got there, only to find he wasn't attracted to her enough to ruin his relationship with Ashley. They had a few drinks and called it a night.

He lied to Ashley.

As he told Jenny about it, he admitted he knew it was wrong and he shouldn't have, but felt cornered by Ashley's assumptions and didn't think he had any other choice at the time.

Jack told Ashley they'd never met. That she'd talked about it, but he always brushed her off. That she was willing to come up and meet him, but he didn't think Ashley would approve.

Ashley wasn't buying it.

She pushed. She quoted emails she'd found from several of the girls. She called them by their screen names and always returned to Candy1972. She asked why someone would send a picture like that to anyone. Ashley pressed the issue and asked if he'd bothered telling them he had a girlfriend—fiancée if you wanted to get technical about it, since they'd been discussing marriage, and planning the date sans official proposal and diamond. He claimed he didn't know. He dragged it out further than he should have.

When she told him she'd done her own online research and knew

Candy's phone number, he stalled, trying to figure out where to go with his argument. When Ashley revealed she'd finally cracked the password on his new email, he conceded defeat. Yes, he'd been talking to the girls in ways that could be seen as inappropriate, but that was an outside opinion. He *knew* these girls and could joke around with them without anything being taken wrong or too seriously. The Internet was a two-dimensional world and if you didn't know the person well enough, you could misinterpret all kinds of things. He claimed that's what she was doing. The closest he got to admitting he'd done anything remotely wrong was when he referred to them as "safe flirtations" because both parties knew it was just for fun.

He continued to tell her he'd never met up with any of them, just talked about it. Even as she quoted emails and began dialing the number to Candy's house, he tried to reason with her and tell her he'd done nothing wrong. As Ashley dialed the final number and hushed him so she could hear, he reached over and hung up the phone—looking directly into her eyes as the truth came to the surface.

Yes, he'd met up with Candy. No, he hadn't met up with any other—which he claimed only because she didn't seem to have any proof of his previous meeting. He said it was just a drink or two at the bar. He swore on everything he could think of that was important to either of them that he hadn't touched her. Just drinks.

Ashley said if that were all it was, then he wouldn't have hidden it from her. He claimed he had hidden it because he knew she'd react like this. She explained she reacted like this because of his lying about it. The argument went back and forth well into the early morning hours. Through tears and screaming, Ashley continued to belittle him and ask for details at the same time. She threatened to leave, he threatened to leave, and they both verbally kicked the other out on several occasions during the battle.

After saying he'd done nothing for the hundredth time, he slipped. Jack said he made the right decision and came home. That wording cost him a night in a motel and a week on the couch.

Ashley argued that going with intentions was as good as cheating, whether or not he followed through. Ashley yelled that entertaining the idea enough to even show up at the bar was as good as cheating. She asked him if whatever had stopped him this time would still be there next time.

Of course, he disagreed. Jack claimed men saw women all the time on the street they were interested in—the difference between him and a cheater was he didn't act on it. But Ashley continued to scream, continued to call him a liar and a cheat. She forced him to go over the entire evening—made him recall every email that *might* have been misinterpreted by anyone. Repeatedly demanded to know which of them he was interested in but hadn't met yet.

Admitting he'd been intrigued with the girl before their meeting was the beginning of the end for the relationship. It never fully healed after that. He could see her distrust. He heard it every time she got a little upset over anything. She called him every name in the book, demanded he get medical tests for her peace of mind, and continued to tell him it was cheating. Ashley watched his every reaction to every person, and glared whenever she imaged she saw something inappropriate.

They fought almost nonstop. They stopped going out with friends because the atmosphere was so heavy with bitterness everyone commented on it. They stopped going to family functions for the same reason—and either of them going alone to a gathering didn't solve the problem. The rumors started. The gossip didn't help the situation.

When they weren't fighting, it was only because they weren't talking. In the end, it was the same fight they'd had a few hundred times over the past few months. She finally followed through and left—*left him to his other women.* If she wasn't the only girl in his life, she wasn't going to be a part of his life. She threw the snow globe they'd bought on their vacation to Florida at his head and stormed out the door.

Ashley never called him. She never came back and got her stuff. She just up and left, according to Jack. Her friends claimed he'd done something to her, but he denied it. Her family didn't outright say anything to his face, but Jack could tell their thoughts echoed those of Ashley's friends—still did. He could do nothing but stand by and watch as the police searched his house, interrogated him, and closed the case against him for lack of evidence—to the chagrin of Ashley's loved ones. Had they used a different reason for closing the case, it may have helped. As it stood, everyone could still vocalize their opinions and he couldn't do much about it. He helped in any way he could for as long as the case was investigated. He felt there was nothing more he could have done and hated that her family and friends behaved the way they had. Their relationship had gone on long enough that he had expected some allies, and was hurt to find he had none.

In the long run, he didn't stop going to the chat room, but he did change his tone in there. He no longer sent steamy emails to the other women, he received no more playful pictures, and he never met another soul from the group. He knew he was wrong.

"Hindsight is amazing that way."

He stopped and looked at Jenny, waiting for her verdict. He said he didn't have the energy to fight for another relationship and if she didn't believe him, then so be it. He wasn't an abuser or a murderer and hadn't done anything to Ashley. He stared at the ground quietly, expecting her response. He waited.

Jenny said nothing at first. She looked at him and noticed he had a small scar on his forehead to back up the snow globe part of the story. She watched his eyes, his hands—looking for nervous actions, guilty behavior. She saw nothing. She had questions but wasn't sure if she should ask them now. Jack was in the zone of his story. He was immersed in his side of what had happened. If he were lying, she wouldn't trip him up now. She patted his hand across the picnic table they sat at in her backyard, and said nothing. Detective Johnstone's firm belief helped her keep quiet, but didn't quite dowse her anxiety at some of the things Jack had brought up afterward.

The week seemed to go by very slowly, time dragging her along while she waited for an opportunity to question him. Friday finally arrived and she looked forward to their night out. She practiced what she was going to say. She wrote thoughts out on paper to help her keep track of the questions she had. Jenny planned to use the comfortable setting of the restaurant and cozy atmosphere of her living room couch to grill him a little bit further about the extenuating circumstances around Ashley's disappearance.

Instead, Jenny defended Ashley.

Jack took her off guard by asking Jenny if she believed Ashley was right about cheating without actually touching.

"Do that with me and you'll get the same treatment," Jenny told him flat out.

"Really? It's not overreacting just a little?" He leaned back against the couch and watched her intently, seeming fully interested in her response.

"Absolutely not. Men are physical. It's their nature. Women are very emotional." Jenny hated the word, but it worked for the direction she planned to go. "A woman can have an emotional affair, never touch the person, never be too close to the person, and still have guilt because they know deep inside they were as good as with that person."

"So even though I didn't touch any of them, my guilt is on that level?"

"Yep, and even though men don't think that way—normally, or until it's pointed out like Ashley did in her arguments—women do, and therefore, we hold the actions of men to the rules of women—on several topics." Jenny had explained this to male friends in the past that hadn't understood, and she expected Jack to follow suit, but he surprised Jenny and seemed to get it.

"See now, if Ashley had explained it that way... Instead, she's gone."

The sadness in his tone made all Jenny's questions vanish into the candlelight around them. She didn't care why Ashley hadn't come back. She wasn't concerned with the opinions of people that had no proof. Jenny decided right then and there to trust him. His version and the detective's confidence were cemented by Jack's concern. If anything, Jenny wondered if he'd leave her if Ashley came back to town. But Jenny never doubted Jack again.

Until now.

Now, she questioned that decision more than any other she'd ever made.

A man who could lie to the woman he's going to marry about something as stupid as the Internet—repeatedly—could very easily lie to a new acquaintance. That person could look a police officer in the eye and appear exactly as the circumstances dictated they should—upset, angry, worried. It really wouldn't be that hard if the person was a liar. Jenny wouldn't be able to do it, she knew that. She was a horrible liar. But she didn't know enough about Jack to know whether he could lie—she'd never seen him or caught him in a lie, so she was unable to compare that behavior to his demeanor regarding Ashley.

The more she thought about it, the more Jenny realized she didn't really know anything about him. She knew his name, the names and birthdates of his immediate family, his career résumé, a scattering of childhood friends had been mentioned, but otherwise, he'd done a very good job of only letting out small tidbits at a time.

Could she have been *that* wrong?

She stopped digging. She was tired. Both her mind and body were exhausted from the exertion of survival. She needed to rest. She needed not to think about anything for a while.

"Beth?" She choked out a whisper as dirt fell around her, making tiny noises in the darkness. "Please tell me I was right about Jack. And help me if I was wrong." Jenny leaned her head against the wall of her tunnel and closed her eyes. Nothing in her vision changed.

The only time there had been a difference had been when she'd felt pain and seen the visual equivalent of it in white flashes, or squeezed her eyes tightly and caused a brilliant orange-red wave to dance around like shadows on her lids—shadows that were never where you looked, but always just to the edge of your peripheral vision. She longed for the dimness of Alan's nightlight. That little bit of a glow from the hallway near the bathroom had been an annoyance she'd had to get used to. Jenny had always preferred to sleep in pitch black, and that tiny bit of illumination drove her nuts. Right now, she'd put a high-watt bulb into that Elmo-covered irritation just to have variety in her surroundings.

Jack? Her mind went back to the question at hand far too easily and she knew it was time to shut down or break down. The wear and tear on her body was starting to throb in every muscle, every square inch of her skin. She was a survivor mentally, but just not built for it physically. She was dirty, tired, bruised and hungry. She was lonely, confused, and most of all, scared. She didn't like being scared. And while the idea that she should have been afraid of her boyfriend boggled her, she snapped out of her self-pity and came to the conclusion that it didn't really matter who put her here, or why, or even where here was exactly. What mattered was someone had done it. The only important thing right now was getting out.

She'd lost track of days and didn't know how close to day six she was. Jenny didn't know much about the situation, she knew only that she didn't want to find out why there was no seventh hash mark. Unfortunately, at the moment, the cumulative strain on her system was going to be her defeat. She needed to rest. She needed her mind to focus. She needed her body to function. She couldn't keep a thought going past the first few sentences. She'd called upon Beth to help her and then promptly forgot about her. She'd analyzed everyone in her world because she was too afraid to analyze herself, and was sick and tired of the fear doing it for her.

She needed a nap. Not a knock on the head, not a shock-induced slumber. A consciously relaxed, planned time-out.

She opened her eyes, more out of habit than need—she'd been here long enough now to know on a primal level opening them was useless. Jenny scooted back toward the entrance of her tunnel to judge the distance. She'd gone a little more than her body length inward and a touch more than her arm's reach upward. Grandma's cellar had about a dozen steps to the surface. Most steps were less than a foot. She had seven feet left to dig through by her calculations, maybe less. Jenny made a mental calculation of how long she guessed it might have taken her to get this far through the dirt. She'd never be able to do it. She was too tired, and working over her head was harder than working in front of her.

She crawled back into the deepest corner of her tunnel and leaned against the wall. Jenny pulled her knees up to her chest and hugged them to her for comfort. She concentrated on her breathing, trying not to think about anything else. She couldn't get comfortable and repositioned herself several times.

CHAPTER TWENTY-ONE

She was so tired, she didn't realize it when the exhaustion took her over and carried her weariness into dreams. Her body ached. Her mind continued to search through suspects. She drew maps of her surroundings from the bits of information she'd gathered, both in the dirt and on paper that miraculously made its way to her hand. She was just beginning to ponder the meaning of the paper when her dreams did what they do best—take from the real world, twist reality, and go in directions that made no sense upon waking.

She jumped as a loud thudding noise echoed through her shadowed landscape. She was leaning forward in the tunnel trying to figure out a sudden light source when the sound startled her. The surprise sent her back and up, and Jenny slammed her head into the dirt above her, which turned into a wooden doorway complete with handle. She reached up, frantic with relief, and grabbed the brass knob. The metal was cold and slick in her grip. It felt larger than it should be and she was reminded of the oddly shaped door handles in her grandmother's house. Jenny twisted and turned the ball repeatedly but nothing happened. It was locked.

She began to dig in the dirt for the key, which of course she believed would be right there in her dream, when the echo was refreshed. This time the noise was metallic. The muffled sound of steel hitting steel reverberated throughout and she was drawn again toward the mouth of her tunnel.

Rather than sand, her hand came down in water.

At first she thought it was some type of puddle in the dirt, caused by rain leaking through the soil above her. But the water was clear, and her dream eyes told her it was crystalline. The only thing that could have made it more inviting would have been ice. She leaned down and used her hands to scoop it to her mouth. She drank savagely, spilling almost none down her chin as she greedily gobbled it up before anyone else could come along to take it from her.

The walls around her shook. The water vanished. Her knee began to throb again. Jenny sat up and swallowed back the fear. The moisture in her mouth was gone, replaced with the taste of dirt and she spat the granules from between her lips. She felt her face go flush. Jenny imagined the moisture welling in her eyes would glisten if there had been enough light. In an attempt to stop it from quivering, she bit on her lip—

And woke up to the last resounding beats of a metallic echo.

She was on her stomach. Feeling in front of her, she deduced she was lying down, facing away from her escape tunnel. After realizing she'd woken up, she sighed. She didn't remember falling asleep, didn't have any idea how long she'd slept, and believed the sound that bounced from the dirt and stone around her was one of those leftover dream details that follows you when you wake up. She listened for several heartbeats. The echo wasn't a memory—it was real sound and it had come from the main room.

She opened her eyes, though she'd gotten used to the idea that it did no good. This time, however, they found something to focus on. Something in the distance that glowed and moved. She squinted at the small bobbing orb of white for several seconds before recognition dawned on her. It was a flashlight—and it was heading her direction.

Jenny immediately sat upright and banged her head above her. She wasn't as far into the flat portion of the tunnel as she thought. Dirt and sand showered down on her. She felt it fall beneath her collar and drop down into her bra. The distinct feeling of a many-legged insect ran down the length of her neck and she swatted it away. A light. Rescue?

Or her captor? The light was coming in her general direction, but Jenny was near the spot the plate of food had been left, and he could just be going there to see if that's where she was. Or did he know where she really was. Did he know she'd started to fight for her life and had begun to dig her way to freedom.

Oh God, she thought. *How much time have I lost? Is it day seven?*

She scooted backward, the loose soil still falling in scattered clumps about her. The light swung in and out of her vision, and she couldn't tell if it was panning left and right, up and down, or if he was actually to the side of the tunnel and she was only catching glimpses of it rather than seeing it straight on.

Jenny pushed her back against the dead end behind her, trying to become flush with the dirt wall. She reached above her with one hand and below her with the other, bracing herself for whatever was coming. Jenny thought she'd be more prepared, she expected to react differently, and felt a bitter taste in her mouth as fear held her hostage. She wanted to vanish rather than fight, even though she knew it was the wrong instinct.

She didn't have time to contemplate how to dispute her primal urge to hide, as the sky began to fall.

The hand above her had pushed too hard on soil that wasn't as compact as she'd thought, and a barrage of dirt rained down on her. She pulled her hands to her face and covered herself in the fetal position. The soil continued to fall on her and she crossed her arms in front of her face to keep it out of her eyes. It just kept falling and she cowered lower as it coated her hair and shoulders. The ceiling fell in as she looked back toward the bobbing light and was forced flat to the ground.

This was her chance to attack. This was the opportunity she'd been preparing for. And instead of being perched in waiting with a rock to throw or stick to jab, she lay under at least fifty pounds of dirt, unable to move for fear of more damage to her surroundings. If her choices were starving to death in an underground lair, being brutally murdered by some psychopath, or buried alive, she was taking anything other than the slow suffocation.

She pushed her hands out in front of her slightly. The dirt was mostly on her back and legs—it felt moist in areas and she could feel the weight of it against her clothing. Her shoulders and head were completely covered, but at the outer edge of the cave-in, it didn't feel as heavy on her and she smiled when the small movement of her hands provided an air pocket of dust. She heard shuffling feet outside her grave. Jenny froze.

She didn't know where he was and couldn't risk wiggling out of her dirt cocoon only to find him right in front of her. She needed time to find her weapons. She'd put the bone next to her when she'd leaned back to sleep, but hadn't noticed it upon waking. She didn't recall any large rocks in the last few feet of digging and had left the others at the mouth—which she'd expected to get back to at the first sign of someone approaching. *All the best-laid plans,* she thought.

She concentrated on breathing slowly, deeply. She couldn't

afford a panic attack right now, and panting or whimpering were out of the question. She closed her eyes, her breath shuddered from her chest, and she fought the urge to cry. Jenny knew all about panic attacks—she'd survived several in her lifetime. She knew without a doubt one was coming on. An episode to rival all others. One that could not be stopped by any amount of concentration, willpower, or deep-breathing exercises. She was dead and she knew it.

Jenny still didn't know for sure who might have put her here. She didn't know how long she'd been here. But she knew without a doubt others had been here before her. Others who were now gone, except for a bone or two they had left behind. People who'd gone missing and no one cared, or missed them, or looked hard enough to find them and stop the person that now had her in their underground holding cell of dirt and darkness. She didn't know how many or how long they'd lasted, only that at least one had been there for six days. Not five, not seven.

Her heart pounded and her chest muscles contracted in seizurelike activity. Jenny's thoughts swam. Every hair on her body felt electric. Each tear on the cuticles of her fingers, from digging without concern for her manicure, screamed with torturous pain. Even her hair seemed to come alive, as each and every follicle throbbed to the beat of her heart.

Seven days. It hadn't been that long, couldn't have. Her breath skipped through her teeth and made a slight whistling noise. She gasped and held her breath, afraid the sound had given her away.

Maybe he couldn't see her. Maybe she was covered enough that cowering there was the best choice, rather than the only choice when faced with muscles that refused to move and a mind that refused to react. Her hands began to shake in front of her, as she listened past her own breath and heartbeat to the expanse beyond. Feet continued to shuffle toward her. She thought she heard murmuring.

"Filthy—" Echoed lightly in the chamber. "—me. Goddamned… lesson."

Her imagination tried to fill in the blanks around the syllables, as her mind registered a male voice. Jenny squeezed her eyes shut and willed herself to remain composed, even as the tears snuck through her pinched lids. A tremor started in her lip and quickly spread throughout her body as she lay there sobbing, gasping for panicked breath, shaking against the cold ground.

"Darling—" He sounded closer. His voice was hoarse, but not from disease or habit, more because he was purposely speaking in hushed tones and his tenor vibrato didn't translate well to whispers. The voice taunted her like the refrigerator motor's whirring had. She knew it, but couldn't place it. Jenny tried to concentrate on where she might know it from, but the shaking in her body was leading to a complete breakdown.

She felt warmth on her leg and questioned it before she realized the wetness wasn't a puddle or rainwater. Her body had responded to the fear by squeezing out the last few ounces of liquid contained in her bladder, creating a wet spot on her pants and leaving a burning sensation in her crotch. The voice echoed in her head. Her body shook with such force Jenny both heard and felt the dirt falling from her back to the ground around her. She was shaking off her cover.

A searing pain crawled up her spine and into her skull. The throbbing in her chest moved to her temples and her breath skipped again. She fell into a deeper blackness than that which surrounded her with dirt.

She listened to the minister tell the crowd what a wonderful person she'd been and spin tales of gardens she'd tended and beautiful roses she'd grown. Jenny shook her head in confusion. She'd never grown roses in her entire life. She killed most things that weren't edible and was most proud of what she could do with a tomato sapling. Roses? She tried to look behind her to the source of the voice that spoke lies about her, but found she couldn't turn around. She couldn't move at all. She was stuck and only then realized she was lying flat on her back, surrounded by satin walls.

Jenny willed herself to stand up and found herself standing next to Beth. A gaping hole in the ground at her feet drew her attention and she looked down to the mahogany box at the bottom of it. The brass handles were visible enough to recognize on the side. The top was glass and inside she could see the white satin that surrounded the prone body of a woman. Her arms were folded gracefully over her chest, her pale pink fingernails striking against the soft beige of the dress she wore. Her skin was pale, with a smattering of freckles and makeup that had been applied in harsh lines that lacked blending or skill. Her hair was swept to the sides, fanning out on either side of her head like a halo.

Across the chasm, Dan and Alan sat in folding aluminum chairs. Dan's arm was around Alan's shoulder. The boy looked limp and Dan appeared to be holding him upright. Both of their faces showed great strain and weariness. Their red-rimmed eyes stared at the trench, but they appeared to hear nothing the minister said. Dan was wearing Jenny's favorite suit with the tie Alan had bought him for Father's Day. Alan was wearing the outfit he'd worn to Beth's funeral and Jenny was shocked it still fit him. The pants looked a bit short, but the lines fell right, and while the seams of the jacket looked snug, they were not strained.

A raindrop landed on Jenny's cheek and she looked away from Alan and up to the sky. The gray overcast day was punctuated with several small dark clouds, and she noticed the leaves blowing in the tops of the trees but felt no breeze. She smelled the pile of dirt at the end of the grave before she turned to look at it. Knowing full well what it hid under the faux green grass carpet, remembering the vivid details of her father's funeral. And Beth's. She turned toward her best friend and opened her mouth to question the somber occasion. Beth shook her head and pointed back down into the hole in front of them.

Jenny took a closer look at the woman lying there. The familiarity slipped her conscious mind and she questioned Beth with furrowed brows. Beth raised her brows in response and nodded again to the pit. Jenny squinted at the face behind the glass. The scar on her jawline, only visible from this angle, reminded her of the one she had, and she absently ran a finger across the bottom of her chin. She pushed her hair behind her ear and reached into her pocket for a Kleenex. Instead, she found a handful of dirt.

On impulse, she pulled the soil from her pocket and stepped forward. Holding her hand above the open grave, she turned her wrist and let the dirt fall to the coffin below. The woman inside opened her eyes, her hands slamming against the glass above her. The milky, unseeing orbs bulged with terror just as Jenny's widened with acknowledgement. She looked herself in the face. The prone version opened its mouth and screamed to the oblivious crowd around them.

~

And dirt filled Jenny's mouth as her lips scraped across the ground. "Damn!" the muffled voice of her captor barked from nearby and Jenny heard the faint tones of a beeper going off.

Jenny realized she'd passed out and froze, afraid of his proximity. She held her breath, letting out tiny streams of anxiety through her lips with measured caution. When her lungs were empty, she counted to three and then began pulling in another deep breath. She listened for him.

His shuffled steps seemed farther away than his voice had been. Jenny heard something clatter and flinched.

"Not worth it— Bon appetite."

Metal on metal clattered again in the distance, and she dared push the dirt away from her face and looked out. The flashlight beam bounced haphazardly across the dirt floor twice and then vanished as a thud sealed her up once again in silence. As the sound resounded into the thick walls, the beeper went off again in a short burst of alarm and she froze.

No, she thought. The sound hadn't come from out there. The sound had come from nearby. From her. Confusion fled as she remembered the broken watch in her pocket, not broken after all. *It must have an alarm set on it. That must be how the owner knew how many days they'd been here.*

She tried to remember hearing that sound and could recall two other times when she'd thought the noise had chased her from unconsciousness. That would make three times it had gone off. *But how often did it go off? And how many times did it beep while I slept?* She realized she could analyze how long she'd been down there, using this new information, and waste more time, or she could get the hell out before she learned what happened after six days.

She put her palms flat on the ground on either side of her head and pushed up against the weight of the dirt above her. She moved, but not enough. Jenny tried another tactic—frantically wiggling as if she were a little kid being tickled. She could feel the dirt shift and slide off her lower back and legs. She felt more dirt fall and replace it. She scissor-kicked, as if doing laps in the pool, and sloughed the remaining soil from her lower half. She pushed again with her hands and shook her back at the same time. She felt relief when the heaviness was gone and only the dampness remained.

Jenny sat there for a moment, breathing heavily and without fear of being heard. Panting from exertion, she decided it was a good thing she hadn't tried that while he was down here—there was no way he wouldn't have heard all of that.

She opened her eyes and immediately closed them again. They burned. The searing made her think she'd gotten sand in them and scratched the corneas. She paused, the pain blazing behind her lids. Flashes of white and yellow streaked like fireworks in the reddish black. Her eyes watered and she let the liquid clean the surface of her eyes for a few moments before she tried opening them again.

She peeked through the narrowest of gaps in her lids as they fluttered almost imperceptibly at the darkness around her. On the dirt floor beneath her, the small pebbles and finer grain mix she'd been digging through looked fertilized with its dark color and small dots of white. She wondered who used good planting soil to fill—

She could see—

The darkness was gone.

Her chest muscles constricted, as she sucked her breath in with shock. Without hesitation, the watering of her eyes changed from pain to relief. Jenny had no control over her body, as her heart pounded and her shoulders shook with racking sobs. An onlooker would think she was upset. Her quivering mouth was agape. Her breath came in the great staccato beats of hyperventilation. Tears ran down her face in streams of liquid happiness, meeting up with the spittle that ran from her mouth as she cried. She collapsed to the floor and let it out.

She rocked herself back and forth while the jubilation ran its course. Powerless to stop the flood of emotions, she was reduced to a quivering child. Only after several minutes of adrenaline-induced elation was her logical mind able to get her attention—make her understand. Celebration happens in all forms and this was acceptable considering the situation, but she could do this later. She had to control the adrenaline, use it to her advantage. She swallowed back the sobs and spit, wiped her face with the heels of her hands, and sat up.

Jenny opened her eyes a sliver and looked around. She could see the dirt. She opened her eyes completely but had to shut them again. The burning had not been dirt to begin with, but daylight. She felt above her, attempting again to look through her lashes, and squinted her eyes at the ceiling of her tomb. The collapse had broken through to the surface in an inverted funnel shape. Through the center of it, a thin beam of light shone down.

Oh, God. Elation at escape and anxiety at her captor's approach wrestled for attention in her mind. It was there. Daylight. Out. She could see it through the small tunnel her hand had put in the roof.

But the light was bright. Her captor's voice had been close. Had he seen the beam of light that was blinding to her? Was it there before the final bit of dirt fell on her after he left? Or was it there while he was, shining in the distance like an echo of his own bobbing light? Did he know what she was up to? When would he be back to make sure she hadn't succeeded—or would he be sitting outside waiting for her when she broke through?

Beth's voice echoed in her head and bounced off the walls around her. "Go!"

CHAPTER TWENTY-TWO

Jenny sat up on her good knee, reaching above her head, and began pulling the dirt down toward her. She kept her mouth closed and tried to pattern her breathing with her actions so she would exhale as each handful of soil fell—preventing her from inhaling the loose dirt.

She kept her eyes closed most of the time. In part, because the sunlight still hurt, but also to keep the dirt out. She was getting very good at working in the dark, her eyes closed just mimicked that reality. Jenny felt the air above her—cool, fresh, intoxicating. She was almost there, almost free. Jenny could taste freedom. It tasted like sunshine after a long gray winter. The joy in her bubbled over and she began to hum while she worked.

Around the cave-in, the ground was packed a bit harder and she realized how lucky she'd been to put her hand where she had. Otherwise, she'd have never known how close she was. Jenny knew she had teetered on a breakdown that could have immobilized her and kept her there—left her a helpless victim to whoever put her here. Whoever had left her food and come down with a flashlight to— She refused to let her mind contemplate what his plans were any further. She was free and that was all that mattered.

While she worked, she continued to wonder who he had been. Who he was. No matter how unimportant she convinced herself it was, it kept coming back at her. Sometimes in her own voice, sometimes in the voices of her memory, friends or family. The question was a constant, even when she didn't want it to be, much like a child when they first begin questioning the why of life of itself.

But this time the inquiry was different. This time it had more purpose, more immediacy, more impact. She'd known that voice, but not intimately. Or perhaps she didn't recognize it at all. Maybe she was just so desperate to figure out the who and why, she'd filled in the blanks with familiarity because it was easier on some level to imagine someone you know turning evil and hurting you, than a total stranger picking you at random. At least someone who knows you might have a motive you could agree with, even if you didn't condone it, you might at least understand or sympathize with their anger. But a stranger? That was luck, or fate. Neither of which had been her friend through the last few decades, and she didn't want anything to do with either of them in a life-threatening situation.

It wasn't Jack. It wasn't Dan. Those two were the most important suspects to cross off the list. Jack because she needed to know not only was she right in trusting him, but everyone else was wrong. She needed to justify her stupidity in not listening to her friends, and her ignorance of town gossip that might actually have had some truth to it. She needed it not to be Jack. Dan had been too big a part of her life for too long. It would not only hurt her, but also destroy Alan, if Dan had trapped her here. He wouldn't do that to her, he wouldn't do that to Alan, and, well—

Did she still love him?

Jenny wasn't sure she could answer that, and if she could, she knew she'd never say it to another person, not even to Beth during her conversations with the dead. A part of her ached because she couldn't answer that question. Another part of her hurt. She hadn't tried hard enough to keep him when he decided they were done. She'd just let him have his way, like she always did. She didn't argue her side, she didn't fight for the years they'd already had together, and the time they'd invested in each other, in their family. She didn't stand her ground and stick up for Alan. She let it fall apart. She let Alan be ripped from the security he had always known. Was there still something she could salvage?

No, it was too late. In his mind, he had moved on before he'd told her he was leaving. To prove that, a different blonde was at his apartment every time Jenny dropped off or picked up Alan. Funny—he had never dated blondes women before and professed to dislike them, but there they were, lounging on furniture that was never hers, and swooning over someone she still considered hers on some level.

The hole above her had widened to almost six inches across when she reached up for another groundbreaking pull of dirt. Her finger struck something hard and when she pulled it away, pain coursed through her like lightning—not in a straight line, but with a distinct path. From her finger, it jumped up her arm and across her back. It registered immediately. Wave after wave of pulsating shocks followed the initial sharpness. She put her finger in her mouth. The copper-tasting blood leaking from it was garnished in dirt. Her tongue felt a sharp point where the nail bed should have had been and she feared she had pulled an entire fingernail from its housing.

She rocked back and forth a few minutes, using every ounce of strength left in her not to scream and announce her presence this close to the surface. Sucking the blood from the wound, Jenny felt the flow lessen and explored the edges of the sharp area again with her tongue. It hurt, but not unless she put pressure on it. She could feel her fingernail and knew it was still there. She withdrew her finger from her mouth and opened her eyes enough to examine it—thankful for the ability to see again, even if it hurt like hell.

Jutting from the side of her finger, protruding from under the edge of her nail, was a large splinter. She was reminded of the stories of torture she'd heard throughout her life, where prisoners had bamboo shoots shoved under their fingernails—yeah, she had to agree upon feeling the pain, she'd tell someone just about anything if they did that to her. She'd sell herself right now to stop the pain. This wasn't bamboo, though. If she had to guess, the color and grain reminded her of the entertainment center she'd purchased and put together for Alan's bedroom. Pine? She gripped the end of it and pinched. It was soft, but she wasn't sure if that was from weather wear, sucking on her finger, or the wood's natural state. Without a doubt, it had enough strength to ram into her flesh.

The skin around the puncture was very sensitive, the lightest touch sending shivers of pain through her again. As she pulled, with care and a stalled trepidation, the pain threatened her fortitude and she tasted the beginnings of bile at the back of her throat. She swallowed hard and jerked the wood free in one quick motion—deciding it was best to get it over with, like pulling a Band-Aid off a drying scab that stuck to the nonstick padding.

A sudden but silent intake of breath was as close as she got to releasing the scream that leaped into her throat. She wrapped her fist around the throbbing digit and waited for the heat to wash through her. Warm tears ran down her face and left clean streaks in the smudged dirt and grime she wore like foundation. Jenny didn't bother to wipe them away. She let them run free and swallowed back the rising lump in her throat. After a few moments of allowing the pain to ebb and flow, she released her grip on her hand and looked at her finger. It was bleeding again, and when she wiped the blood away, it was still quite tender. Most of the splinter was out, lying on the ground beneath her. The length of a toothpick but the width of a pencil at its thickest point, the small piece of wood looked like a miniature stake. A small fragment was still under her skin—bulging it just a bit and creating a pressure spot of white on the side of her finger.

Jenny looked at it and chewed on her lip, thinking. If she'd been at home, she'd have used a safety pin or something similar to put pressure against the deepest end and force the shredded bits out. She didn't have a needle or knife. She had light to see, but her eyes still hurt too much and she could barely open them enough to see the wound, let alone pinpoint where she should push on it. She needed something hard, not necessarily metal, to rub up her finger toward the entry point and see if she could get it out. Jenny put her finger back in her mouth and moistened the area further, hoping to coax the particle loose, while she looked at the ground around her.

The plates were too thick and cumbersome. The rocks in this part of her prison were too small to get a decent grip on. The larger portion of the shard would work, but she would risk giving herself smaller splinters. She continued to filter the loose soil around her with her free hand. The sunlight glinted off her index finger and she stopped. She didn't have her watch anymore, but he hadn't taken her ring. She could use that.

She pulled the plain silver band from her finger and gripped it firmly. She pulled a knee up toward her chest and placed her injured hand on it for stability. Putting the edge of the ring against her knuckle, Jenny pushed it forward along her skin toward the bead of blood that had collected at the point of puncture. Nothing other than clear liquid and blood came out on the first sweep and she bit her lip against the pain to repeat the motion. Several tries later, she'd succeeded in removing three small slivers of wood and a broken tip. The tip made her think she'd gotten to the bottom of the wound and she relaxed, releasing her lower lip from her teeth.

For the first time, she understood how raw her lip was. They were dry and cracked in general, from the dirt and dust and lack of water, but she'd been chewing on the lower one a lot and didn't realize it until she felt the swelled lump where she'd damaged the tissue. She didn't normally have that nervous habit—she didn't think—but thought perhaps she should try *not* to bite on her lip anymore. For that matter, she should probably not lick them either. She could feel the signs of chapping beginning on the left edge of her upper lip.

She licked the wound on her finger one last time and briefly thought about tearing off a strip of shirt to tie around it like she had with her other finger, but decided it was unnecessary considering how close she was.

Jenny smiled and looked up. She was close. She could hear the small sounds of nature outside and reveled in the blinding sunlight. The sun was high in the sky and she guessed it to be midafternoon. While that was a wonderful aid to her sight, it also meant anyone outside could see as well. She squinted. Her eyes almost shut against the brightness, and reached up to where she'd gotten the splinter and been forced to stop digging.

Gingerly, she explored the area, peaking occasionally with a barely open eyelid but relying more on her touch, as it had been sharpened over the last few days and she now trusted what she couldn't see, so long as she could feel it. The board she'd pulled the sliver away from was a few inches under the surface and it wasn't alone. Another board ran parallel to it on the other end of the hole she'd created.

It seemed her captor had thought about this possible escape, or maybe that was giving him too much credit. Maybe it had some other purpose at conception. Whatever the case, there were twin boards blocking her progress. The thickness was no more than an inch and Jenny presumed they were one-by-fours put down after most of the hole was filled in, perhaps to give it strength or maybe to keep animals from digging. Two narrow planks, with six inches of air between them, meant she would have to not only dig away all the soil around them, but bust through at least two of them—if there were more she hadn't uncovered, and logic said there were—to make the hole big enough for her to crawl through.

She sighed an exaggerated breath through her nose and teeth, and wondered what would be the best way to work past this latest hitch. She removed the dirt from between them and searched for the opposite end of each one, probing with tender fingers and fearful of more splinters or other hazards.

Jenny had looked at her hands after pulling the majority of the wood out of her finger. They were a mess and couldn't take much more damage before they'd be useless. The backs of both hands were scraped and bloody. A few of her knuckles were missing more than just the top layer of skin, and Jenny was sure bone showed in a few places she'd been too nervous to prod. Dirt mixed in with the varying stages of drying blood and made a thick, clumpy maroon paste on her skin. Fresh blood ran across her hands and highlighted the fine lines and scars on her skin. It looked like her veins were on the outside of her skin, and they had turned to a bright crimson rather than the usual blue-green that showed underneath. A thick coat of grime and dusting of fine grain soil across the tiny hairs on her hands made Jenny look like a gorilla rather than a girl. Jenny's nails and cuticles were reminiscent of a nail-biter's, and she remembered the battle Beth had waged against that habit in middle school. Edged in the brownish red of the clay, dirt and blood she'd been digging through, the nails that weren't frayed to the point of pain were tipped in what looked like a black version of a French manicure. She was sure it would take several washings, a serious soak in hydrogen peroxide, and a trip or two to the salon, before her nails were back to their former plain state. Two cuticles were torn and another was cracked. They no longer seeped blood or pus, but the crust of healing wasn't allowed to stay in place either. She knew they felt bad, but seeing the state her hands were in just confirmed they felt as bad as they looked.

She kept an eye out for sticks and rocks as she continued to pull the hard-packed soil down. Jenny kept her eyes closed when working between the planks—she'd had enough dirt in her face for one lifetime. The side of her left hand brushed against the one-by-four and she stopped, waiting for the sting of a splinter to come. It didn't and she continued pushing her way toward the surface. The circle of light she sat in grew wider until sunlight enveloped her, and Jenny could no longer keep her eyes open against the glaring sun. By feel, she judged the hole above her to be at least a few inches more than she needed to squeeze her shoulders through, but still had the boards to deal with to fit her ribs and hips past.

She hadn't located any rocks or sticks to use to pry the wood out of the way or break through it. A fist could maybe break them up, but it would take a lot of beating and she wasn't sure she had the strength in her arms, or enough skin left on her hands. She crawled back toward the beginning to fetch the second plate she had put to the side when she had reverted to using her hands only. It didn't seem like she'd been digging very long since the cave-in and brief visit from her captor. Then again, time was confusing at best and dangerous at worst—

Time!

Jenny used the dim light of her tunnel to glance at her wrist. Full of the same filth that covered her hands, she understood how she'd forgotten it was even on her wrist. After wiping it free, she saw it was just after two o'clock in the afternoon. She scolded herself for her preference of simplicity in timepieces—the analog face had no small square with the day or date in it and she still didn't know anything. Then she remembered the other watch.

She squirmed to flip and expose her hip pocket, pushing her damaged hand into it and retrieving the broken watch. The crystal was definitely cracked, but the digital face beyond it was visible. She knew it had an alarm. She'd heard it go off. Jenny pushed the buttons on the side in several combinations before she figured out the sequence to get the date to appear. It still didn't help her. The numbers flickered in their damaged state and she couldn't tell if the watch said six or eight. If it was only the sixth, she'd been there for four days. If it was the eighth… Six days.

Jenny prayed silently to no one and anyone, and returned the found watch to her pocket. She had to move. She had to get out. She had to… Could it really be the sixth day? Had he been coming in to show her what exactly that meant when his beeper went off and interrupted? Jenny scurried forward to the opening, as she hoped the plate would do the trick and help her bust out before he came back.

Sitting below the opening she'd created, plates in hand, Jenny allowed herself to bask in the warmth of the sun for a few minutes while she planned. She barely noticed the tear in her jeans and the raw meat underneath it. Somewhere in the back of her mind, she realized, this was the wound she had woken up with, and she now understood why it had been so tender. Rather than exploring it in the light or contemplating how she'd gotten it, Jenny continued to plot her escape. She would use the edge of the plate at the weakest point on the boards and break them in half. After that, she'd use her weight to pull them down toward her and break them off where they met the undisturbed dirt. It was a solid plan, it should work, and afterward—

Then what?

She didn't know where she was. If she was in town, then there would be other houses, businesses, or buildings of some sort to run to for refuge. If she was in the country, she'd have no way to get her bearings and know which direction to even run. If she—

"If," she voiced, but continued the thought internally. *If is a term used by losers and whiners—by victims.* She'd worry about if after she got out of the hole.

Sitting up on her knees, she inspected the wood lying across her escape hatch like bars holding a prisoner in his jail cell. There was water damage on both of the planks, and what appeared to be insect burrows. She pushed on the wood with the edge of the plate, testing the softness to see if it was as pliable as the sliver she'd had in her mouth. It wasn't. The wood neither budged nor dented under the pressure. Jenny hoped that meant it would snap under sudden, sharp force and reared back down toward the ground, planning to strike the center and hope that was the weakest point since it had no soil holding it in place.

Springing upward with the plate firmly gripped in both hands above her, she struck the wood slightly off center. A squealing followed the dull thud, as the metal plate slid across the wet wood and shot past it into the open air above it. She halted, holding her breath, and stared at the wood—expecting it to fall or crack or show some proof she'd damaged it. It remained where it was.

Jenny pushed against it with the heel of her hand and noticed the slight give it had. *Did the water damage mean it had more give? Would it be harder, rather than easier, to break it this way?* She tried to think back to her college physics class and drew a blank. She chuckled under her breath. She couldn't remember ending up here but hoped to remember a class she had hated, almost ten years ago? She sat back on her knees and gripped the plate for another attack.

And then changed her mind.

How could I be so stupid? She put the plate down and lay on her back underneath the sky. Looking straight up was blinding and she shut her eyes against the harsh midday sun. She counted to ten in a controlled, steady pace and singsong cadence, and then cracked one eyelid enough to squint and double check she was directly below the left board. She tucked her knees to her chest and put her hands against the walls of her tunnel. The dirt felt slippery but she knew it was the combination of sweat and blood on her hands.

She closed her eyes again, and took a deep breath. With every ounce of strength she had left in her, Jenny kicked outward. Her feet met the wood with force. Her left foot went past the board and her leg straightened. She thought she missed it. But a loud crack echoed past her.

Rather than feel the wood give under the pressure and snap to the power of her leg muscles, she felt the small shards enter her foot. In the excitement and adrenaline of the moment, Jenny noticed the contact but didn't feel the tiny punctures as pain. Instead, she felt white-hot throbbing in her left foot. In her drive to escape, she'd forgotten about the tooth puncture on the sole of her foot. She'd been on her knees for so long in the tunnel—and hadn't walked or stood on it for so long—Jenny had completely forgotten what pressure against her arch felt like and cried out before she could stop herself.

She threw her head back against the dirt floor and gritted her teeth. Touching the foot would do no good, and she grabbed her knee instead, pulling it close to her, and pumped it in a rocking motion tight to her chest. Tiny droplets of spit shot out between her teeth as she panted in pain, careful to keep any further urges to shout in check. She blinked in rhythm to her heartbeat, pounding at an accelerated rate, but eventually coming back down to a normal pace. She didn't lie there long. She knew she couldn't. But she allowed herself several minutes for the exaggerated frustration and pain to build to a crescendo in her chest, before sobbing back into a more controlled state to push herself forward.

She felt abused. Beaten. She hadn't been in a fight since she was a child on the playground, and even then had come out of it looking better than she imagined she did now. What she could see—arms, legs, hands, feet, and torso—were bad enough. She dreaded what a mirror would show her. How badly scraped up was her face? How much blood ran through her hair, and dried into a dirt-covered mat thicker and more unforgiving than any amount of hair spray she may have used in the '80s? Jenny knew her lips were chapped and cracked and chewed to hell, but what else marked her face? What kind of damage was now evident in her eyes and how long would it take that haunted, defensive look to go away? How much of that appearance was from environment, and how much was from reliving her past?

She had plenty of questions, but didn't want any of the answers. Not yet. She just wanted out. She'd deal with whatever consequences came from this later. Now, right now, she needed to let go of her knee, bite a stick if need be, and break that other board so she could crawl out of here.

"Okay then." She spoke to Beth, Alan, Dan, and anyone else who had helped her get this far by staying in her thoughts. "Out it is."

She reared her legs back, clamped her jaw against the pain she knew would be there, and aimed at the other board. One more moment of hesitation could turn into an hour and she knew it. She was tired, she was sore, but she was too close to quit. Jenny shot her legs straight up at the sun and aged wood that stood between her and freedom.

The anticipation of pain stopped her from putting all her strength into the kick, but the proximity was close enough not to be affected by it. Braced for agony, she felt it, but more important, she heard the board snap. Jenny flipped over onto her knees and sat up toward the opening. Both boards were broken in the middle. Now she just needed to get them out of the way and wiggle through.

She grinned. The smile was nothing short of a child's eager Christmas morning expression. Listening to the tunnel for a moment, to make sure the racket she'd made didn't attract her captor's attention, Jenny reached above her and grabbed one side of the first board. She wrapped her arms around it and crossed them over, hugging it. Jenny felt the difference in temperature between her dirt-wall tunnel and the open air above her and thought how amazing that just a few feet below the surface, surrounded by cold soil, there could be such a difference.

The grin was still on her face as she jerked back down with the board in her grasp, her butt landing on her feet in a sitting position. The board creaked with resistance but gave, breaking away in one big piece and coming down with her. Just as she'd thought, it broke where it met the wall, the weight of the dirt above the rest of it holding that side of it like a fulcrum.

The wood didn't snap like she had expected, but it did break. The water damage must have given it enough extra pliability, and while it could take some abuse, it could not withstand her full body weight and determination.

The other side of the first board, and both halves of the second, came away in the same manner. She felt a few slivers slide into her forearms and wrists throughout the process. She ignored them. Sunshine was far more important and it beckoned to her.

CHAPTER TWENTY-THREE

With four broken boards beside her, Jenny reached up and grabbed the top of the hole. For the first time in days, she felt something other than dirt and wood. She felt grass. It was rough and scraggly, not soft and lush like a well-kept lawn, and it jabbed at her already battered flesh, but the sensation on her skin was amazing, and she allowed herself a moment to enjoy it.

She could feel different types of grass in just that little handful and noticed the blades were dry, not moist like the earth had been. If it had rained while she'd been in the tunnel, the ground soaked up the majority of it and the sun dried the rest from the leaves and grass.

The sun.

God, how she'd missed the sunlight. Even artificial light would be appreciated at this point, but sunlight was especially amazing. Anything other than darkness was a welcome change, and she yearned to climb through and run. But the logic that had gotten her this far nagged her—told her to be careful. Be cautious. Be smart. And she decided to check out her surroundings first. She needed to know her captor didn't lie in wait for her outside the hole. She needed to know it wasn't a trap. And a look at the outside might tell her where she was, so she'd know which way to run to find help the fastest.

She pulled herself up in a smooth, restrained motion, careful not to put pressure on her injured foot. The hole would have opened up at chest height if she had stood straight up, but she didn't need to go that far. Jenny raised herself up until her eyes were above the mouth of the hole, like a hunter peeking out from a blind, and surveyed the area around her prison through tight slits that kept out the glaring sun. She wondered how long it would be before bright light no longer hurt her eyes. Was it possible to have permanent damage from a few days in the dark?

The grass was exactly what she'd expected from the blind handful—country grass.

Crap. Unless she was in a very bad part of town, help was not going to be right next door on a city block. She was outside the city limits and would likely have a trek in front of her before she found another house. She examined her surroundings, hoping her fears were unfounded..

Not seeded, not fertilized, weeds and thistles spotted the grass around the hole. It was shorter than wild growth but taller than a trimmed yard. It led her to believe it was mowed, but not very often, or due soon.

Her eyes roamed across the grass and found the edge of what might look like a small patch of woods. The gentle roll of the landscape prevented her from seeing beyond the first few rows, halting her ability to judge the density of the trees. The poplar and pine were no indication of where she was, as they were common everywhere up north, and used to replenish areas that had been logged or damaged by fire. The trunks were thin. They were young trees, and stood no higher than a two-story house—great for hiking or hunting in, but no help for someone looking for rescue.

To her left, the trees tapered off into an open field surrounded with a barbed-wire fence. The boundary was in dire need of repair and apparently not kept up for active use. Jenny saw no cows or horses on the other side, and blew it off as an abandoned field, or farmland in its down year for cycled crops.

To her right was more flat land, but this wasn't fenced and had the look of wear to it. Scrub brush and wild grass led to what looked like a path. A road? Jenny squinted in the sunlight, straining to get a good glimpse of the ground without standing up farther for a better angle. The grass was still green enough that stark differences between it and the gray of the path were obvious. Her eyes burned as she tried to get them to focus in the bright light, but she couldn't tell how wide the trail was, or whether it was gravel or just worn. She turned to continue surveying—

And saw the house.

Behind her, underneath her, she had crawled and clawed and dug her way this far—strove to put distance between her and the structure she felt was above her. Now, in the bathing glow of daytime, she could see the building that had been her ceiling. Jenny took in the full view of the house that had a refrigerator running in it somewhere. A refrigerator that had echoed through her prison walls like breath and reminded her of what civilization was—what normal included.

Looming over her, the off-white three-story home was intimidating and she imagined it would somehow let its owner know she'd found a way out—that it had allowed her to escape.

The house was old. The paint peeled along the corners and underneath the windows from weather and age. The wood beneath looked dark and rotted and she was reminded of her grandmother's habit of calling anything in need of repair a fixer-upper, no matter if it was just a broken railing or collapsed roof requiring attention. This house was definitely worthy of the term. However, the age of it also meant it was sturdy, built to last, and it had.

Several of the windows looked newer, with fancy energy-efficient insulated double-pane slides. Others were old and stained, a dirty, almost opaque milk color. She counted ten in total—two on either side of the door, four spaced at even intervals above, and two smaller half-circle versions above those. One of the third-floor windows had a crack through it she could see against the drawn shade and wondered why it hadn't been repaired yet. The front door was foreboding, not welcoming. The dark oak door looked thick and consisted of four equal panels, the top two with stained-glass inserts. It looked out of place. Like a grand mansion door had been slipped onto the poor farmer's house when he wasn't looking. Or perhaps the door weathered better than the house, and they had matched when first constructed.

The front porch ran the length of the house. Four steps led up to the ledged shelf, and a broken swing hung from its single remaining chain at the far end of it. Wide rails—the kind she'd always wanted, the kind that would be great for sitting and reading on during a lazy summer afternoon—were broken up by pillars every five feet or so that rose to meet the ceiling above. One of the pillars was bare, having been either replaced that summer, or stripped of the decaying paint, and it stood out against the dirty white backdrop. Had Jenny been driving along this road, she'd have thought the house quaint and valuable for its age and size. Coming from underneath it, she only saw the evil the structure housed—the windows were nothing but prison bars, the porch a locked cage.

She tilted her head, cocking it to the side like a quizzical dog staring at its master, as she saw how far away from the house she had come. Jenny didn't think she'd dug that far away from the root cellar door, and wondered if she hadn't been inside some sort of tornado shelter connected to the basement. She was horrible with distances, but would guess at least thirty yards separated her from the house. Perhaps she hadn't been under the house after all, but underground near the house instead.

The yard in between was devoid of personal possessions that would give her any hint to the person who had kept her hostage. Two tires lay near the side of the porch. Across the distance, both seemed to have what looked like decent-looking dark tread on them, and were neither flat nor mounted on rusted rims. A garbage can with a lid held down by a yellow bungee cord sat next to the tires. It was pristine. The silver of the metal sides still shined, and from her vantage point, showed no dents, scratches or other signs of abuse and age. It was either new or this person was extremely careful with his trashcans. There were no old cars, no toys, not even a clothesline with articles to help her judge his size or style. Nothing marred the landscape or littered the yard other than two newer-looking tires and a garbage can—and her.

No signs of life came from within the house or the surrounding land. Jenny's warden was either very quiet or not present, and she ducked back down into her hole. She should run. She should pull herself out of the tunnel while she still had adrenaline flowing and run—in any direction. It didn't matter that she could barely stand on her left foot, it wasn't important that she needed sleep and water. She'd get those things and let the paramedics deal with her injuries as soon as she located a phone and called the police. All that mattered was she go—remember every detail about the house, so she could describe it to authorities, and get the hell out of there.

So why was she still squatting in the dirt and darkness? Why was the nagging at the back of her mind telling her to stay put? It wasn't Beth's voice, or Alan's. It was Jenny's own.

The sunlight. The beautiful, wonderful, warm sunlight. As much as Jenny yearned to reach it and reveled in its mere existence, she also feared it on some level. If she could see, so could her captor. If he was home, he'd see her no matter what direction she ran. If he wasn't home and she found the road, she'd be right there on it when he drove up it to come home. No, the cover of darkness was what she needed. Or at least until the sun passed the thin line of trees to the side—it was past noon and it would be there soon enough. She could hide among the long shadows toward the end of the day. She could take her time and be careful of her foot and the terrain. She felt she would have a better chance to make it if she waited—just a little longer.

But the hard part was over. She'd survived the futility of her underground tomb. She'd suffered through her own imagination and recollections, and battled the demons within herself. No jury of her peers could do to her what she did to herself. Jenny had looked inside, even when she didn't want to, and come away knowing she'd done the best she could in any given situation. Even if she'd have changed things she had done, knowing then what she knew now, she could still justify her actions at any time. She could live with herself and the choices she'd made over the years. Looking at her wrists, and the fresh scrapes and bruises surrounding old scars, she knew she could carry those scars forward and wear them with pride. She was strong. She was a survivor.

Jenny squatted back down out of sight. She grabbed one of the broken boards and held it like a weapon at the ready. She was alert and ready for whatever else could be thrown at her. She would wait. She would think of those she longed to see, those who would be looking for her, and wait. Patience was a virtue, but on a more important level, it could be a lifesaver right now. Closing her eyes, Jenny tilted her head back and let the sun wash over her face, warming her inside and out.

A noise outside her hole pulled her back to reality and she snapped her head upward. Holding the stick with a firm grasp, ignoring the sharp pieces poking her hand, she stood and peeked out. Careful to show only what she needed and not give herself away.

The yard looked the same in all directions, though the grass was losing its glossy appearance as the day continued to wane. A small clump of tall weeds rustled and she drew back a little, staring at it. A light gray rabbit jumped out from behind it and paused, twitching its nose and ears in the breeze. Jenny relaxed. She figured it caught her scent and huffed in disgust, *God, I probably smell awful.* She was genuinely surprised she couldn't detect the stench she was convinced covered her after several days in a dank hole.

"Jesus Christ." She admonished herself, her behavior. If a damn rabbit could scare the crap out of her, and remembering her captor's earlier proximity had frozen her to the point of uselessness, she knew she couldn't linger. She couldn't sit here and wait for death to come home and finish her off like a patient with a terminal diagnosis. She needed to get out.

She'd dug her nails to shreds. She had kicked numerous injuries into her feet. Yet, here she sat, with freedom palpable on the thin breeze around her. No. This was fear, this was victim—this wasn't her. It was out of character, and she wouldn't concede to whatever voice had told her to stay put. She fought to get out. She was free to go. It was time to leave.

Jenny realized she had her eyes open and looked up at the sky.

The sun had moved close enough to the tall trees to her left that it didn't hurt her eyes with the same tear-inducing intensity. She was amazed she'd somehow lost track of time, while sitting in the glow of the sunlight, and snapped her head in the direction of the house, to make sure she hadn't missed hearing anyone come home or wake up. She licked her lips and stood to her full height, leaning against the edge of the hole.

The house still loomed over Jenny like a boogeyman, but now it cast long, dark shadows across the yard, as if reaching for her. What she thought was a driveway was still clear of any vehicles—unless it was just a path and the vehicles were on the other side of the house, or parked in a garage she couldn't see from here. But from what she could see, what she could presume, she was still alone. It was time.

She ducked back down into the hole and grabbed the plate and another board. Jenny stood and placed all three objects on the ground outside her tunnel. She turned to her right and put her palms flat on the grass above where the broken boards would be—figuring they would make the ground sturdier and she wouldn't push straight through the dirt when she put her body weight on it. She took a deep breath and squatted as far as she could without changing the position of her hands. She thought of Alan, Jack, Dan and Beth and jumped up, extending the leap by using her arms as they straightened to push her farther into the air. She cleared the grass and leaned forward. Her upper body lay across the ground. Her legs dangled in the hole below her. The broken edge of the board still embedded in the dirt dug into her lower abdomen, scraping her skin as it tore through her shirt. She gasped as pain pushed the breath from her lungs.

She lay for a moment, brows furrowed and eyes squeezed tight against the anguish. The wood hadn't penetrated, she could tell, but it hurt like hell. Jenny cursed herself for not thinking of the possibility of ramming into the broken end, and rolled over to her back. The accumulated wounds, both physical and mental, past and present, seemed to pour their scars into her abdomen, and she lay with her eyes closed as the warm pain washed over her. She didn't swallow back a gasp. She didn't blink back the unwanted tears. Jenny was getting used to being battered and something about that made her smile, and then frown.

Before she had a chance to ponder the conflicting reaction in her, Jenny's ears picked up the far-off sound of a motor. Even before the noise had finished registering as an engine, she knew it was not a refrigerator. She pulled her legs up and out of the hole, and rolled back over, scrambling to her feet but remaining low to the ground.

Squatted down, with one hand on the ground for stability, she looked like a football player waiting on the line of scrimmage. She scanned the horizon around her, turning her head to accommodate her peripheral vision and track the scenery in one steady gaze. Searching completely around the left until she was looking behind her, she found nothing. To her right was the same, and she started over again. Jenny held her breath and stared at the strip of gray she thought might be a road. The sound grew louder, closer, but she saw nothing on the horizon. Half a step into a sprint for the trees, she realized the sound came from behind her and she spun, losing her balance and falling onto all fours.

The abandoned field behind her was still empty. The wire fence still hung in neglect. Nothing in view would make that noise, but it clearly came from this direction. She was stumped, and prepared to turn and head for the cover of the poplars, when it occurred to her to look up. There, flying low over a neighboring strip of land, a small plane turned away from her and continued sweeping the field it was tending. A puff of billowing white powder blocked the plane as it dropped its payload and dusted the crops below it.

She cursed her timing. Had she turned earlier, had she looked up sooner, perhaps she could have waved the pilot down. Then again, he was quite a ways away. Her sense of distance had never been good, but this wasn't an immediate neighbor and he wouldn't be watching the land around him. He'd be concentrating on getting his job done.

"Damn." She turned away as the small plane grew more distant and the sound of its single engine began to fade. Jenny looked back and forth between the tree line and the path, before deciding on splitting the difference. If she stayed parallel to the road, but off it, she could duck down to hide if trouble came along, and still be close enough to flag down help if it drove by. *If I can recognize friends from enemies at this point,* she thought, before pushing the negativity to the back of her mind.

She looked at the ground and the various tools she had dragged through her ordeal in case she'd need them. It was time to decide what needed to come with her and what should stay behind. Jenny could think of no use for the plates on the run and the rocks would likely be replaceable if she ended up needing to toss one. The bone was still below in the hole and she wanted to neither retrieve it, nor carry it with her away from this place. That left the broken planks. Fine enough weapons for an alley melee, they'd be lightweight and easy to swing. If she found a nice big stick, she might trade in on her way, but for now, that was all she needed to feel somewhat protected. She reached down and grabbed the longest one. At just under two feet, she thought the solid wood with jagged edges would make a fine weapon indeed. Jenny slapped it against her hand like a bully looking for a fight, grinned and took her first tentative step away from the hole.

She paused. Nothing happened.

No alarms went off. No one came running out of the house. *Am I really free and clear?* She took several more steps and could see the other end of the porch. The edge of a garage peaked out, and Jenny crouched as she moved forward. The garage's proximity to the gray path led her to believe it was indeed a road and she veered left, avoiding the unprotected line of sight it would provide to anyone on it.

She limped along in a careful half crouch, keeping the trees to her left and the road to her right. She headed for the long grasses of the fields in between—slowly, taking cautious almost fearful steps at first and then picking up the pace until she was somewhere between a fast limp and a slow jog.

She bounced along on the balls of her feet, not giving her heels time to touch as she went. Jenny could feel the weight lifting from her shoulders, almost taste the energy growing in her core, and she put more distance between her and her prison. The pain began to subside throughout her body, as jubilation took over, and she wondered why in the hell she even toyed with the idea of sitting there waiting for the cover of evening.

A hundred yards from the hole, she paused, turned back toward the house and looked around the opposite side of it. Now she had a clear view and could see the open garage door, its gaping maw devoid of any vehicles. Relief washed the remnants of fear from her and she turned back toward the trees and resumed her tiptoe jog.

At the crest of the small hill, she saw the trees were just an outcropping and did not lead into a chunk of forest. Beyond it was open grasslands, dirt and brush, unkempt country fields. And no houses. Either the road to the right of her was a long private driveway branching off the main road, or the road itself really ended here. Either way, she'd have to follow it to find people, help. Jenny took a deep breath of the fresh air and pushed forward, keeping the road several dozen yards away from her and hoping what looked like a bend in the road, wasn't a trick of the landscape.

For the first time since she'd woken up, hope was back. It hadn't been swallowed, beaten or battered by the oppressive darkness of either her prison or herself. Hope was at the end of the road, possibly around the turn, and held firmly in the hands of someone she couldn't even be sure existed out there.

CHAPTER TWENTY-FOUR

The brush beat against her exposed flesh, and the terrain pounded under her stocking feet. Jenny noticed neither, as she loped through the field like a wounded animal running from a predator. She kept her mind busy, averting thoughts of pain and exhaustion by committing to memory the details of the house she'd left behind, and recalling happy tidbits of the life she strove to find around the next bend.

Alan. She thought of her son, and ached at how much she'd missed him. A twinge of guilt ran down her spine, as she realized she hadn't concentrated on him the entire time she'd been trapped, but just as quickly forgave herself—she'd had other things on her mind. He was her first thought and that counted for something. After that, he had been tucked into a safe place in her subconscious, and kept as a reminder to push her forward, without being intrusive and breaking her down out of worry.

Ced Dan, however, had been in her thoughts more than she'd expected. Jack was in and out, Beth was in and out, but Dan seemed to hover in the darkness around her, as she juggled strengths and weaknesses inside herself.

Jenny knew she'd always love him in some respect. After all, she'd spent a good portion of her adult life with the man. But she never expected him to remain so firmly seated in her brain as to be the face she returned to over and over when in trouble. On some level that bothered her—on another, it gave her comfort. Her father had been dead for so long, Jenny had no guilt at forgetting what he looked like. Jenny's mother had been buried in both the ground and her psyche for long enough she thought of her only when she was mentioned. Beth was gone and yet still fresh enough to hurt Jenny on a daily basis. But Dan, Dan wasn't gone—just removed.

Or replaced, she thought. Jack had slipped into the position quite easily. He helped her pass the time, made her laugh, intrigued her with conversation and reminded her what it was like to be happy again. She had crossed him off the suspect list when her captor's mumbling hadn't registered as Jack's voice. Now, her mind roamed over their various nights out on the town and dates spent sitting on the couch in silence, either alone or with Alan. Some days it felt like they were a cohesive unit, other days it felt like Jack was a stranger intruding on their family time. She was sure it would get easier. Alan had never once tried to push Jack out, never played the part of wicked stepson or sabotaged his mother's life. For that, Jenny was grateful. She appreciated them both, and their roles in helping her move forward toward escape. As she daydreamed, her muscles relaxed, her anxiety started to clear. For the first time in days, Jenny was content and she drifted haphazardly through her recent past. Until searing pain shot through her leg and she skidded to a stop.

She looked down at her knee and saw the fresh scrapes and scratches that ran through and around the deeper, older injuries, but nothing that should have stung. Jenny huffed as she caught her breath and ran a finger lightly over the various wounds. Her fingertip touched something she didn't see and the pain returned. She could feel it but not see it, and scowled at the invisible intruder, her lip curling in anger and confusion.

Looking behind her briefly to see how far she'd come, she realized what had happened. The house was no longer in sight, the road was still to the right of her, and she had stopped in the center of a wild blackberry patch. She was happy to have escaped even the view of the house, but surprised she hadn't stepped on any of the thorny berry branches. She looked back to her knee and felt for the thorn she was certain had embedded itself.

Locating it with ease, Jenny used what remained of her fingernails to grip it and pull it free. Only then did it dawn on her—blackberries. Her mouth salivated even as the thought solidified and she looked up, eager to risk thorns in her already torn fingers to get a few fresh berries.

Unfortunately, the season had yet to come, or had already come and gone—bare branches and exposed thorns was all she could see in the brush patch. Jenny never could remember when the berries were ripe in the wild, and always seemed to miss roadside picking's peak season, the bears and other wildlife beating her to it.

Bears? Did they eat blackberries? How far out in the country was she? What kind of animals could there be out here? Would her injuries cry out to them?

A disgusted grunt escaped her lips as Jenny grimaced. It was the middle of the day. She wasn't in any danger. At the moment. However, when nightfall settled, then yes—she would be exposed to nature, and could very well be in danger. Escaping a lunatic, only to be hunted down and eaten by a mangy, rabid, wild animal was not an option. Her only alternative was to hurry up and find help before the sun set.

Jenny looked up to the sky, squinting, and then back to her watch. It was almost five, but she still had a few hours of light left. How far could she get in an hour? How far did she have to go still? The questions, like all others before them, were unimportant and sitting here debating it was just a waste of time. Not only did Jenny need to continue forward to get to safety, she needed to keep putting distance between her and the house. No amount of space seemed safe, until she found another person and had a witness. Then and only then would she feel comfortable enough to relax.

If he'd seen the beam of light above her earlier—if he knew Jenny was clawing her way out through the dirt—would he go straight down to the basement and after her? No, he would have stopped her without delay. What had dragged him away before, and was it something that still held his attention or would his attention be focused on her? What would he do when he realized she was gone? Did he have dogs? No, she would have heard them or seen proof of them. Would he chase her? He couldn't let her just escape and tell the authorities to raid his house. She could still lose this battle and the thought scared her more than the darkness had.

She used the board to push the branches out of the way and pushed her way out of the berry patch and into field again, ignoring the occasional scrape or stinging that marked her progress. When she cleared it, she saw the curve of the road ahead as it stopped abruptly at a T intersection. It was a driveway. It did meet up with a main road. But there were no visible signs, either directional or street names, and she had to make a decision. Left or right.

She limped her way to the intersection and squatted down low in the ditch. The one she had followed this far was gravel, little more than a path—it looked homemade with its center strip of weed growth and lack of shoulders. The side road was paved. The blacktop was covered in cracks, great chunks were missing, two distinguishable grooves marked the well-traveled path of most vehicles. But it was paved. Paved meant civilization. People meant rescue.

The faded black asphalt stretched for as long as she could follow to the right of her. There were no turns, no hills or valleys, and no marked side roads. A few hundred yards down, she could see trimmed bushes at the edges of the shoulders on either side, but no mailboxes. If there were houses down there, they were rentals, vacation homes or cabins, and didn't require a weekly shopper or daily mail delivery. Or maybe they just used post office boxes and help was right there, just a few football fields away from her.

To her left it extended as well, but not as linear. The first hundred yards were flat and boring. After that, texture speckled the landscape in the form of small dips, a short S-curve she could see both ends of but not the middle, and the road itself suddenly disappeared, leaving nothing but horizon where it dropped off. Jenny could see only field beyond the road and presumed the road turned off at the bottom of the hill that crested at the edge of her view. This route held no mailboxes either, but it also didn't have the hopeful sign of cultivated greenery.

She looked back the other direction and squinted at the bushes in the distance. Which way?

Right. She had nothing more than bushes, rather than a twist in the road, to lead her that direction, but thought back to the food in captivity. If she'd have gone right in the darkness, she would have found it before it had spoiled. She'd go right this time, if for no other reason than that. She turned toward the straight stretch of road and sidestepped back into the weeds, away from the ditch again, returning to the practice of keeping distance between the road and her.

Jenny walked, rather than continuing her hobbled jog, and listened intently to the sounds around her. She hadn't noticed the wind in the grass or the occasional cricket or bird before. They seemed to surround her now. She looked around, but saw no sign of the birds, and presumed they were chirping from the safety of cover.

She felt alone in the scrub brush and overgrown grasses of the ditch and field—as if the rest of the world had died while she'd been underground, and now Jenny was cursed to wander it in search of other survivors. Her mind twisted around that thought and recalled the doomsday and disaster movies she enjoyed so much. Generally, the characters found other survivors, but they didn't always end the film on a happy note, so she decided she'd be better off not thinking of things like that.

Beth. She could think of Beth. No, that would depress her, and Jenny needed to keep her adrenaline going, keep her hopes high. Thinking of mortality, even if only her friend's and not her own, would bring her down. If she crashed again, she may not find the reserves to get back up and continue.

Alan worried her. Or rather, she was worried about him. What must her disappearance be doing to him? She knew Dan would be doing everything he could for the boy, but hoped he was keeping the faith strong as well. Were they searching for her? When had they reported her missing? Were teams of townsfolk and dogs looking in the outlying woods? Did they dredge the lake? Hell, for that matter, did they know where she'd been taken from yet? If her kidnapper left her car in the parking lot, they would know to start there—maybe find an eyewitness. If he'd sunk her car in the lake, they'd spend a few days searching the nearby waters and shorelines, and then close the case, declaring her dead. Was she already dead to her loved ones?

"God!" She barked at her surroundings but aimed the anger

inward. She couldn't think like that. She had to stop coming up with worst-case scenarios. A little hope went a long way, and she had just a touch of it in the trimmed brush up ahead. She needed to absorb that glimmer of optimism into herself somehow and hold it tight, let it fuel her forward. She had to think of good things, she had to stay positive and keep moving.

The sculptured hedges were close enough now, she could see them for the manicured evergreens they were. The height and width were not something you would see in the wild and the surroundings were desolate enough they were obviously not planted as some taxpayer-funded, beautification campaign. These were kept, cared for, and planted by landowners. Someone owned that property. The only question was whether they were currently on it.

She'd been staring straight ahead at the bushes, watching the road for signs of life and ignoring her peripheral vision. Movement to the side caught her attention and Jenny saw beyond the squirrel that had scurried past her in the tall grasses. Ignoring the animal, she stopped her forward motion and took in the changing landscape. The field gave way to rolling hills on the other side of the road. The hills were slightly lower than the ground she stood on, but she could see the sparse new tree growth and winding driveway—and house.

The modest ranch-style house looked far more modern than the one she'd escaped, but she couldn't tell if it had been built on the land, or manufactured elsewhere and put together here. And she didn't care. It was a house. Complete with curtains blocking her view of the interior, a freshly painted garage and a bicycle lying abandoned on the unnaturally green lawn. A house.

Looking back to the road, Jenny judged the distance to the bushes and then estimated the length of the driveway. She compared that to the length it appeared to be if she cut across the rolling hills, moved straight at the house from here. She looked skyward while she thought.

The sounds of the dying day surrounded her, as she studied the clouds above her and tried to work through the logistics. Leaves rustled from somewhere and random chirps from unseen birds punctuated the breeze. The sound of a car engine interrupted nature, and she snapped her eyes open, blocking out all other sounds in the process.

CHAPTER TWENTY-FIVE

The noise grew louder—she knew it was getting closer, but the sound echoed over the fields in an odd pattern, and she couldn't pinpoint the direction it came from.

Jenny studied the road in front of her for a moment. The strip of road she could see went for at least a mile, and she was sure, if she could hear it, she'd be able to see anything on the road. Unless they were coming from the side road up ahead, but she dismissed the idea and spun around to check the other direction.

The short length of road before the dip that swallowed the asphalt showed no signs of a vehicle. Before she could consider the curves beyond the horizon and below the visible tarmac, she panicked and twirled in the direction of the house, losing her footing briefly and stumbling forward a step before catching herself. She could no longer see the house, but the faint gray path was still visible as it cut a path through the grasses. It too was empty, and she wondered if she was hearing things.

She squinted toward the homemade road, and worried there may have been a car on the other side of the garage she hadn't seen.

Did he realize she was gone and was now on the chase to return her to the darkness? Would he bother, or would he mow her down on the road, wandering off the shoulder and into the weeds if need be? Jenny didn't want to know the lengths he'd go to, to finish what he'd started, but needed to keep a clear head, and that meant considering all options.

She ducked down, using the tall grass as cover as she'd intended, and checked the T-road again. Looking past the presumed driveway for the house she'd just spotted, she searched with her eyes, but relied on her ears more, as she tried to pinpoint the direction the noise came from.

The rumble of the vehicle told her almost nothing. It wasn't a quiet luxury vehicle, made to be silent, inside and out, and glide along while holding the passengers in perfectly measured suspension to hide every bump and crack in the road. She'd never seen or heard of a Lexus that roared as it ran, even in the high idle of a midwinter start, which ground on the gears for a moment before turning over. No, this was something else.

On the opposite end of the spectrum, the engine was nothing even remotely close to the throaty growl of a motorcycle. The guy she'd dated right before her mother's death had had a motorcycle, as did his friends—which was a major thorn in her mother's side and therefore gave Jenny every reason she'd need to date him. It only lasted two months, but during that time, she'd spent enough afternoons with the boys and their toys to be able to distinguish certain makes. A decade after the fact, she'd never forget the sound of a motorcycle. This was not a bike, not even a high-pitched foreign version.

The sound bounced off the landscape around Jenny and she continued to turn her head to each of the three possible directions in a methodic, almost robotic check for movement. The options narrowed, leading her to believe the vehicle in question was either a car in dire need of a tuning or a larger vehicle—an SUV or truck perhaps.

The engine revved as the driver drew closer, and she looked back toward the ranch house. What if it was her captor? Should she just run across the ditch and head for the house, forget the car, and find help. Jenny hadn't seen anyone wandering the grounds. There were no lights on in the house, but it wasn't quite dusk and they weren't necessarily needed yet. But there were also no vehicles outside the garage or in the visible portion of driveway. It didn't matter. If the owners weren't home, she'd break a damn window to get to the phone that had to be inside.

As Jenny readjusted her feet under her, in preparation for a sprint across the road and down the ditch on the other side, movement from the edge of her vision caught her attention. She snapped her head to the left and waited for it to register.

There. Past the crest of the hill that swallowed the road in the opposite direction, plumes of dust rose above the horizon. Someone was coming up the hill.

The billowing cloud made her wonder if the asphalt turned to dirt on the other side, or if there were other private roads down there and a neighbor was traveling. A country resident owning a truck or utility vehicle made sense, and part of her tried to reason it was a neighbor. But were they coming her direction or were they going away from her? She couldn't be sure and her legs twitched with a subconscious desire to run to the edge and check. Her balance teetered and Jenny put the other hand on the ground in front of her to steady herself. The cloud of dirt dissipated but the sound grew louder—the vehicle was heading her way.

Help was coming.

"Run!" The voice in her head was neither her own nor Beth's. It was everyone's she knew, blended together and sounding like no one in particular. Jenny ignored it. She needed to be sure before she exposed herself, and she stared at the cracked edge of the blacktop.

She duck-walked closer to the asphalt, keeping the majority of her body hidden in the tall grasses, but daring to keep her head above the weeds. Her eyes remained focused on the road as she waited, counting the seconds by the beat of her pounding heart. The small sounds of nature around her seemed to stop, as her ears remained perked and intent on hearing only the vehicle's engine. Even the rustling of the grass, from both the wind and her own movements, seemed to be done so in pantomime. She watched. She waited.

As Jenny's shoulders began to loosen in resignation the vehicle had actually been going in the opposite direction, headlights lit up the air above the horizon as the car itself came over the hill and became visible. In the fading daylight, she couldn't tell the make of car or even the color, only that it was a dark sedan, and not a truck or utility vehicle, that had rumbled into her escape route. It continued up the darkening strip of road in front of her, getting larger as it drew closer. Her breathing turned to crackling gasps as her mind spun out of control. Her knees twitched, wanting to sprint forward. Her feet refused to move and felt like they may have fallen asleep in their statuesque position. Jenny battled the logic of both desires.

The car slowed at the strip of road that began the S-curve. Just as her legs were trying to take over her mind and spring into action without her consent, the side of the vehicle came into view and something reflected off the door at her.

Jenny couldn't see what it said, but could make out the distinct shape of the shield on the door of the car and the thick strip of contrasting color along the side of the vehicle. It was a cruiser. The cops—

Her legs relaxed, her right knee falling forward and landing on the ground. Jenny's arms began to tremble as the realization hit her. Rescue. She'd survived. She was home free.

The cruiser pulled to a stop at the intersection, the well-worn engine much quieter in its idle state, but the night cooling enough she could see exhaust and knew it was still running. She couldn't see the driver, couldn't tell what he might be doing in there, and didn't care. It was the cops. She needed to get there. She was standing and running before she'd even realized she wanted to be, needed to be. Her lopsided, half-limp stumble had turned to a pained jog, as she cut diagonally across the ditch, gaining on the car and heading for the road at the same time. She waved her hands above her head, like they were on fire, and prayed she'd catch the driver's attention.

The cruiser's right blinker began to flash and Jenny tried to scream. A raspy half syllable escaped her lips and nothing else. She tried to whistle—she'd always been very good at whistling and had been asked to do it from the stands of football games by other kids when she was younger. But again, there was just no moisture left in her, and her pucker produced nothing but a heavy exhale.

Her feet hit the road and two things struck her simultaneously. The pavement hurt her feet more than the dirt had, and the blinker stopped flashing. She was close, he had to have seen her. Her jog started to slow, her adrenaline leaking out of her, as help loomed in front of her.

She was only thirty feet away when she noticed the plumes of exhaust had stopped. She couldn't see the door open but heard it creak as the officer exited and slammed it shut again behind him. The silhouette pulled a long shaft from his side, and she realized it was his flashlight as the spot of light hit the pavement. The cone of white rescue moved smoothly across the ground to her feet, and then up her legs.

She watched, willing her vocal cords to work. They ignored her. She had stopped without realizing it and now lunged forward, finding her feet in lieu of her voice, and continued to limp toward him.

With a hand outstretched in front of her, reaching for the assistance that was so close, she opened her mouth and screamed. It came out as a cracked exhale, and she whimpered.

He walked toward her, stopped on the third step, holding her captive in the beam of the flashlight. They were ten feet apart and Jenny felt she was going to collapse and never close that last gap in her bridge to freedom. She pulled herself along, no longer feeling the pain in her foot, but rather the weight of everything on her shoulders, as the true exhaustion began to hit home in the light of rescue. She tried to speak again and it came out a whisper.

"Help."

"Ma'am?" His flashlight blinded her for a moment before it swung back toward the ground and she heard his feet scrape across the pavement as he walked forward. "Ms. Schultz?"

Jenny smiled as she fell toward the ground. The officer lunged toward her but was a moment too late and she landed on buckled knees. Pulling her up from the ground and allowing her to collapse against him, he asked, "My God, are you okay?"

"I—"

"It's okay. I got you. Just relax." His voice was soothing and welcome. She'd heard nothing but her own thoughts and the sounds of memories for too many days.

"Help." She couldn't think enough to say anything of substance, and simply repeated her plea again softer, her voice fading as her strength waned in the face of safety.

"How'd you get out here?"

She looked up to him, trying to figure out where to start and find the words to explain it. In the shadow of dusk, his eyes were darker than she remembered, but his facial structure was unmistakable.

"Officer Johnstone?" She hadn't seen him for months but would never forget those kind eyes and reassuring attitude.

"Yes…" He pulled her away from him, and looked down at her. "Ms. Schultz? Yes, it's me. I've got you."

"Oh God." Tears rolled down her cheeks, "Help me."

CHAPTER TWENTY-SIX

Jenny woke to the rumbling of a car. *Oh no! Was that even real?* Relief washed over her, as she realized she was inside the car. Lying back against the seat with Officer Johnstone driving. It had been real. She had been rescued.

"Welcome back." His eyes never left the road.

"How long was I—"

"Only a few moments. It's to be expected. You've been through a lot. How'd you get out here?"

She stared at his profile for a moment and then turned toward the side window. "I escaped." Her whisper bounced off the glass and left a small frosted mark that quickly evaporated.

"Escaped?"

"A house, back there." She nodded behind them. "I don't know who or why. I just woke up there."

She paused, remembering the house and thinking she should describe it, rather than her escape. She should ask him to call the station and have them call her house, let Dan and Alan know she was okay. She should start jotting down or babbling off details before they were lost to her. She needed to do something, and everything came at her at once, confusing her and pinching her chest.

"Ms. Schultz?"

"Yeah, the house. An old farmhouse. Detached garage, new front door—on the house not the garage—and really clean yard. It could use paint—not the yard. Two garbage cans. And there's a field, a fenced-in empty field and a plane— There was a plane…" She sat in stunned silence for a moment.

"Ms. Schultz." He put his hand on her shoulder and she jumped. "It's okay. Slow down. Calm down. I wasn't prodding or pushing, I was just checking to see if you'd passed out again. You were quiet."

"I— I— I don't know where to start." Her face twisted into a grimace, and she looked at him, her eyes welling with relief. "Details, I should tell you the details. Can you call my ex-husband? I think I need to go to a doctor. Where's the nearest hospital? Where are we anyway?"

"Okay, okay. Slow."

Jenny had been unaware of his police radio spitting bursts of static until he reached over and turned it down. "We'll get all the details. We'll contact your family. And yes, you look like you definitely could use some medical attention."

"Okay. Sorry, it's just—" Her voice trailed off and she noticed the bumps in the road.

"We're about fifteen minutes southeast of Harding, just past the White River and the old gravel pit." He looked at her, his eyes widening as he waited for a response.

"Oh." She knew the area but didn't feel anything she'd seen today looked familiar to her. Another bump in the road jostled her, and she looked out into the headlights. The pavement she'd been rescued on had turned to potholed gravel. "Where are we now? What do we do first? The police station or the hospital? And when can I call my son?"

"I've just got to check something out up here and then we'll be heading back to the station. Do you want to relax and I'll wake you when we get to town?"

"No. I could sleep for a week, but I've relaxed enough." She watched the shadows on the side of the road give way to complete darkness, as the sun dropped behind the horizon. "There were others."

"Pardon me?"

She swallowed nothing and felt her stomach acids rumble. "Others. Before me. There were signs. Do you have anything to drink? My throat is really dry and I feel like I'm going to throw up." Jenny felt like she'd jumped out of her body and sat in the backseat. The woman in the front seat used broken language, incomplete sentences, and babbled as she bounced between subjects. "There were bones. And food. Well, what was left of it."

"Here." He handed her a half-full bottle of water and kept his eyes on the road. "Sorry, it's all I've got."

"I had to dig. It was like a grave and I had to dig my way out." Jenny looked at her hands in the dark interior of the car. The dashboard lights were turned down low and the yellow glow from the CB radio didn't illuminate anything other than itself. "I don't know how long— What day is it?"

"Sunday." His voice jumped as they bounced over another pothole.

"Sunday?" She stared at the barely visible Chevrolet emblem on the glove box in front of her. "Day six." She heard the fact clear as a bell in her mind, but it barely registered to her own ears.

"Pardon?"

She looked back toward him, his profile full of shadows and angles in the dashboard lights. His starched collar peeked over the lapel of his jacket. His wide arm adorned with the official patch and something she couldn't make out underneath it. She couldn't answer. She couldn't find the words to describe the hash marks on the wall. Jenny could only turn away from him and look out the windshield again. "Others. There were others."

He opened his mouth to speak but closed it again, as he let off the gas and followed the slight curve in the road as sparse trees passed by Jenny's window. The outcropping was thin but healthy and looked to be mostly poplar and pine. She was wondering if that was all they planted out here when the house came into view.

Jenny pushed herself back into the seat with such force she felt the springs against her spine. Her arms wrapped around her and tightened, even as her eyes widened. The farmhouse.

He pulled to a stop and turned the car off. Grabbing both his nightstick and Maglight, he flashed a toothy smile at her. "Stay put, I'll be right back."

She couldn't speak but didn't plan on getting out. Why would they be here? This was what he had to check on? How'd he know? Did someone call in? Did someone hear her screams, or see her wandering? Her mind was flooded with questions she couldn't hope to answer, when her hand reached for the handle and opened the door. She didn't want to be back here, but she didn't want to be alone in a dark car either. She'd had enough of both solitude and darkness. She headed toward the bouncing orb from Officer Johnstone's flashlight.

She limped, ears perked for noise other than the two of them, eyes scanning the windows for any sign of life. The house remained as still as it had been that afternoon when she'd left, and the surrounding area offered no sounds—even the crickets and night birds had gone silent. Jenny limped slowly toward the officer as his light scanned the front steps and door before turning toward the ground around the house. She caught up to him just as his light crossed the area she'd dug up from the inside out.

"That's a first." He scanned the ground with his flashlight, pausing on the plate and broken boards before inching forward and shining the beam on the open hole in the ground. He moved the flashlight beam back across Jenny and grabbed her arm. "You're more resourceful than I gave you credit for."

CHAPTER TWENTY-SEVEN

"But—" Jenny's eyes grew wide, as his words sunk in.

"They usually lose willpower by day five. You should have been reduced to nothing but a shell yesterday, or even the day before." He grinned—the charm of his gaze melted and reformed. His expression had never been one of sympathy, but of planning and determination. She hadn't seen it, hadn't thought to look for it the entire time she'd been in the car with him.

"No…" she wailed as she turned away from him.

"I'll have to reinforce that old doorway before I go hunting again."

She twisted her arm out of his grasp and ran. Bile rose in her throat, as she kicked up grass and dirt, her feet slipping occasionally as the evening dew began to settle. She ran for the trees and hoped she could hide in their shadows or fallen branches. Jenny heard him shout behind her.

"Halt! Police officer." His words faded into laughter, as she heard the pounding of his steps behind her.

She dared not turn and see how close he was. Jenny kept her vision focused on the trees in front of her, only twenty more yards and she'd be over that hill. She'd be out of plain sight and prove more difficult to see or find. She tried to block out the sound of his proximity and continued running.

Beth coaxed her forward with unspoken words of encouragement. Alan appeared at the tree line and waved at her to come to him. Exhaustion, thirst, and hunger threatened to take her, but she ignored it all, and kept going. Her body took care of itself and fed her the adrenaline she needed more than the food she wanted.

She didn't hear him when he stopped running after her. She didn't stop and consider what that could mean.

And she didn't feel the bullet tear through her side.

Jenny heard the echo of the gunshot from the trees in front of her, as birds scattered with a noisy chorus of squawks.

She stumbled, caught herself, and took several more steps before her knees refused to listen to her fight-or-flight command. Jenny watched the ground come rushing up to meet her and her muscles gave out. Her hands, reflexively shooting out in front of her, skidded along the grass as she landed on all fours.

The night promised to be cold, as the temperature had dipped down with the sun. Her breath became visible as it huffed from her mouth. She looked down at her stomach and saw the dark stain spreading through the fabric. She knew she'd been shot—the wetness on the front of her shirt told her it had gone straight through her. Amazed she didn't feel it, she touched it to see if it was real, or imagined as Alan had been in the tree line. Her hand came away wet, warm liquid dripping from her fingers.

She pushed herself up to crawl forward if she had to, but he was already there. His boot connected with her spine and sent here sprawling. Something hard pushed her down into the grass as it dug into her back. He twisted the nightstick there, and she let out a yelp that startled her.

"There, there." His voice was soft and reassuring, like he was talking to a child awoken from a bad dream. "It'll be all right soon."

She turned her head so she could see him peripherally, and pleaded with her eyes. "Why?"

"Why not?" He shrugged, the innocence of his question echoing lightly into the tree line. "They'll accuse your boyfriend—they would normally, but with his questionable history, well— You couldn't have been a better gift if you'd tried. Regardless, 'Why?' is such a boring question. Is that the best you've got? You'd be surprised what women will offer up in exchange for their freedom." He sounded excited and she stared at him, speechless that someone could be so empty, yet put on such a show for the public.

Jenny was scared by the extent of torture someone like this could be capable of—someone who could grin while shooting you and laugh while chasing. What had he done to the others, and how many more bones had lain in the dirt she didn't find? She sobbed, but she was out of tears. She stopped thinking about Alan and Beth, Jack and Dan. She could only think of herself, and what this meant.

"Come on, now." He grabbed her arm and pulled her upright in a sudden motion that yanked her arm from its socket and made her shriek. He half dragged and half carried her back toward the house.

Jenny could feel her strength draining out of her, as blood continued to seep from her stomach and grow cold against her skin in the night air. It wasn't a killing wound if treated—would he treat it?

Her mind spun. She could see the gun in his holster and reached for it. Her arm fell back uselessly, her strength flowing out of it, and she cursed her weakness. She was sore, injured and tired. She needed to get away, but defeat had made a home in her physical abilities and she would need to recoup before attempting to get away again.

Jenny told herself she would get away—eventually. He had said no one else had crawled out before. She was the first. She'd be the first to fully escape, as well. She just needed a little rest. Maybe, when he put her down, she'd be rested enough and ready. She needed to rest and gain some strength.

The darker side of her consciousness wondered if he would stitch her up and feed her, if for no other reason than to bring her back to the brink of healthy to torture her some more. If so, she could escape then. She knew the lay of the land now, and could plan it better. She would stop being cautious and just flee at the first opportunity. *Yes, that's what I'll do.*

Her head lolled to one side. Exhaustion threatened to drag her into unconsciousness. Stress volunteered her up to fear and pain. He said something, but she wasn't coherent enough to grasp it. She needed to remain awake, to calm her heart rate, to slow her bleeding, but felt reality darken at the edges of her vision.

Jenny justified closing her eyes, just for a moment—telling herself she was letting him do the work of carrying her. She had been fighting since she had first woken up in that basement. She was tired of fighting, and her adrenaline was tapped. As she slipped back into the blackness she'd fought so hard to escape, she heard Beth call her name and couldn't find the strength to answer.

Jenny opened her eyes expecting darkness. Instead, the glaring light of a high-wattage bare bulb greeted her. When she reflexively closed them again, the intensity of the room followed her, and her eyelids lit up in a burned orange.

Her pants pocket issued a muffled beep and she realized he hadn't take away the watch she'd found. Jenny wondered briefly if she should start counting days again.

One.

As the weight of sleep lifted, she realized she was tied to a chair. The rough threads of rope held her hands behind her, aided by the sharp edges of something tighter. A quick scan of herself, through downcast eyelashes, showed her rib cage wrapped in dirty bandages and her socks now gone. The wounds she could see dripped clear liquid and blood from beneath the shine of drying flesh. Her stomach hurt where he'd shot her, but it was a bearable, dull reminder of her need to flee. *Gut shot,* she thought. *How long can I survive with one of those?*

Underneath her was a white tile floor—dirtied and stained in colors she couldn't find the ambition or energy to contemplate. The walls around her had been covered with some sort of reflective paint, and the light emanating from the bulb that hung from the ceiling bounced off them, blinding her further. She could see no doors or windows and presumed they must be behind her. Straining her neck as far as she could in both directions, she found nothing but an old wooden chair against the nondescript wall. She wasn't concerned. She had found a way out before, and she'd do it again.

She kept her determination close, but the tray of items on her right worried her. The promises the sharp metal objects and unknown instruments whispered frightened her. She didn't know their purpose but she could guess, and wished she hadn't looked that direction. Jenny tried to push them from her mind, pretending she hadn't seen them or their unspoken intent. Her hands began to writhe as she worked the rope, soaking her wrists in the blood of desperation as her restraints cut into her flesh. She debated her choices—wait for opportunity, or create one.

She jumped at the subtle creak of an unseen door behind her and stopped struggling with the ropes, frozen in anticipatory dread. The footsteps were casual, slow and steady, but echoed ominously in the all-but-empty room. He scraped the chair across the floor, placing it in front of her before straddling it. Jenny refused to look up. She forced herself to keep her focus on the floor, rather than let him see her fear.

When she heard the metal clang on the tray to her right, Jenny glanced sideways and saw his outstretched hand rummaging through the instruments. Her eyes danced as her imagination ran wild. The heat of fear built behind her eyes and a single tear fell to the dirtied floor below her.

Awake for only moments in the brightness of the room, Jenny missed the oppression of her previous prison. There, at least, she had been alone and had had time to figure out her surroundings, and find her strength. Here she hadn't been given that opportunity.

He spoke with a calm tone, but she didn't comprehend his words as she drifted into the only escape she could find—the blackness of her own mind and safety of removed catatonia.

Jenny wouldn't see pure darkness again for several days. When it came, she would welcome it, and its release. The darkness, for all the mystery and memories and madness it had provided her, was never the threat.

True monsters lived in the light.

ACKNOWLEDGMENTS

Thanks to Amanda and Mark for everything, nothing, and the dark closets in between; Bob Ford and Ron Dickie for their eyes; Jenny "JFB" Brown for her ears; Mrs. Honz for sharpening the pencils; Todd Keisling and Kevin Lucia for bringing it back to the light.

ABOUT THE AUTHOR

KELLI OWEN is an American author, editor, reviewer, podcaster, and indie film producer, who has spoken at the CIA Headquarters in Langley, VA regarding both her writing and the field in general. While her nonfiction has appeared in various places—including the Bram Stoker Award-winner *It's Alive: Bringing Your Nightmares to Life*—she is primarily known for her fiction.

As a member of both the Horror Writers Association and the International Thriller Writers, she has published over a dozen books, including *The Headless Boy*, *Teeth*, and *Wilted Lily* (a YA series). Her short fiction has appeared alongside Neil Gaiman, Stephen King, Robert McCammon, F. Paul Wilson, and Josh Malerman, among others, and was in both Bram Stoker Award-nominated anthologies *Arterial Bloom* (2020) and *Lost Highways: Dark Fictions from the Road* (2018).

A logophile from a young age, Kelli spent a decade as a reviewer and editor, while running a large genre website, before returning to her roots behind the keyboard. Born and raised in Wisconsin, she now lives in the dark woods of Pennsylvania. For more information, please visit her website at kelliowen.com

CEMETERY DANCE PUBLICATIONS

We hope you enjoyed your
Cemetery Dance Paperback!
Share pictures of them online, and tag us!

Instagram: @cemeterydancepub
Twitter: @CemeteryEbook
TikTok: @cemeterydancepub
www.facebook.com/CDebookpaperbacks

Use the following tags!

#horrorbook #horror #horrorbooks
#bookstagram #horrorbookstagram
#horrorpaperbacks #horrorreads
#bookstagrammer #horrorcommunity
#cemeterydancepublications

SHARE THE HORROR!

CEMETERY DANCE PUBLICATIONS PAPERBACKS AND EBOOKS

IN THE SCRAPE
by Mark Steensland and James Newman

Most kids dream about a new bike, a pair of top-dollar sneakers endorsed by their favorite athlete, or that totally awesome videogame everyone's raving about. But thirteen-year-old Jake and his little brother Matthew want nothing more than to escape from their abusive father...

"Stories like In the Scrape don't come around as often as I would like. This is exactly what I want to spend my days reading about forever and ever and ever." —Sadie Hartmann, Mother Horror

THE EATER OF GODS
by Dan Franklin

Dan Franklin's debut supernatural thriller is a tale of grief, of loneliness, and of an ageless, hungry fury that waits with ready tooth and claw beneath the sand.

"This neat little book, Franklin's debut, is much fresher than its B-movie premise might suggest. Franklin is a horror writer to watch."
—Publishers Weekly

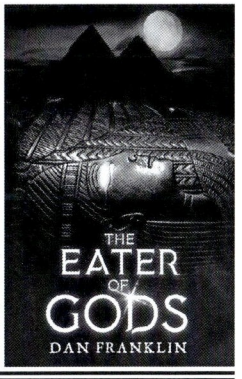

IN THE PORCHES OF MY EARS
by Norman Prentiss

LEAN CLOSER. Let these stories whisper poison into your ears...

This debut full length collection from Norman Prentiss opens with the Bram Stoker Award-winning title story, where an overheard conversation in a movie theater has unexpected effects on a couple's relationship.

"I've never forgotten a Norman Prentiss story. He builds his nightmares gently, word by word, sentence by sentence, working his way into your subconscious so that you are never sure again if it happened to you, or you dreamt it, or it was a Prentiss story." —Kaaron Warren, Award-Winning author of *Through Splintered Walls*

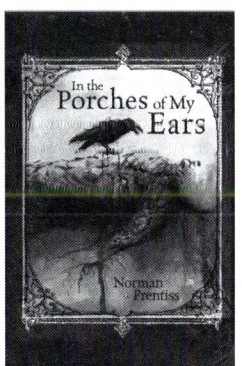

Purchase these and other fine works of horror from Cemetery Dance Publications today!